KA STEAMSHIP CO.
TY OF SEATTLE".

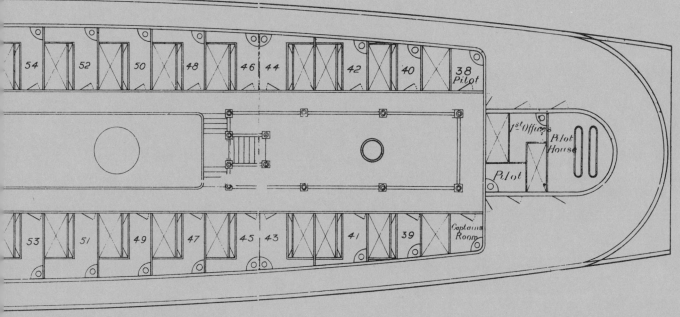

54 52 50 48 46 44 42 40 38 Pilot

1st Officer
Pilot House
Pilot

53 51 49 47 45 43 41 39 Captains Room

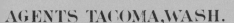
NE DECK

AGENTS TACOMA, WASH.

STEAMSHIP "CLEVELAND"

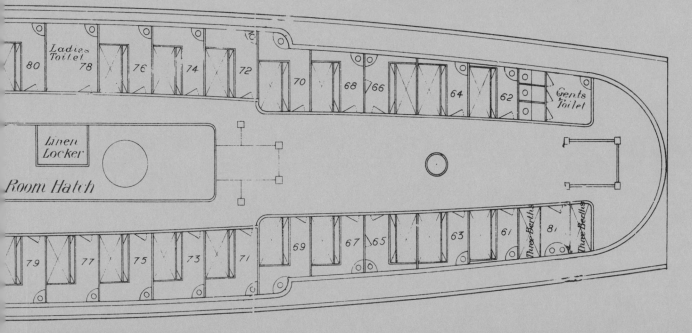

Ladies Toilet
80 78 76 74 72 70 68 66 64 62 Gents Toilet

Linen Locker

Room Hatch

79 77 75 73 71 69 67 65 63 61 Three Berths 81

Steamer's Wake

Steamer's Wake

by JIM FABER

With a Foreward by MURRAY MORGAN

ENETAI PRESS • SEATTLE

3

Steamer's Wake

First Printing.

Printed in U.S.A.

Printing: Arcata Graphics/Kingsport,
Kingsport, Tennessee

Design: Bill Johnson

Production: Eulah Sheffield

Typography: Thomas & Kennedy, Seattle

Published by:
Enetai Press
105 South Main Street
Seattle, Washington 98104

Library of Congress Catalog Card Number:
85-81527

ISBN Number: 0-9615811-0-7

Bill Greer

Table of Contents

Foreword by Murray Morgan **6**

Preface **10**

Prologue
the *Tacoma:* World-Class Loser **13**

Rivers of Gold
and a Sound of Steamers **23**

Trivial Pursuits
and Other Steamer Getaways **115**

Epilogue:
The Course Ahead **235**

Appendix:
Racing, Gold, Fires,
and Other Dramas **243**

Maps and Index **255**

Foreward

Long before the July day in 1787 when Captain Charles Barkley of the *Imperial Eagle* detected the waterway between Vancouver Island and the Olympic Peninsula, before Manuel Quimper in the *Princess Real* charted the Strait of Juan de Fuca in 1790, before George Vancouver turned the prow of the *H.M.S. Discovery* south at Point Wilson and entered the waterway he named Admiralty Inlet, even before the evening when a credulous English traveller in Venice heard a Greek seaman's yarn about sailing for Spain under the name of Juan de Fuca and discovering a passage from the Pacific to the North Sea—in short before the coming or rumored coming of any European to the Pacific Northwest—the inland waters were nature's highway.

The natives of Puget Sound, the Strait of Juan de Fuca and the Strait of Georgia were of many nations—all Indian. They spoke diverse languages. Their cultures were variations on the common themes of hunting, fishing, gathering. Some tribes were blood enemies, others allies. All shared a heritage of tidal waters sheltered by the crests of mountain ranges thrust up from the eastern edge of the Pacific; shared the swift, short, salmon-rearing rivers; shared beaches abundant with mollusks fed by the ebb and flow of the tides; shared the easy mobility of seafaring peoples. For them the cedar canoe meant what the horse meant to the Indians of the interior, what the automobile means to Americans today.

Fishing, whaling and seal-hunting took them out into the Pacific; commerce took them north and south. They paddled, too, for pleasure: to see the shoreline change, to visit relatives, to meet new women. Such ventures might lead to marriages that cemented tribal alliances, or to kidnappings that led to wars of vengeance. The inland seas in the evergreen forests, opening onto the oceans of the world, offered both gateway to new places and the threat of intrusion.

They were paddlers, not sailers, the tribes of the tidal waters. Though over the centuries they must have come across hulks with masts and canvas—Japanese fish boats swept east by the *kuroshio,* Spanish galleons driven off course on the annual voyages between Manila and Acapulco—there is no evidence that the coastal Indians experimented with sail or keel or outrigger. Canoes sufficed. Nor did the Indians quickly take up sailing after seeing the ships of the explorers.

Some of the merchant vessels that came in the wake of the explorers were better designed for sailing in constricted waters. Indeed, the first two ships built in this area—the *Northwest America* by the Englishman, John Meares, in 1788 and the *Adventure* by the Yankee, Robert Gray, in 1792—were small, single-masted craft built especially for work in shallow waters and narrow coves. These early commercial voyages were made in a specialized branch of the fur trade. The whites came to barter trinkets with Indians for the skins of sea otters; the fur was a status symbol in China and commanded extraordinary prices at Canton. But Puget Sound had few, if any, sea otters (they like rocky shores better than clay banks) and was seldom visited by the trading vessels.

More than a quarter century passed between Vancouver's discovery of Puget Sound and the next recorded visit by whites, though some captains must have ventured into its waters. The first to report on their visit were employees of the Hudson's Bay Company who were sent north from Fort George (Astoria) on the Columbia River to see if a small-boat route to the Fraser River could be found that would not involve crossing the Columbia River bar. The party, which included William Cannon, the first American known to have been on the Sound, came in York boats — large row-boats with auxiliary sail. Although they made it to the Fraser and back, nothing about their trip encouraged the Indians they encountered to forsake paddles for sail or oars. In 1828, when the Hudson's Bay Company's Governor, George Simpson, visited the Sound, he travelled in a birchbark canoe.

Sail did not become familiar on the Sound until after settlement, and slowly even then. In 1833 the Hudson's Bay Company established Fort Nisqually (Nisqually House) as a way station between Fort Vancouver on the Columbia and Fort Langley on the Fraser. The settlers came north overland, by canoe down the Columbia then up the Cowlitz to Coltz Landing, then on horses rented from the Indians to Sequalitchew Creek on the Nisqually prairie. Most of their supplies were shipped by water around the Olympic Peninsula. The land and sea parties left Fort Vancouver on May 18. The overlanders reached Nisqually in twelve days but the *Vancouver,* a 60-ton schooner built on the Columbia, didn't show up for two more weeks, the captain explaining that he had been "bedevilled and becalmed."

Calms were a curse for sailing vessels but storms a calamity, especially for ships on the coastal run. Crossing the Columbia River bar was the major problem. The Hudson's Bay Company lost the 161-ton brig, *William and Ann* there in 1829, and the 195-ton brig *Isabella* the following year. Entering and leaving the Strait of Juan de Fuca was often a problem and sometimes a disaster. The farther north the vessels went, the greater the danger, with the powerful northern tribes adding to the threat posed by storm and fog. A year after visiting the Nisqually, the *Vancouver* impaled itself on Rose Point in the Queen Charlotte Islands. The hulk was plucked clean of metal by the Haida Indians. (A later Hudson's Bay Company bark named *Vancouver* was lost on the Columbia bar in 1848, and in 1853 the third *Vancouver* was wrecked on the same spit as the first *Vancouver.*)

Of the masters of sailing vessels sent to this farthest reach, only a few — for example Aemilius Simpson, a spit-and-polish Scot who wore white gloves in dreariest Alaska, and Henry McNeill, a turbulent Yankee who challenged subordinates to bare-fist combat — won reputations for skillful navigation. More frequent were complaints about skippers' diligence in disposing of available alcohol.

The Chief Factor at Vancouver complained in a report to the H.B.C. Governor of one such officer:

> *I have several times perceived he made free with Liquor before Breakfast, often I have seen him intoxicated before dinner (the noon meal), seldom have I seen him perfectly sober after dinner.*

Governor Simpson was not unacquainted with his problem in navigation. He had sailed on a Company ship captained by a man "whose talent as a grog Drinker I understand to be without parallel and I shall be agreeably surprised if he and his ship ever reach the Port of Destination."

And, indeed, some ships did stray. A notable example was a brig that sailed from the Columbia with lumber for Chile and wound up in Tasmania, south of Australia. The captain blamed compass error.

Small wonder that the Hudson's Bay Company board of directors decided changes must be made. Meeting in Beaver House in 1834 they decided to export the Industrial Revolution to the wilderness. They ordered that a steamboat be built, at the Green, Wigrams and Green yard on the Thames, and sent to combat the powerful current of the Columbia and the fickle winds of the Pacific Northwest.

Chief Factor McLoughlin objected, complaining:

She is not required and the expense incurred is so much money thrown away .... Though she could go up the Inlets and Bay yet what she could get by doing so would not pay her increased expense and she could only be required for two or three months in the year on the coast and would be laid up for the remainder of the time.

Christened the *Beaver,* the steamboat was launched in May of 1835 and proceeded, under sail, to the Columbia, anchoring off Fort Vancouver 225 days out of Gravesend. Her 13-foot diameter paddles, which had been brought around the Horn on deck, were quickly put into place. To McLoughlin's delight, the *Beaver* proved underpowered for work on the great river of the west. He exiled her to Puget Sound, never to return to Fort Vancouver, but to serve for more than half-a-century on Puget Sound and in British Columbian and Alaskan waters as trading vessel, tender, warship and ultimately towboat. Thus came steam power to the inland waters.

Though the *Beaver* failed to arouse enthusiasm in Factor McLoughlin, she stirred first wonder, then the competitive instinct, among the Indians of the coast. John Dunn, a trader and interpreter who went on her first northward voyage, recalled that the Bella Bella Indians called her "She Who Walks on Water" and said she could do anything but speak. Dunn wrote:

But before long they told us they would make a similar vessel. We listened and shook our heads incredulously; but in a short time we found they had felled a large tree and were making the hull out of the scooped trunk. Some time afterward this rude steamer appeared. She was from twenty to thirty feet long, all in one piece, a large tree hollowed out, resembling a steamer. She was black with painted ports; decked over and her paddles painted red and Indians under cover to turn them round. The steersman was not seen. She floated triumphantly, and went at the rate of three miles an hour. They thought they had come up to the point of external structure, but the machinery baffled them.

The reaction of the whites on Puget Sound to the *Beaver* was somewhat similar. They admired the sturdy little steamboat but continued to move between the new-born communities of Olympia, Steilacoom, Port Townsend and Seattle by canoe or rowboat. Sails had appeared. John Low and David Denny, scouts for the party that eventually settled Seattle, came up from Olympia in 1851 on a sailing scow used by a merchant who bought salmon from the Duwamish Indians, and several enterprising settlers had built small sailboats, known as "plungers" from the rough way they took waves. Governor Isaac Stevens rented one of these, the *Sarah Stone,* for his first inspection tour of the Sound in 1853, an experience which may be the reason he came to the treaty grounds at Medicine Creek the following year in a dugout canoe.

In 1853, the year of Steven's arrival, a tiny sidewheel steamer called the *Fairy* arrived on the Sound aboard a brig from San Francisco. First owned by Captain Warren Gove and A.B. David, she passed into the hands of A.B. Rabbeson of Olympia, who operated her with a conspicuous lack of patronage on runs to Steilacoom and Olympia until she disappeared in a puff of steam while pulling away from the wharf at Steilacoom on October 22, 1857.

The *Major Tompkins* went into service in 1854 but the following year made a monument of herself on a British Columbian ledge. An Olympia liquor dealer, in San Francisco to refurbish his stock, bought a 60-foot iron steamer that had been built in three telescoping sections in Philadelphia and shipped around the Horn. He changed her name from *Kangaroo* to *Traveller,* re-launched her at Port Gamble, and gave her the distinction of being the first steam-powered vessel to venture up the Duwamish, the Snohomish and the Nooksack. She sank off Foul Weather Bluff in 1858. A wooden-hulled, propeller-driven steamer came up from San Francisco under her own power in 1857. She was called the *Constitution* but proved so expensive to operate that she was amended into a sailing vessel, her machinery being deployed to the cutting of lumber.

Not until the graceful *Eliza Anderson,* grande dame of early steamers, and the hulking, lumbering *Wilson G. Hunt* were dispatched from the more developed Columbia to the third world farther north in 1859 did the Age of Steam solidify on Puget Sound.

What happened then, when the steamboat served the hopeful and hopeless settlements of the inland waters not merely as hauler of freight and transporter of passengers, but as the means of communication for the isolated, as fire-department, ambulance and even, in great emergency, as banker, is the story Jim Faber tells here with affection, accuracy, and a healthy dose of salt.

The days he recalls, the era when the steamship linked neighborhoods and provided people on isolated farms with word from a larger world, is gone, killed by the internal combustion engine and electronic communication. The surfaced road has replaced the liquid highway. The Puget Sound waters that linked communities now serve as moats, serving those (like me) who cherish island life, as protection against over-development.

The Age of Steam is a memory clouded by heavier vapors. Those who never knew it may not miss it. But for those who remember, like Jim Faber, there is the dream, the faith, that some new technology will bring back the day when the most travelled highway is one that ebbs and flows and ever enriches those it carries.

Murray Morgan

Preface

My previous book, *An Irreverent Guide to Washington State* (Doubleday, 1967), was a sentimental tour of the state I have called home for almost 70 years. *Steamer's Wake* is a trip down those forgotten marine highways of the past. Here I have volunteered to serve as guide, attempting, as Ivan Doig wrote of James Gilchrist Swan, "to lead us back to where we never have been."

Friendships have provided me with some excellent mentors. My tillicum of 30 years, Murray Morgan, not only enriched the book with his Foreword, but with the eyes of a true historian warned me off many shoals (including an admonishment not to overwork the salty metaphors.) Paul Dorpat, whose books have captured this region's past with lens and text, has provided leads, and some of the volume's best photographs. Captain Bob Matson has dipped into his memories to review copy and into his personal collection to provide illustrations, including the remarkable wide angle photograph of Port Blakely.

I'm appreciative of the efforts of others who checked copy: British Columbia's marine historian and author, Bob Turner; Larry Gilmore, curator of the Columbia River Maritime Museum; Mary Kline, co-author of *Ferryboats,* the best of its kind since Harre Demoro's *Evergreen Fleet,* and other aids, including my much-used copy of Gordon Newell's encyclopediac *McCurdy's Marine History of the Pacific Northwest.*

A special thanks for the cooperation of Dr. James Warren of the Museum of History and Industry, and to Bob Monroe, who several years ago when chief photo curator of the University of Washington Library opened the drawers of the Northwest Collection and thus helped launch this book.

Many of the best photographs in *Steamer's Wake* are stamped "From the Joe Williamson Collection." That's the imprimateur of a tireless and talented marine photographer and collector. For the past 40 years his efforts have delighted us. Now his photos, from their permanent repository at the Puget Sound Maritime Historical Society library, will reward generations to come.

My first introduction to historic photos, one that led to writing *Steamer's Wake,* was during the years I was publishing a ferryboat newspaper called *Enetai* (which means "crossing" in Chinook). It was then that I discovered the rich store of history captured in this region's photo collections. Seattle and its environs must be among the few settings that have been encapsulated on film almost from their very beginnings. I also became aware of how those priceless collections are neglected—not by their dedicated custodians, but by those who set their miserly budgets. Storing and cataloging facilities are primitive. Many collections of old negatives remain boxed in storage awaiting the day when sufficient funds are provided for their development. The Joe Williamson Collection must rely on volunteers for cataloging and storing, and the Puget Sound Maritime Historical Society library is closed most of the time due to lack of funds.

Several years ago I introduced a friend, Ivar Haglund, to the U of W's Northwest Collection of photos. He was so impressed at the breadth of the collection and so dismayed over the paucity of funds allocated for their preservation, he provided a substantial donation to further the Library's work, thereby setting an example worthy of much broader adoption.

I share that admiration and concern, which is one reason why I have made arrangements for a portion of *Steamer's Wake* sales to go to the support of the University of Washington's Northwest photo collection, and to the Puget Sound Maritime Historical Society and its photo section.

Finally, a salute to the designer of *Steamer's Wake,* Bill Johnson, who has produced a book of photography that is a visual pleasure.

I hope you enjoy the writing, too.

Jim Faber
Seattle, 1985

Joe Williamson Collection

11

This book is for Ann

Prologue

The *Tacoma:* World-Class Loser

Prologue

More than a century ago there was born on Puget Sound a marine transportation system artless in concept and splendid in operation.

It included proud sternwheelers, their paddle boxes encased in carved fretwork resembling lace doilies; shallow-draft river steamers capable, it was said, of "floating in a heavy dew," and slender propeller-driven steamers so numerous and maneuverable they became affectionately known as The Mosquito Fleet.

They operated year-around with virtually no navigation instruments or accurate charts, and in some cases were manned by men who understood neither. They churned up stretches of river hardly deep enough to accommodate a spawning salmon and poked their bows into inlets strewn with logging camps, homestead farms and the huddled huts of sodden mill-towns. The steamers hauled farm wives laden with baskets of eggs and produce; beachcombers carrying sacked clams; Indians hauling vats of fish oil to grease logging camp skid roads; land promoters and lovers, preachers and con men. They bore the machinery, crops, supplies, passengers and dreams which were to carve towns and cities out of the forests and farm lands of a great inland sea.

Unregulated, financed by loans and gall, fueled by cordwood and fierce competition, they were to forge a mass transit system that for 70 years made inter-city travel on Puget Sound a delight. Delight ended in the 1920s when the automobile arrived with a more seductive lure, sending the steamers off to the ship wrecker's yard. Within a decade, nearly all had disappeared, leaving only bright memories in their wake.

Among the last to head for the boneyard was the crack steamer, *Tacoma,* a world-class steamer, born too late.

The launching on May 13, 1913 of the *Tacoma,* heralded to become the queen of Puget Sound steamers, had all the flutter of a coronation. In retrospect, it was a wake.

The maid of honor, Miss Florence Lister, daughter of Washington's governor, Ernest Lister, arrived at Seattle midmorning from Tacoma aboard the ex-Great Lakes steamer, *Indianapolis.* The 180-foot *Indianapolis* was to become the *Tacoma's* consort on the 28-mile run between Washington's two largest cities.

Surrounding Miss Lister, whose parents were Tacoma Blue Book entries, were a dozen of her best friends from school. Like her, they wore white linen ankle-length dresses and wide-brimmed hats. The other guests, numbering around a thousand, were drawn from the most select of invitation lists.

The press paid note with deference. The *Seattle Times* moved the advance story of the *Tacoma's* launching onto page one. It featured, not the new steamer, but the beauteous Miss Lister, her figurehead profile captured in a three-column pen-and-ink sketch.

Amid the sheds and ways of the Seattle Dry Dock and Construction Company shipyard on Seattle's Harbor Island, work stopped on two submarines being built for Chile as the smartly clad guests, led by the Governor and Mrs. Lister, picked their way to the bunting-draped platform. Miss Lister clutched two bunches of red roses.

Just prior to the launch, May 13, 1913.

The workers shared a strong pride in the big yard, founded by a self-educated New York machinist, Robert Moran, who had arrived in Seattle in 1874 with the legendary dime in his pocket. By the turn of the century, he had become mayor of Seattle and a rising builder of ships, including a steam-powered whaler, four compact Sound steamers, a dozen mass-produced Yukon River sternwheelers, a torpedo boat, and, in 1904, the battleship *Nebraska*.

At the *Tacoma's* launching, the yard crews were about to share another prideful accomplishment. They were not only delivering another speedy and smartly appointed steamer, but were completing the assignment in record time. The 221-foot steel-hulled vessel, with plush accommodations for more than a thousand day passengers, was built in only ten months. Now, on launch day, she was so near completion wisps of smoke were curling from her raked-back twin stacks.

The *Tacoma's* owners, the Inland Navigation Company, a subsidiary of the Puget Sound Navigation Company, foresaw a bright future for their new greyhound, now ready to join the flotilla of passenger craft that was making Puget Sound one of America's busiest marine highways. Already on the drawing boards was the *Tacoma's* consort, the *Seattle*. This running mate, her designers vowed, would best the *Tacoma*, cutting the Seattle-Tacoma run to but one hour. But the king was never to be crowned, for other engineers were on the verge of perfecting the mass-produced automobile. It would take only another 20 years for the autos to depose the *Tacoma* and send the Mosquito Fleet off to the ship wreckers. The *Tacoma* was to be the last steel-hulled steamer built on Puget Sound.

As the 3:00 p.m. launch time neared, none of these clouds were apparent to the *Tacoma's* owners, the dominant P.S.N., which with the arrival of the auto ferry was to fly its Black Ball Line flag into every nook of Puget Sound.

The company's president, Joshua Green, retrieved Miss Lister's roses, and with a courtly bow befitting his Mississippi origins, handed her the beribboned champagne bottle. The platform shuddered as workmen began loosening the launching chocks.

Now as the last of the chocks were pounded lose, the *Tacoma* inched forward.

"I christen thee *Tacoma!*" Miss Lister cried. She smashed the champagne bottle against the *Tacoma's* sharp nose. With a triumphant blast from the *Tacoma's* own whistle, echoed by a hundred more in the harbor, the black-hulled steamer slid down the tallow-greased shipway and cleaved the waters she was to ride for the next two decades. Miss Lister turned and shook hands with the jubilant Green.

Now 45, Green at 19 had signed on as purser aboard a nondescript Skagit River sternwheeler, the *Henry Bailey*. He quit within a year and together with the *Henry Bailey's* captain, mate and engineer borrowed enough capital to buy another wooden paddlewheeler, the *Fanny Lake*. Green was a prudent and thrifty man—his only recorded act of violence was when he fought a fist fight with a crewman he caught throwing a slightly burned pie overboard. Within three years, the *Fanny Lake* was paid off.

Green had awaited this moment ever since four years previously when

he clocked the newly-launched Puget Sound steamer, the *H.B. Kennedy,* over a measured mile. Other railbirds on hand included J.V. Paterson, head of the Moran yard. En route back from the trials, Green and Paterson agreed they could do better. Green pledged the $200,000 price of a new steamer, stipulating she must be capable of cruising at 20 knots. Paterson himself went to work designing the rakish lines of what was then known only as Hull No. 73.

Three weeks after the launch, Green and Paterson congratulated each other as the *Tacoma,* on her first test run, easily achieved her required 20 knots. After her shakedown, she routinely logged 21-knots on her Seattle-Tacoma run. Impressed, Lloyds of London rated her as the world's fastest single-screw vessel.

The *Tacoma's* fast pace was not without its penalties. Departing and arriving, she loped like a merry-go-round horse. Not until she hit 19 knots did her tendency to vibrate lessen.

Green likened the *Tacoma* to an English cross-Channel packet. While she never achieved the elegance of the Canadian Pacific mini-liners already starting their reign on the Seattle-Victoria-Vancouver run, she did have a touch of class, or at least enough to make her a favorite both for business and recreational trips.

The *Tacoma's* 77-minute ride was a welcome relief from the mud and dust of Seattle and Tacoma streets perennially under repair and realignment, and less disarraying than the sooty trains and rackety interurbans, both of which made the run in less time.

Young Captain Coffin
George Bayless

Aboard, lady passengers could relax in wicker chairs in the observation lounge or sip tea at a window seat in the mahogany-panelled dining room, hoping for a chance meeting with the *Tacoma's* dashing captain, Everett Coffin. The men were more likely to congregate in the oak-lined smoking room and bar.

Nantucket-born Captain Coffin was an imposing figure suited to his role as master of the Sound's fastest steamer, having graduated from the pilot houses of the *Fleetwood* and the *Flyer,* both with reputations for speed and endurance.

In Captain Coffin's saline bloodline were enough seagoing Coffins to crew a barkentine. His great-grandfather was Captain Hezekiah Coffin, under whose command, the British ship *Beaver,* was one of three vessels that acted as the stage for the Boston Tea Party. Two other relatives served with John Paul Jones. Another, Captain Isaiah Folger, was skipper of the tiny schooner *Exact,* which carried Seattle's first settlers. Sir Isaac Coffin was governor of Massachusetts and an honorary admiral.

Captain Coffin was something of an adventurer himself. He served as a deckhand on a New Bedford whaler and later earned his fare as a ship salvager. During the Klondike gold rush, he made it all the way to the Yukon, returning only with the wages he picked up from temporary duty as a river-boat skipper.

Fresh from the wheelhouse of the *Flyer* and buoyed by a munificent pay scale of $125 a month, he found the slender 209-foot *Tacoma* not only fast but extremely responsive.

"She could be depended on to the second… like landing a rowboat," he said. "Her reversing power was wonderful and from full ahead to a dead stop required 17 seconds."

Captain Coffin also knew how to avoid a collision. While skipper of the *Flyer,* he once escorted the mate's wife to her husband's cabin. As they entered, he noted a pair of lady's gloves lying on the errant mate's bunk.

"Ah, my wife's gloves," Captain Coffin said, picking them up. "She has been looking everywhere for them."

By 1928, the *Tacoma* had logged more than 1,200,000 miles, carrying more than six million passengers without a single fatality. That year, a ribbon was cut, opening the Seattle-Tacoma highway, 24 miles long, cutting ten miles off the valley road, and soon to be among the nation's first to offer the safety of four-lane traffic. The mass desertions that followed soon left the steamers sinking in a sea of red ink.

On December 15, 1930, just off Three Tree Point, the *Tacoma's* running mate, the *Indianapolis,* blew three long blasts as the steamers passed for the last time. Among those aboard was marine photographer Joe Williamson. He recalled:

We passed the Indianapolis *off Three Tree Point. It was the* Indianapolis' *last run also. There was a full moon and as the ships passed, they exchanged three blasts of their whistles. Everybody on the* Tacoma *was standing around the stacks on the upper deck singing* Auld Lang Syne. *It was quite a moment.*

The *Tacoma* then followed a course leading to the boneyard. Her older compatriots like the Great Lakes-built *Chippewa* were remodelled into auto ferries — disdainfully termed "steam-powered garages" by Captain Coffin. But the racehorse lines of the *Tacoma* precluded any such reassignment. For a time she operated on the Seattle-Bremerton run. There, accompanying the *Kalakala* on her maiden run, Captain Coffin suffered the indignity of being instructed not under any condition to pass the highly-touted ferry, billed as "the world's first streamlined ferry." This was a bit of Black Ball Line hyperbole that concealed the fact that despite the *Kalakala's* teardrop configuration she could do but 15 teeth-jarring knots. On the return trip, running unaccompanied, Captain Coffin opened the *Tacoma* up and set an all-time record.

Then, like an aging trouper the *Tacoma* slipped into the role of a summertime entertainer on excursions to the San Juan Islands and Victoria, B.C. Finally, joined by the *Indianapolis* and other rejects, she came to rest in the wrecking yard. There, even her faultless engines were put to the burner's torch and carved into scrap metal.

In 1950, at age 85, Captain Coffin died in the house he had bought for retirement, one located within earshot of the Alki Point lighthouse he had sighted daily for almost two decades from the *Tacoma's* pilot house. A piece of that wheel house railing graced his retirement snug. From this vantage point, Captain Coffin could watch Puget Sound ship traffic and possibly sight the wakes of steamers past.

When the interurbans made their debut, the Businessman's Express was inaugurated to speed commuters between Seattle and Tacoma. They proved much faster than the steamers, but failed to dim their popularity.
Frank Maslan

It's Finished with Engines for the Tacoma *and four other steamers awaiting their last voyage to the wrecking yard. Moored alongside the* Tacoma *is the* Kulshan, *built at the Moran yard just two years prior to the* Tacoma's *launching. The 160-foot* Kulshan *was one of the few vessels ever constructed with Puget Sound steel, rolled at the short-lived Irondale mill near Port Townsend. Others shown are the* City of Bremerton, *the* Indianapolis *and, at the far end, the circa 1907 sidewheel ferry,* West Seattle. *Above, the skeleton of the* Tacoma, *picked bare, awaits the final burner's torch.*

Williamson Collection

Nearing the end, the Tacoma *was reduced to the role of a day-excursion steamer, plying the various Puget Sound ports. Here she docks at historic Coupeville on Whidbey Island, just north of Seattle.*
University of Washington

Rivers of Gold and a Sound of Steamers

The Yosemite *leaving San Francisco*
Bancroft Library, University of California

The Argonaut Saga Begins on the Sacramento

The role of the railroad in the opening of the West is part of America's folklore. Spanning a continent, the rails created fortunes, built cities—and ruined a few—planted the prairies and denuded the forests. Their movement westward led to the immigration of tracklayers from China and sod busters from Scandinavia. They became celebrated in song, poem and fable.

Along the empty, roadless coasts of California, Oregon, Washington, British Columbia and Alaska, the steamboat was to play a similar role. Unlike the railroads, the steamers were drawn west not by the land tillers, speculators and developers, but by an hysterical and often witless passion that was to create another gaudy chapter of Americana: the series of gold rushes that sent almost a hundred thousand adventurers into incredibly hostile frontiers.

The frantic search lasted from the big strike at Sutter's Mill on the Sacramento River in 1849 to the bonanza uncovered on the beaches of Nome in the early 1900s. Without the lure of gold, the steamers never would have come west as trailbreakers, homesteaders and engineers of industry and commerce. The steamer's wake became a highway to development.

The whole country from San Francisco to Los Angeles and from the seashore to the base of the Sierra Nevadas resounds to the sordid cry of Gold! GOLD! GOLD!! The fields are left unplanted, the houses half built. Everything is neglected but the manufacture of shovels and pickaxes and the means of transportation to Captain Sutter's valley.

A few days after the editor of the *California Star* set those words in type, he shut up shop for good and headed for the gold fields. He had plenty of company. Discovery of pay dirt on the Sacramento River 130 miles upstream from San Francisco was to send 40,000 adventurers racing west, some by overland routes, others traversing the Isthmus of Panama to gateway ports on the Pacific, or enduring the agonies of sailing around the Horn.

First to make this foul weather passage through the Strait of Magellan was the handsome new sidewheeler, *Senator.* Her elapsed time from Boston to San Francisco—eight months—was disappointing to her investor. But once on the Sacramento the *Senator* prospered indecently. She completed her upriver run in but nine hours, a considerable improvement over her predecessor, the tiny (37-foot) *Sitka,* an absurdly underpowered steamer that was beaten by an ox team in her first downriver race to San Francisco in 1848. Running unopposed during her first year, the *Senator* piled up a million-dollar profit.

Pay dirt discoveries continued to create new gold camps along other northern California rivers including the Yuba, Feather, American, and San Joaquin, where the steamer *John A. Sutter* cleared more than $300,000 in profits in a few months. In 1850, the rivers yielded $41 million in gold and double that amount the following year. But for most of the 40,000 gold

The Suzie *leaving Dawson for Cape Nome*
University of Washington Library

The Tenino *in the upper Columbia rapids*
Oregon Historical Society

seekers, the glitter of the California gold rush had dimmed. It was time to move on. There was ample fuel for the migration. For the Sacramento gold stampede had made the term, "strike it rich," a siren's call, one translated into nearly every language. A year after the discovery at Sutter's Mill, a new gold fever began sweeping up the West Coast of North America to as far north as the beaches of Nome.

Thousands of prospectors, each possessed of his own version of geology, fanned out in all directions from the Sacramento with a gold pan and a phial of mercury to examine the riffles of every promising river and creek within earshot of a rumor. The flood was swelled by a stream of greenhorns who headed west to trade the plow or the bookkeeper's stool for the unlikely prospect of discovering pay dirt. In the years ahead they were to uncover some of the world's richest gold fields, more golden by far than Sutter's strike on the Sacramento. (One of these, the Klondike's Bonanza, which became a watchword among prospectors, was the discovery of George Washington Carmack, an inheritor of gold fever from his father, who had died broke on the Sacramento.)

The exodus from the Sacramento has been described by Pierre Berton in his classic, *Klondike:*

> *… a kind of capillary action that saw men with pans and picks slowly inching their way along the mountain backbone of North America from the Sierras to the Stikines, up…through the wrinkled hide of British Columbia, through the somber canyons of the Fraser and the rolling grasslands of the Cariboo to the snow fields of the Cassiars at the threshold of the sub-Arctic.*

In less than 50 years, the epic search was to uncover major discoveries that shaped the destiny of the Pacific Northwest, British Columbia and Alaska. Most bountiful were a series of strikes on the Fraser River in the Cariboo District of British Columbia and shortly after, a rash of rich mineral discoveries in regions of Idaho and Montana reached via the Columbia River.

The Wild Fraser Yields Millions in Gold

The stampede to British Columbia's Fraser River was a re-run of previous sagas.

Wrote a correspondent for the *Daily Alta Californian* in 1858:

> *We are crazy with gold fever! Everybody that can get away is off to Frazer's (sic) river after gold!*

Coming close on the heels of the celebrated California stampede in 1849 and soon to be overshadowed by the Civil War, the Fraser River gold rush was almost ignored by the world press. Yet it produced more wealth than the Sacramento (some put the total yield as high as $100 million) and drew more gold seekers. One Canadian historian, Clinton Snowden, estimated the prospectors and camp followers drawn to the Fraser gold fields numbered between 75,000 and 100,000. Almost 30,000 of these sailed north from San

Francisco to entrepots like Victoria and New Westminster, and a smattering of improvised anchorages scattered from Bellingham Bay to the San Juan Islands.

By mid-summer, almost 10,000 were camped along the shores of Bellingham Bay. Lots in the pop-up tent town of Whatcom (now Bellingham) were selling for $600. New arrivals included Oregon Territory's best known wagon team pioneer, Ezra Meeker, who did less well in a rowboat, peddling milk to arriving sailing ships. Other noteworthies included a Frenchman, who landed with carriage horse and a poodle and demanded to be shown the road to the Fraser River. The entire crew, except for the captain, of the U.S. Revenue Cutter *Jeff Davis*, which had arrived in July just to keep an eye on things, promptly deserted to seek revenues more rewarding than government pay.

Whatcom's $600 lots were a bargain compared to those at Victoria, rapidly being transformed from a quiet settlement of British emigres into a boisterous capital of prospectors and ruffians. There, lots which had attracted no buyers at $50 were selling for as high as $3,000.

(It was not until the gold fever subsided that Victoria regained its colonial cool. This was signalled by the arrival in 1868 of the new Governor General, Frederick Seymour. Victorians noted with approval that among his first actions was to order a chain gang working on badly needed street repairs to halt their work and give top priority to laying out a croquet course at the official residence.)

Riverboat captains soon discovered that in contrast to the Sacramento, which flowed broad and serene through lush meadows and tule marshes, the Fraser was a killer cataract, surging through black canyons clogged with snags, submerged rocks and shoals. Charts were non-existent, guides were few.

First to complete the 400-mile ascent of the Fraser to Fort Hope, the portal to pay dirt, was the Brooklyn-built sidewheeler, *Surprise,* in 1856. She had been brought around the Horn to the Sacramento in a four-month journey so stormy her skipper, Captain Edgar Wakeman, solemnly maintained he had sat for two weeks on the smokestack with his feet touching the swells.

The B.C. Express *in the Upper Canyon of the Fraser*
B.C. Archives

The arrival of the *Surprise* at San Francisco failed to startle that urbane community. But her later debut on the Fraser inspired this fervid accolade from the British Columbia correspondent of the *Alta Californian*:

She first woke the echoes of the grand mountain gorges in the wild region of Fort Hope with the shrill scream of the steam whistle and astounded the natives with her wonderous powers in breasting successfully the now world-renowned Fraser River.

Actually the upriver trip of the *Surprise* party had been uneventful. The sidewheeler had left Bellingham Bay on a May morning, reaching the Fraser at 1:30 that afternoon and after running upriver to a point 16 miles above Fort Langley, anchored for the night. The next morning, she picked up a barefoot, blanket-clad Indian guide, Speel-est, whose knowledge of the tricky upper river was so impressive he was rewarded with a fee of eight twenty dollar gold

A trio of sternwheelers that left their wake on the Fraser and Columbia rivers. At top, the 162-foot Minto *is shown in around 1900 on one of British Columbia's Arrow Lakes. She was built for the short-lived Stikine River "all-Canadian route" to Dawson City during the Klondike Gold Rush. A companion vessel, the* Moyie, *has been preserved as a museum at Kaslo, B.C. At top right the* Western Slope *lets off steam as she unloads along the Fraser shortly after being launched in 1897. Note the sail rigged on the foremast. She, too, was built for Stikine River service, and was owned by Capt. William Moore, whose sternwheelers were among the first to serve every gold field from the Klondike to the Queen Charlotte Islands. Above is the* Lot Whitcomb, *shortly after she was launched on the Columbia in 1851, becoming the first substantial stern-wheeler on the river. She carried the twin stack arrangement familiar on the Mississippi, and was capable of 12 knots.*

University of Washington Library

British Columbia Archives

Oregon Historical Society

pieces at its conclusion. Speel-est promptly bought a suit, a white hat and a pair of California boots, and resumed his navigational duties as Captain John, thus joining the ranks of colorful Fraser River pilots who were to include Volcanic Brown, Rattlesnake Pete, Stuttering Bailey, Blue Dick Berry, Wake Up Jake, Twelve-Foot Davis and Gassy Jack, the latter notable leaving his name to grace Vancouver's contemporary gold mine, the old town shopping district that bears his nickname: Gastown.

Like her counterparts on gold streams from the Sacramento to the Yukon, the *Surprise* proved a bonanza. During her first year she made 15 round trips, carrying 500 passengers at $25 a head (one-way, with meals and berth extra) and charging up to $45 a ton for freight. At season's end in 1858 she was sold to interests in China, being replaced by the *Wilson G. Hunt.*

Gold strikes in the wild regions served by the Fraser and its satellite rivers continued throughout the Sixties, spreading into the Thompson, Okanogan, Peace, Stikine and other streams and creating steamer routes on a network of Canadian lakes. The waterways were ideal proving grounds for the sternwheel steamers that replaced the less maneuverable sidewheelers. By the turn of the century, almost 300 were churning the lakes, rivers and coastal waters of British Columbia and the Yukon Territory.

The whistles were not stilled until the 1950s, when rail and road finally ended the steamers' dominance; the Canadian Pacific's *Minto* operating on the Arrow Lakes until 1954, and the *Moyie* on Kootenay Lake until 1957. (The *Moyie* has been preserved by the Kootenay Lake Historical Society and is on display at Kalso, B.C.)

The Enterprise *on the Columbia above Wenatchee*

The Columbia Hailed: A New El Dorado

The big winner on the Columbia River was a Mississippi riverboatman, Captain John C. Ainsworth. Christmas Day 1850 found him sharing a platform with the Oregon Territorial Governor, the mayor of Oregon City, a brass band and numerous celebrants. All were on hand at the Willamette River hamlet of Milwaukie to launch the *Lot Whitcomb,* the first big paddlewheel steamer on the Columbia, and to toast her skipper. Up to that bunting-wrapped day, Captain Ainsworth had been a loser.

As a youth he successfully piloted two flatboats from Louisville to Memphis, but lost all the profits when slickers paid him off in worthless paper money. Backed by an uncle, he then bought a small steamboat, and worked his way up the ship's ladder from purser to captain. In the pilot house, he took time to instruct a young pilot candidate named Sam Clemens, giving him a

Captain J. C. Ainsworth
Oregon Historical Society

barely passing grade. After five years, Ainsworth was broke again. Like many failures of that day, he drifted west to the California gold fields. In Sacramento he met a wealthy businessman who was building a riverboat on the Columbia named the *Lot Whitcomb.* He was looking for an experienced riverboat skipper. Captain Ainsworth signed on.

The *Lot Whitcomb* prospered no more than the hapless captain's previous commands. But the knowledge Captain Ainsworth accumulated of Columbia's shoals — including those fashioned by its pioneer bankers — was to prove an invaluable asset. When the *Lot Whitcomb* was sold to San Francisco interests a few months after her brassy launching, Captain Ainsworth bought part ownership of a 110-foot paddlewheeler, the *Umatilla.* Then he headed for the Fraser's wild canyons. The *Umatilla* already had proved her toughness. Shortly after being launched on the Middle Columbia, she was swept over the rapids at the Cascades, surviving intact with the loss of only one life.

After learning how to separate the Fraser gold from the Fraser gold seeker, Captain Ainsworth returned to the Columbia. There, that talent was to make him rich. Signing on a few fellow steamboatmen, he began assembling a collection of a dozen paddlewheel steamers and laid plans to gain control of the vital portages at the Cascades and The Dalles, two barriers that divided the river into Upper, Middle and Lower Columbia. In 1860, he incorporated the Oregon Steam Navigation Company which was to become one of America's most successful steamboat monopolies, controlling river shipping all the way from Astoria on the Pacific to Lewiston on the Clearwater River.

Gold was discovered along Idaho's Clearwater River in 1860, and a few years later on the Salmon, a branch of the Snake. Nearby, the Boise Basin was to yield even richer strikes, producing in the next 20 years $250 million in gold. The newly-hatched Oregon Steam Navigation Company moved quickly to establish steamer routes on the Columbia, Snake, and other rivers tapping these regions. In 1861, it laid out the gateway town of Lewiston at the mouth of the Clearwater. The rivers soon became roads to riches — at least for the O.S.N. monopoly.

During its first year, investors doubled their money. Aboard steamers like the *Okanogan, Spray, Tenino, Nez Perce Chief, Kiyus, Owyhee, Webfoot* and the *Yakima,* pursers ended downriver rus with up to $4,000 in fares, plus additional revenues from the dining room, staterooms and bar.

Having corralled the market, the O.S.N. moved to fence off any competition. Usually, all it took was a ruinous rate war, such as that unleashed against an early upstart challenger, The Merchant's Line. The Oregon Steam Navigation Company met this intrusion into its domain by dropping freight rates from $15 a ton to $5 a ton. When The Merchant's Line surrendered, O.S.N. pushed rates up to $25 a ton.

Where competition persisted, the O.S.N. simply bought off the owners or resorted to less orthodox tactics. Some read like the script of a grade-B Western. For example, when angry Idaho mine owners and businessmen started their own overland freight lines to avoid the monopoly's exhorbitant river rates, the O.S.N. stirred up renegade whites and hostile Indian tribes to

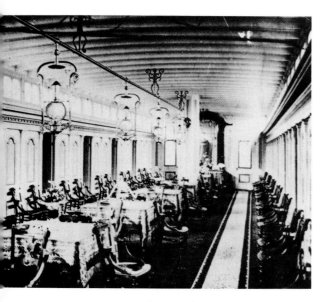

Dining saloon, Wide West
Oregon Historical Society

harass the wagoners. (The O.S.N. also profited by hauling men and supplies to Columbia River Army posts established to quell other hostile tribesmen.) Despite these lapses, the O.S.N. under Captain Ainsworth had its virtues. No man without funds was denied passage. Hard up settlers were granted deferred payments on their freight bills, often unpayable because of grain crop failures. He was a fair man on payday, insisting on "a fair wage" for all hands, not just the captains, five of whom on one occasion were presented gold watches.

(When Henry Villard's Northern Pacific bought out the O.S.N. in 1879, the line's Midwestern officials showed less enlightenment. They promptly wired instructions to cut the pay of masters and engineers. The result was a strike—one of the first among steamboatmen—that tied up every steamer of their fleet on the Columbia and Puget Sound. The Northern Pacific threatened to replace the striking officers with men recruited on the East Coast, but prudently capitulated when Portland agents reminded them this would require years of expensive training.)

Some of Captain Ainsworth's sympathetic concerns for his crews may have stemmed from his memories of steamboating on the Mississippi. There, deckhands were on duty 24 hours a day, seven days a week, slept on cotton bales and ate on deck from scraps. Because of the steamers' penchant for explosions, Irish immigrant hands were assigned sleeping space closer to the boilers than slaves—who cost more.

Whatever his motives, Captain Ainsworth's probity did not go unnoticed. One editorialist of the time, Thomas Merry of *The Dalles Inland Empire* wrote of him:

> *Captain Ainsworth has been at all times a gentleman public servant, a faithful custodian of the interests of his fellow stockholders, and the most equitable and merciful of employers.*

If the ex-Mississippi skipper was, as another biographer claimed, "a firm friend of the laboring classes," he was even kinder to his fellow stockholders.

By the time Ainsworth and company had sold out in 1879 to the Northern Pacific, the Oregon Steam Navigation Company had paid out dividends of nearly $5 million in 19 years on a capitalization of $2 million. O.S.N. stock had become the Xerox of its day. When Captain Ainsworth brought R.R. Thompson, owner of the steamboat *Colonel Wright,* into the fold, he gave him an $18,000 bonus to sweeten the deal.

The Oneonta *on the Columbia*
Oregon Historical Society

In his journal Captain Ainsworth wryly noted:

Here Mr. Thompson made a great mistake in not taking this $18,000 in stock instead of money. It made a difference against him of nearly half a million dollars.

Unlike many of his flinty counterparts, Captain Aisnworth revelled in his calling, one that had proven so unrewarding during his youth on the Mississippi. Once in 1858, after piloting the first steamer to probe British Columbia's Thompson River, he exulted:

The sensation to me, of entering a water that had never before been divided by the prow of a steamer, was beyond description.

As the O.S.N. prospered, he indulged himself in realizing a dream: to bring to the Columbia a steamboat with the grace and luxury appointments of those plying the Mississippi. His first attempt came in 1863 when he launched the *Oneonta,* built in 1863 at the Cascades for the run to The Dalles. She was a proud beauty, 182 feet long with two tall side-by-side stacks forward of the pilot house, a Mississippi configuration rare in the West. A housed-in freight deck and a cabin deck extended stem to stern over the guards. Equipped with outside steam escape pipes, she could be heard coming down the gorge well in advance of her arrival. But she proved uneconomical and in 1870, Captain Ainsworth took the helm and steered her through the Cascade rapids and downstream to Portland. There in 1877 she died ignobly, as a barge.

The O.S.N. steamboat that followed the *Oneonta* was a different story, one that Captain Ainsworth's pupil, Sam Clemens, would have appreciated. She was the *New World,* the pride of her New York owner, William Brown, who built her in 1850 for the posh trade on Long Island Sound. Brown equipped her with red plush upholstery, marble-topped tables, brass chandeliers, and a tier of 35 staterooms opening onto a gallery overlooking the grand saloon. He also papered the 225-foot walking beam sidewheeler with debts. To frustrate plans for her departure to the California gold fields, creditors filed attachment papers. A sheriff and three deputies were put aboard at dockside in New York. Here the *New World's* skipper, Captain Edgar Wakeman, took over the con.

After a period of comfortable conversation following dinner in the *New World's* saloon, Captain Wakeman excused himself, explaining to the well-lubricated lawmen that he was about to turn the engines over—just to keep them in proper shape, you understand. The sheriff and the men didn't understand. Too late, they realized the *New World* had surreptitiously cast off and was actually underway. After moving down the channel, Captain Wakeman gave the lawmen a choice: continue on to California or debark in a dinghy. The lawmen took the easy way out, rowing ashore.

The errant paddlewheeler made it around the Horn, surviving 18 of her crew dying of yellow fever. At Rio de Janeiro she eluded a British frigate sent out to check her non-existent papers; dodged another posse at Panama, and arrived in San Francisco on July 11, 1850,laden with 200 prospectors who had

The T. J. Potter *underway*
Oregon Historical Society

31

boarded at Panama. On the Sacramento, far from her home waters on Long Island Sound, the *New World* made a fortune, but whether or not her debts were ever paid off, history does not record.

The *New World* joined the O.S.N. fleet in 1864, Captain Ainsworth purchasing her for $75,000 from the California Steam Navigation Company, a cartel that provided him with a few lessons on how to control a river. At first, she fared well; on one trip hauling out a ton of gold from the Cascades, thus presaging the Klondike gold ship *Portland,* but without worldwide press fanfare that greeted that 1898 accomplishment. When business waned on the Columbia, the *New World* plied Puget Sound before once again returning to California where she served out her days as a reformed old con artist, paddling off to the wreckers in 1879.

In 1877, Captain Ainsworth finally built his dream boat. She was the *Wide West,* 236 feet from stem to sternwheel. Among her amenities were a central saloon decorous "in a delicate tint of lilac," and a ladies' cabin in pale yellow. Brass bedsteads graced cabins equipped with running water jets in toilets. The latter innovation, as one early advertisement soothed, assured occupants that "no offensive effluvia taints these sumptuous cabins."

For 10 years the *Wide West* carried passengers between Portland and the Cascades where, after an overland transfer around this barrier, another O.S.N. steamer would complete the upriver passage to The Dalles. She wore herself out quickly. In 1888, her upperworks were removed and installed on Captain Ainsworth's new pride and joy, the *T. J. Potter.* Here the accomodations were built on an even more lavish scale, including a staircase worthy of Tara, a panelled dining room, and the Northwest's largest plate glass mirror. Even the exterior was elegant, the fretwork over paddle boxes resembling a fan of lacework.

The speedy *T. J. Potter* quickly conquered the Columbia and Captain Ainsworth began casting a covetous eye on Puget Sound. In 1890 he ordered her north. There it was soon established that the broad-beamed *T. J. Potter* was without a doubt a fine riverboat. Wallowing miserably in the winds and the seas of the broad reaches of Puget Sound, she soon retreated to the Columbia. With her departure went the O.S.N.'s dreams of dominating Puget Sound.

Building a Steamer Fleet of Wood: The Puget Sound Story

If the threads of steamer routes along the Columbia were spun of gold and grain, those of Puget Sound were fashioned of timber.

In 1869, only 20 years after Captain Ainsworth arrived on the empty Columbia, more than a thousand men were working in almost a score of Puget Sound sawmills. Sawmills cut 170 million board feet of lumber (a modern two bedroom house requires 10,000 board feet). That same year, arrivals included 113 ships, 491 barks, 45 brigs, and 87 schooners, bound for California, New England, the Sandwich Islands, Australia, China and the

Pictured in 1904 at the helm of the wheat carrier, Mountain Gem, *Capt. William Gray strikes a relaxed pose. The* Mountain Gem *was built for the Open River Navigation Co., formed to compete against railroad domination of Columbia River grain movements.*
Oregon Historical Society

Far East, the East Indies, South America, Europe and Russia.

Wrote Samuel Wilkerson in an 1869 reconnaissance study he conducted for the Northern Pacific railroad: "The world has never seen such a trade in lumber outwards by sea."

Cut off from the outside world by land, the Sound's new milltowns welcomed the steamers that had been drawn north. Those that survived boiler explosions, groundings, collisions and piratical competition found that business was good. The isolated sawmills and their company-owned towns required everything from hay for oxen and horses to milk for millhand children, and it all moved by steamer. More income came from log tows or from helping dock lumber vessels, most of which furled sails shortly after entering Puget Sound from the Strait of Juan de Fuca.

Joining the new arrivals from the Sacramento and Columbia were the first sternwheel steamers built along the Sound, some of them simply sheds riding on scow-like hulls. Designed with no keels, their ability to navigate in shallow waters made seedy ports of call out of such inland hamlets as Snohomish, Mount Vernon, Monroe, Sultan, Kent, Montesano, and Shelton, with a scattering of even smaller whistle stops: Bell's Camp, Birdsview, McKay's Landing, Fir, Skagit City, Six Mile Point and hundreds of other riverside communities from the Nooksak to the Chehalis, all now gone and forgotten.

Forerunners of the larger deep-raft paddlewheel steamers that were to bring a touch of class to Puget Sound, the early riverboats were simply ill-groomed work horses. Lower decks provided crowded space for cargo, stacks of cordwood, boilers, engines, a galley and crew quarters. Crews, numbering no more than a dozen, worked 12 hours or more a watch, seven days a week. An early-day deckhand jibe went like this:

"Where do we sleep?"

"I dunno. I only come aboard three days ago."

For overnight journeys passengers rode in drafty, flea-ridden cabins on the sternwheeler's upper deck. This, the so-called Texas deck, was crowned by a kingpost to which were anchored cables and chains providing fore and aft support in lieu of a keel. Overlooking it all was the high-perched pilot house. Here the captain guided his boat through constantly shifting river channels, dodging sandbars, snags, forest fires and rival steamers. Picking up and discharging passengers and freight was accomplished by nosing into a bank. Installed on the housing at water level, sliding barn doors provided mid-river boardings.

Further upstream, sternwheelers were "lined" over riffles, some so shallow even Indians portaged their canoes. In this process, crewmen would wade upstream carrying a shoulder roll of cable. Sometimes as much as a thousand feet was played out before the cable was looped around a tree or stump. Aboard the sternwheeler, the mate would begin winding the cable onto the steam-powered capstan, pulling the boat over the shallows. This type of bootstrap advancement was not without its perils. Ripped bottoms and explosions of overloaded boilers were commonplace. A spectacular example of the latter mishap occurred when the sternwheeler *Bob Irving* was straining her way over Ball Riffles on the Skagit in 1888. The boiler blew under the strain, killing the engineer and the captain, who was decapitated by the wheel he was manning. But the risks were worth it as the riverboats became the sole outlet for passengers and freight.

One of the first to measure the steamer's future was a young Southerner, Joshua Green. Through the influence of a prominent Seattle merchant, Bailey Gatzert, he got his first steamer job, that of purser aboard a scruffy Skagit River sternwheeler, the *Henry Bailey*. He was 19. As he kept entries, he noted the *Henry Bailey's* comfortable profits — as much as a hundred dollars on a short haul. The chunky riverboat served the Skagit River farmers and loggers, carrying freight that included everything from boom chains to whiskey. On downriver trips she hauled out shingles and crops.

The following year, the *Henry Bailey's* captain, mate and engineer joined with Green and, quitting the *Henry Bailey*, borrowed $5,000 and bought the *Fanny Lake,* a shallow-draft steamer ideal for penetrating river sloughs to load hay and oats for logging camps. Green was a fair but frugal owner. Within three years, the *Fanny Lake* was paid off. Joshua Green was launched on a career that was to make him one of Puget Sound's most powerful steamboat operators.

(Later, having become a millionaire and perhaps foreseeing the approach of the automobile juggernaut, he sold out and bought a bank. He went duck hunting on his 100th birthday and lived until he was 105.)

To accomplish this, Green forsook the riverways and began knitting together the settlements of Puget Sound. For along 2,100 miles of shoreline the Sound's first extractive industries — coal mines, logging camps, lumber and shingle mills, canneries and fish packing houses — were creating communities that relied on the steamers for just about all the necessities and luxuries of life.

By the turn of the century, emergence of propeller-powered steamers announced the arrival of a new day in waterborne transportation on Puget Sound. As they began replacing the paddlewheelers, the propellers, as they were named, took over the role of providing the Sound's farmers with farm-to-market roads. Laden with sacked grain, apples, berries, eggs, poultry and meats, the steamers worked around the clock stoking the appetites of the growing urban belt along the Sound's eastern shores.

It was to be a gaudy period of flashy boats commanded by talented crews ready to race at the wave of a cap. But it also was to be a period when the captain-owners found themselves perilously rocked by combative competitors who thought big. No more of this pick-your-own-route, set-your-own-fares nonsense. The new breed of steamboat operators was up-from-the-ranks men like Joshua Green and Warren Gazzam—and a rich landlubber named Charles Peabody. They went ashore for capital; designed steamers with wooden hulls that slipped through the Sound waters like a knife. They brought others around the Horn, big two-stacker steamers with white hulls of steel and saloons of glitter. Then, raising their Puget Sound Navigation Company and White Collar Line burgees, they began moving their boats around the Sound as if it were a Monopoly game board, which it soon was to become.

The old sternwheeler Multnomah *nears her Seattle dock, apparently being chased out of the picture by the new steamer* Flyer
Washington State Historical Society

The Busy *Beaver*

The opening of the West by steamer created boisterous rivalries that sent whistles echoing up the Columbia and later into the farthest inlets of Puget Sound.

Old Glory placed third in this winning of the West. The first steamer into the Pacific was the tiny Spanish paddlewheeler *Telicia,* plying between Mexico and Central America in 1825.

The *Telicia* played no significant role in history, sinking when her captain committed suicide by torching the powder locker. But the first steamer to enter the North Pacific, the *Beaver,* left a footnote in her wake by keeping Great Britain's flag of empire supreme in waters coveted by Uncle Sam's traders.

The tiny (100-foot) *Beaver* (shown at upper left off Victoria in 1870) with a top speed of seven knots arrived in British Columbia waters in 1835, 13 months after being launched on the Thames. Her construction and assignment had been urged by George Simpson, Governor in Chief of the Hudson's Bay Company. He sagely predicted the entry of an armed British steamer in the North Pacific would "afford us incalculable advantages over the Americans...and bring the contest to a close very soon by making us master of the trade."

Simpson was right. The *Beaver* soon dampened the fur-trading ambitions of the Yankee traders by stretching a trade route between Hudson's Bay Company's Fort Nisqually in southern Puget Sound to the Russian-American capital at Sitka where she showed the flag to the Russian governor.

Entries in her log are not lacking in drama, including a mutiny involving four crewmen, all of whom were imprisoned, and a bit part in the comic opera "Pig War of 1859," carrying a contingent of British troops to San Juan Island. She had one brush with the Indians, but for the most part they welcomed the *Beaver.* For in addition to the usual trading stock, she also dispensed jugs of rum, a practice officially deplored but otherwise actively pursued. Tobacco also was a trading staple and not only for furs such as beaver, fisher, mink, and otter. A *Beaver* ledger of 1838 notes

the price paid for an Indian slave girl obtained for use as a servant: 26 heads of tobacco, 25 blankets, one trade gun, six and one-half gallons of rum, two tin tea kettles and four yards of cloth. The fate of the Indian maid remains unchronicled and awaits the pen of a dramatist.

Clunky in appearance, underpowered and energy inefficient, the *Beaver* was not to be denied her moment of triumph. In 1860, she responded to the challenge of the *Julia,* recently completed at Port Gamble as the first steamer built on Puget Sound. The *Beaver* plodded ahead of the *Julia* during the slow-paced Gulf of Georgia crossing, arriving in triumph 35 minutes ahead of the new steamer. Following the race, the *Julia* retreated to California waters.

As a commercial venture, the *Beaver* was something less than a success. Dr. John McLoughlin, the towering Hudson's Bay Company factor at Fort Vancouver, whose idea of a boat's propulsion unit was a dozen Indian and French-Canadian paddlers, complained that even during one of her best years the *Beaver* drained 960 pounds out of the HBC treasury.

Much of the loss could be attributed to the *Beaver's* engines, for in order to travel a day, the *Beaver* was forced to halt for two while a crew of Indians and Kanakas cut wood. The two side-lever engines, each generating 35 horsepower and built by Boulton Watt, (who fashioned those engines powering America's first successful steamboat, the *Cleremont*) proved to be impressively durable. In addition, her hull fittings of oak, elm, teak and teredo-resistant greenheart were equally sound, as evidenced when during an 1867 refit a 10-pound rock was found imbedded in her bottom.

The *Beaver* underwent several such refits, which may account for the mixed reviews she received from travellers.

Later, after she passed into government hands and no longer was dependent on the thrifty McLoughlin for funds, the refurbished *Beaver* was likened to a "gentlemen's yacht, every knob or gun polished, the deck likewise."

All other factors considered, the *Beaver* proved a wise investment. During her 53 years, she drove out the fur trading competition, established far-flung trading posts, including one that was to become British Columbia's capital, Victoria; pioneered the opening of gold and coal fields; served as an improvised courtroom; surveyed the hazardous inlets of the Inside Passage, and in the words of Canadian maritime historian Derek Pethick, earned her rank as "the most important ship in the history of Canada's west coast." She survived a fire and grounding and was still going strong, towing log booms up to 800 feet long when on July 26, 1888, a careless crew piled her on the rocks at Prospect Point (above) near today's Lions Gate Bridge at Vancouver, B.C.

There she lay for *another* (inset above) four years until another unlucky steamer, the *Yosemite* cleaved a wave ashore that sent the *Beaver* down to her final resting place, 20 fathoms deep.

University of Washington
British Columbia Archives
Bancroft Library, University of California

Multnomah

One of the first steamers to share the river with the *Lot Whitcomb* was the *Multnomah.* This daguerreotype shows her moored in 1857 at what is now the foot of Alder Street in Portland.

The 108-foot paddlewheeler, equipped with an ungainly spark arrestor, was shipped from the East Coast to the Columbia in sections.

Oregon Historical Society

Lot Whitcomb

Lot Whitcomb is coming!
Her banners are flying -
She walks up the rapids with speed;
She plows through the water,
Her steps never falter -
Oh! That's independence indeed.

The *Lot Whitcomb* (right) had few admirers as lyrical as Elizabeth Markham, who composed the above tribute, but they were no less enthusiastic. All were on hand for her launching on Christmas Day 1850: the territorial governor, the mayor of Oregon City, a brass band from Fort Vancouver, and numerous celebrants, including one killed when a cannon blew up.

The most effusive praise came from the *Milwaukee Western Star,* a not unlikely bit of coverage since the publisher of the pioneer newspaper was the steamer's owner and eponym, Lot Whitcomb. A cautious contemporary described the vessel as "simple and unostentatious, but tasteful and elegant."

For wagon-weary river settlers, she was a welcome sight. Bereft of the usual carpenter-gothic trim, the 160-foot sidewheeler was powered with two New Orleans-built steam engines capable of pushing her along at a 12-mile-an-hour clip. Unlike her successors, she was designed with twin stacks set forward of a mid-section pilot house, with two "scape pipes" for exhausting steam.

Well-fashioned interiors included a ladies' cabin and a dining room. Altogether a satisfactory improvement over the stubby *Columbia* which preceded her by a few months, clunking along at four m.p.h. with passengers sleeping on decks and packing their own food.

The *Lot Whitcomb* touched just about all ports along both sides of the river on her Portland-Astoria run (fare $20) nosing into Fort Vancouver, Milton, St. Helens, Cathlamet and Cowlitz Landing. At the latter settlement, passengers bound for Puget Sound made connections with the Cowlitz River Canoe and Bateaux Line, which provided muscle-powered river

craft, and trails traversed by relays of horses and later Wells Fargo stages and wagons.

These and other offerings failed to attract much in the way of freight or passengers and the *Lot Whitcomb* soon assumed the role of a loser. Her decline was aided by ill feeling between the riverboat's owner and her first captain, John Ainsworth, who sniffed at the publisher's use of the title "captain." (He was equally disdainful of the abilities of a Mississippi riverboat pilot he had tutored, Samuel Clemens.)

After several other assignments, Ainsworth bought an interest in a tiny paddle-wheeler, the *Umatilla,* and boldly headed up the North Pacific Coast for the wild Fraser River, where gold had been discovered. Here he learned how to separate gold from the gold seeker, an art that was to make his fortune on the Columbia.

Obtaining a few additional small steamers, Ainsworth and his talented company began their monopoly-board moves, wangling mail contracts, and entering additional steamers on the Middle and Upper Columbia runs. In 1860, they crossed the river briefly to incorporate under the Washington Territory's permissive laws, and the Oregon Steam Navigation Company was launched.

As on the Fraser, Ainsworth's timing was right. In 1861, gold was discovered in Idaho, with lesser strikes in western Montana and Eastern Washington. For the next six years, the Columbia and Snake Rivers became roads to riches — at least for the O.S.N. During the first 12 months, O.S.N. investors doubled their money. Freight, everything from mining equipment to cattle and whiskey, moved at premium rates. Pursers on newly-added steamboats like the *Okanogan, Spray, Tenino, Nez Perce Chief, Kiyus, Owyhee, Webfoot* and *Yakima* turned in cash fares up to $4,000 a trip. Coming downriver from Lewiston in the fall of 1863, the *Nez Perce Chief* docked at Celilo with almost $400,000 in gold dust. The O.S.N. had struck it rich.

Oregon Historical Society

Senator   When gold was discovered in California in 1849, the owners of the *Senator* quickly pulled her from a sedate Long Island Sound run and dispatched her to the Sacramento River. The 220-foot brigantine-rigged sidewheeler wallowed her way around the Horn, defying seas never anticipated by her builders. The tumultuous sea voyage took seven months and 17 days from New York, including a pause at Panama. There she took on water, stores, fuel and 200 adventurers who were willing to bet $500 she would reach the California gold fields. She did.

Once on the Sacramento, the *Senator,* the only steamer on the river, filled up with gold seekers eager to pay from $45 to $65 for an eight-hour ride up the river from San Francisco to Sutter's Fort. Freight rates were equally high — $40 to $80 a ton for machinery, foodstuffs and such nuggets as crates of eggs then bringing $1 each at Sutter's Fort; $40-a-quart whiskey and crates of cats that sold for $25 each in the rat-infested gold fields.

The *Senator* was not the first steamer on the river; that mantle had been worn briefly and ignominiously by the tiny (37-foot) steamer, *Sitka,* which arrived in San Francisco aboard a bark in 1847. The plodding *Sitka* required six days to cover 125 miles between San Francisco and Sacramento. On her return trip she was beaten by an ox team. The following year

she sank, unmourned.

For a time, the *Senator* grossed up to $50,000 on a one-way trip. But by 1850 there were so many competitors — 28 of them — that profits dwindled. At that point, the operators united and, setting their own fares and freight tariffs, formed the California Steam Navigation Company, the forerunner of a similar combine soon to dominate the Columbia River.

In 1882, the *Senator* was stripped of power and ended her days in New Zealand as a coal hulk.

Mariner's Museum, Newport News, VA.

Wide West

Unlike most of their counterparts on the Mississippi and on Eastern coastal runs, most paddlewheel steamers serving the Pacific Northwest were plain Janes. An early exception was the *Wide West,* a 236-foot palace built in Portland in 1877 by the Oregon Steam Navigation Company and placed on the Portland-Cascades run, connecting with the *R. R. Thompson* for those en route to The Dalles or points further upriver. Ten years after her launching, her ornate upperworks and machinery were installed aboard the new *T. J. Potter.*

The *Wide West's* interiors (right) were bright with mirrors, brass grillwork and oil lamps lighting the carpeted corridors. But comforts often were minimal, as evidenced by the photograph of the stiff-backed Gentlemen's Cabin with spitoon at the ready for card players who congregated around the circular table (lower right).

Oregon Historical Society

William Irving   The *William Irving*, owned by Captain John Irving, at Yale in about 1881. Yale, 100 miles up the Fraser River, became one of the main gateways to the Cariboo and other British Columbia gold discoveries. The *William Irving* was named after Irving's father, a veteran captain of the gold-rush vessels on the Columbia. His sternwheelers were among the first on the Fraser in the 1850s, when gold was first discovered, peaking in 1858 when the river produced more than $2 million in precious metals. By 1864, the Fraser's bars were cleansed of gold. Merchants and steamer operators were bankrupt. The boom revived with discovery of gold on the Cariboo.

British Columbia Archives

Lily   To meet the needs of traffic on the Yukon and Fraser Rivers, sternwheelers were constructed as far away as England. Pictured is the Hudson's Bay Company *Lily* being built in 1875 at the Isle of Dogs yard near London.

Glenbow Archives, Calgary

Ann Faxton

The *Ann Faxton* loads wheat at a Snake
River landing

Oregon Historical Society

Mary Moody

Flagship of the short-lived Oregon & Montana Transportation Company's entry into gold rush traffic, the *Mary Moody* is shown loading mules for another stop along Pend Oreille Lake where she was built in 1866. Passengers reached the Idaho lake on steamers that ran from Portland to the Cascades, then on to the Snake River, with a final leg via stagecoach. But the Montana gold rush subsided in 1867 and the *Mary Moody,* along with two other O. & M. T. Co. steamers, was dismantled and shipped back to Portland.

Columbia River Maritime Museum

Bailey Gatzert

Among the first paddlewheel steamers to bring a touch of class to the Columbia were the *Bailey Gatzert,* shown at her launching at Ballard in 1888. Both the *Bailey Gatzert* and the *T. J. Potter,* built the same year at Portland, were perennial racers on the Columbia River and Puget Sound for the mythical "golden broom" and were among the most popular excursion steamers of their day.

Oregon Historical Society

Harvest Queen

The serenity of this scene as the *Harvest Queen* moves out of her Portland slip heading for the Columbia (leaving behind our old friend, the *T. J. Potter* at right), is in sharp contrast to an earlier run of the *Harvest Queen*—one that took her over Celilo Falls.

In 1881, hard times on the Middle River above the rocky barrier at Celilo Rapids had prompted the passage. It was a risky one. To breach the falls meant a 20-foot drop over a basalt ledge. Then followed the hazards of rock-strewn Tenmile Rapids. This churning gutted into a mile-long caldron that compressed the Columbia between sheer rock walls less than 300 feet apart.

Running the Celilo Rapids was first accomplished in 1866 when Captain Thomas Stump threaded the *Okanogan* through the hazardous chasm, followed by other sternwheelers of similar size: the *Nez Perce Chief,* the classic *Oneonta,* the *Hassalo (II),* and now one of the river's finer steamers, the *Harvest Queen.*

At the helm was Captain James Troup, 29, who six years earlier had entered the *Harvest Queen's* pilot house as her first skipper. Peter DeHuff, a veteran riverboat engineer, manned the engine room throttle as she moved from her Celilo slip. A slight rise in the low river had prompted the young captain to make his move. For a few minutes it seemed as though it might be his last for, as the *Harvest Queen* swept into the narrow chute, she was unable to clear the ledge.

The rocks tore into the stern of the 200-foot steamer, ripping off her rudders and disabling the engine supports. Legend has it that Captain Troup picked up his speaking tube and shouted:

"Back her, Pete! Back her if you love me!"

"I can't. Everything's busted," came the doleful reply.

Captain Troup, with the skill of command that was to make him an outstanding riverboatman on the Columbia and the Fraser, left his useless wheel. Anchors and kedges were dropped to pull the drifting *Harvest Queen* out of the whirlpools and away from the threatening rocks into the eddy. The worst was over. Defying the chill waters, the steamer's crew completed repairs. Within two days, the *Harvest Queen* was ready and defiant, sweeping at railroad speed through the remaining rapids to be greeted by cheering crowds at The Dalles.

Oregon Historical Society

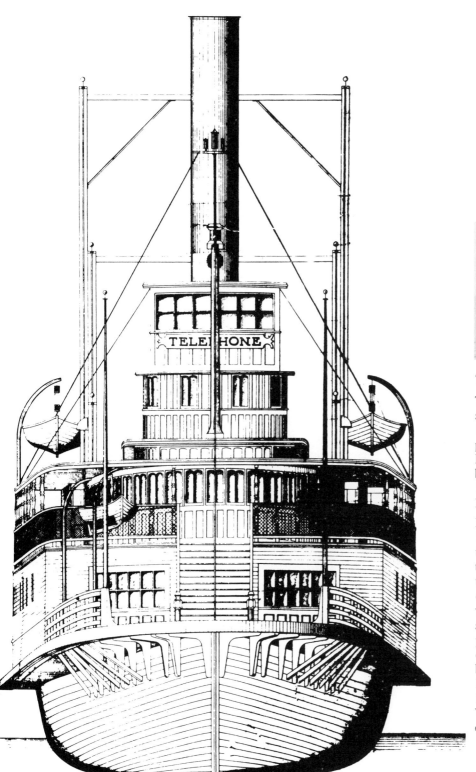

Telephone

This drawing shows ample evidence of speed in the lines of the sternwheeler *Telephone*. Built and operated by that perennial Columbia River speed challenger, Captain U.B. Scott, she raced and beat such swift riverboats as the *Hassalo, T. J. Potter, Charles R. Spencer* and others. Her exploits became river legends.

Included was the time in 1887 when the *Telephone* burst into flames while racing toward Astoria. Captain Scott opened the throttle and headed the *Telephone* toward the bank at an estimated 20 m.p.h., her engine-room fire now engulfing the wooden superstructure. The steamer successfully grounded and the singed passengers jumped ashore. Captain Scott dived out of a window just minutes before flames engulfed the pilot house. Five years later, the rebuilt *Telephone* hit a revetment in a fog and sank in the Willamette, but rose to race again.

Oregon Historical Society

Lurline Engine Room

Shining brass, gleaming paint, wall mottos
and a strategically placed spitoon provide
a setting for this proud photograph of
John (Long John) Epler, engineer of the
Columbia River sternwheeler *Lurline*.
Such care undoubtedly contributed to the
Lurline's longevity. Built in 1878, she
survived until 1930.

Columbia River Maritime Museum

Kootenay Engine Room

The development of electric illumination
on sternwheelers produced control
boards which in their day were as impressive as the cockpits of today's jet planes.
Pictured in the inset is the electrical
panel and the dynamo from the Arrow
Lakes (British Columbia) sternwheeler,
Kootenay, built in 1897. The 184-foot
vessel remained in service until 1919.

British Columbia Archives

Almota

The *Almota* is pictured at Lapwai Landing shortly after joining the Oregon Steam & Navigation Company fleet in 1876. She was built at Celilo, not far from the Cascades, a barrier of rocky gorges and rapids, daringly breached by Captain Troup and other veterans. Troup was one of the *Almota's* first officers.

Twenty years prior to this peaceful scene, this stretch of the river erupted into a brief but bloody battle during the Indian wars that were flickering across the territory.In March of 1856, Indians attacked a settlement near the Cascades, burning cabins and a warehouse. In the battle, 11 civilians and three soldiers were killed. Three more died later of injuries. Indian losses are not known. The warriors were routed after troops from The Dalles, 42 miles away, responded. Among them was a contingent headed by Lt. Phil Sheridan who raced to the scene aboard the steamer *Belle*. The *Almota* was dismantled in 1901.

Oregon Historical Society

55

181 AT THE FERRY, COLUMBIA RIVER

Sheep On Columbia

Ben Gifford, pioneer photographer from The Dalles, captured this shot of early day commuters awaiting a tow across the Columbia to greener pastures.

Oregon Historical Society

Selkirk Prior to the 1900's, Wenatchee became an active port and boat-building community. Among the larger Columbia River steamers built at Wenatchee was the 111-foot *Selkirk,* shown here on a calm summer passage upriver. The steamer was wrecked in 1906 while attempting passage through Rock Island Rapids.

Ice and rock-riven rapids took their toll of Columbia River steamers. At points, ring bolts were driven into cliff walls to help vessels winch their way upstream, pulled by cables.

University of Washington Library

Columbia Freeze When not dodging snags and wicked currents, Columbia River steamers were seasonally threatened by freezing weather. Here, two sternwheelers are frozen in at Cascade Locks during the winter of 1909. A thaw freed them after six weeks.

Columbia River Maritime Museum

Regulator on the Rocks The *Regulator,* best known during the spirited competition for wheat cargoes on the Columbia, is pictured impaled on the rocks below Cascade Locks in 1898. She survived, just as she weathered her river freeze-up.

Oregon Historical Society

Harvest Queen

Passengers bound upriver from Walla Walla or on to the Idaho gold fields changed riverboats at the Cascades for transit to The Dalles, 12 hours or more out of Portland. Here they overnighted at the Umatilla House (shown at right in the foreground just ahead of the *Harvest Queen*) where they shared a room with three others. But the hostelry boasted two baths, and a trencherman's dining room where as the boast went, "you could always get your shirt filled." The smaller Cosmopolitan was not as grand.

The following day at 5 a.m. passengers boarded a train that carried them 13 miles where they boarded another riverboat, arriving in mid-afternoon at Umatilla, approximately a hundred miles from The Dalles. Here stages provided bone-wrenching connections with Boise, Salt Lake City, and points east.

Next stop on the river was Wallula where awaited a single passenger car on the narrow-gauge Walla Walla and Columbia River Railroad. It provided even less comfort than the stage. It took almost two hours to cover 32 miles to Walla Walla, jolting over wooden rails covered with strap iron and held in place by rawhide strips. Nearing its stops, the locomotive was preceded by a barking collie, the Indians having stolen the cow catcher. It made so much money for its founder, a dropout Walla Walla doctor, that he could afford to smile at the name the locals hung on the line's one passenger car — The Hearse.

Columbia River Maritime Museum

J. N. Teal

The *J. N. Teal,* built in 1908 to compete with the Union Pacific wheat trains, pauses at the Cascade Locks with a load of excursionists and two smart limousines.

Columbia River Maritime Museum

Kaslo and Kokanee

The Pacific Coast's greatest concentration of riverboat steamers was on the rivers and lakes of British Columbia and Yukon Territory. Seeded by gold discoveries, by the turn of the century almost 100 were pounding their way up rivers like the Columbia, Fraser, Kootenay, Okanogan, Peace, Skeena, Stikine and others. Pushing even farther into the wilderness, the steamers served a scattering of lakes: the *Arrow, Kootenay, Okanagan* and others.

Here in 1900 the *Kaslo* and *Kokanee* meet on Kootenay Lake, one of the many routes to the gold fields. The *Kaslo* provided a dining room "affording passengers a perfect view of the passing scenery while at the table." Staterooms were trimmed in mahogany, with ground-glass transoms displaying "photographic transparencies of local scenes."

Such luxurious appointments befitted the Great Northern Railroad's ownership of the *Kaslo* and *Kokanee.* British good living also was in evidence. As early as 1876, Lady Dufferin, wife of Canada's Governor General, wrote of boarding a tiny side-wheeler at Kamloops:

> We got on board a steamer and as usual found every comfort and luxury surrounding us: pictures in our cabins; books of poetry on the tables; rocking chairs, and good beds.

A prospector heading up the Stikine on the riverboat *Hope* was not so enthusiastic. Complaining to the *Victoria Standard,* he wrote that the passengers, after paying $25 for passage, were forced to "sleep in one's own blankets, cook for self, pay $1 for inferior grub and occasionally cut wood." The crowning indignity came when passengers were asked to surrender their blankets to help plug a hole in the hull.

Columbia River Maritime Museum

Colfax

Before the sternwheelers literally ran them out of business, two propeller-driven steamers successfully engaged in serving lumber communities along the St. Jo River and Lake Coeur d'Alene in Idaho. The two, the *Colfax* (pictured above) and the *Flyer* (modelled after a Puget Sound counterpart) served the lumber industry until 1903 when the 147-foot sidewheeler *Idaho* was completed. At the peak of river traffic, dominated by the *Idaho's* owners, the Red Collar Line, some 50 passenger and freight boats linked river and lake communities. At Coeur d'Alene, electric interurbans met steamers at dockside for the fast run to Spokane.

Duchess

The *Duchess* may have looked like a tramp, but she had certain royal attributes while serving pioneer settlements on the upper Columbia in British Columbia, starting in 1887. She not only boasted staterooms and a dining saloon, but for a time offered settlers mail service. The postal delivery service included stamps which the captain had printed and sold for five cents each — until Canadian authorities cancelled his all-too-private enterprise. Posed at right with his crew is the skipper, Captain Bacon.

Vancouver Ferry

Cross-Columbia commuters and shoppers debark from the ferry *Vancouver* around 1895. The 108-foot sidewheeler was built in Portland for the Portland and Vancouver Railway Company. Her Portland terminus was at the foot of Washington Street.

Oregon Historical Society

7:00 A.M. Portland Ha

About 1900

Portland Harbor Scene

Three Columbia River steamers "pour
on the wood" as they move out into the
Willamette at Portland in this 1900 morning scene. In the foreground, the *Tahoma,*
headed for the Cascades, carries a deck
load that includes two wagons and, piled
atop them, a buggy. Other steamers were
not identified.

Edith, Maud and *Josephine*

Pioneer settlers utilizing the Pacific Northwest's riverways achieved the historic mien of those who moved West aboard the covered wagons.

Little is known about the *Josephine,* and *Edith* other than that the rivers pictured are probably either the Snohomish, Skagit or Nooksak.

The *Edith,* pictured above on the Nooksak on a May day in 1888, was a family-run affair as evidenced by the mother and babe in arms. Judging by the ox team just visable at far right, this steamer included logging camps on her rounds.

The rakish-looking steam launch *Maud* (upper right) was one of the most learned vessels on Puget Sound during the 1890's. She was operated by members of The Young Naturalists' Society — which included Charles Denny and Edmond Meany — to collect marine specimens for their museum on the downtown U of W site. The patriarchal skipper is not identified.

The *Josephine* (lower right) is more typical of early shallow-draft sternwheelers which nosed their way through the Sound's by-waters.

T. C. Reed   The *T. C. Reed* was typical of the second generation of paddlewheelers serving the gritty lumber towns scattered along the Chehalis River and the deep-sea ports of Aberdeen and Hoquiam. Here the 116-foot sternwheeler is pictured passing the four-masted lumber schooner *William J. Patterson* and the smaller *Gleaner.* The time is 1897, almost 50 years since the Willamette-built sternwheeler *Enterprise* became the first steamer to work the Chehalis. But the *Enterprise,* which earlier had cleaned up $25,000 in a single day during the Fraser River gold rush, found poor prospecting along the debris-choked Chehalis and retired.

Port Blakely

By 1881, outpacing the sawmills of Gray's Harbor country, Port Blakely on Bainbridge Island was boasting that it had, within the space of but two decades, become the "world's largest."

Fed by vast prime timberland holdings, a fleet of sailing ships and tugs, and 35 miles of logging rails, the Port Blakely Mill Co. employed more than a thousand workers drawn from the seven seas: Scandanavian, Japanese, Chinese, Spanish, Irish and Hawaiians.

"We were all foreigners and newcomers," recalled Freda Adams, a Norwegian immigrant living at Port Blakely, "the only natives were Indians."

Most mill hands were single. Those without a specialty were paid slightly more than $20 a month "and found." The latter included huts with running water and a supply of firewood, all for a dollar a month.

The panoramic view, from the private collection of Capt. Bob Matson, was taken prior to 1907 when a fire levelled the mill for the second time in less than 20 years. It was rebuilt at half its previous size and abandoned in 1914.

Presumably, the photo was taken on a Sunday, which would account for the almost complete lack of people visible, including on the decks of the schooners and the company-owned steamer, *Monticello.* (A strong magnifying glass is able to disclose three people standing on the porch of a millworker's house at far right.) Not visible are either of Port Blakely's two company-owned saloons.

Named after a War of 1812 hero, Johnson Blakely, the town and mill sites were located by Capt. William Renton and another early day lumberman, Theodore Williams. They surveyed the harbor depth from a skiff, entered a township claim, built a mill for $80,000, and the following year, in 1864, shipped their first cut to San Francisco.

The mill flourished and the town soon offered a post office, company store, livery stable, a 75-bed hotel and a jail. Brothels were forbidden on the island, providing a dependable source of revenue for Seattle-bound steamers. A board sidewalk led to a nearby resort, Pleasant Beach, which also drew steamer loads of Seattle and Tacoma rakehells drawn by such sporty diversions as boxing matches, dancing, and overnight accomodations, some with an unusually high turnover. More acceptable Port Blakely attractions included tent meetings, picnics, a May Day fest, a community Christmas tree, and an annual operetta that drew a boatload of supportive Seattleites.

Later, as a leisure time class was attracted to Bainbridge Island, Fletcher Bay provided tent houses, cabins and a picnic grounds, as did nearby Wing Point. By the early 1900's, the Puget Mill steamer *Monticello* hauled golfing addicts to the island's four-hole course, located not far from where Capt. George Vancouver had landed a hundred years earlier.

After the mill's closure in 1914, Port Blakely clung to life from revenue created by a ferry terminal, but it died in 1937 when the Black Ball Line moved the terminus to nearby Eagle Harbor.

Bob Matson

Chester

Captains Orin, Ed and Joseph Kellogg (left to right in front of pilot house) were the skipper-owners of the *Chester* which, they boasted, "floated like a shingle on a pond." The comparison was apt, as evidenced by this photo of the 101-foot sternwheeler loading grain on the Cowlitz's shores. She was launched in 1897 in Portland at the yard of Joseph Supple. It was an appropriate name for her builder, for the *Chester* was noted for her flexible hull, supported by hog chains and planked with cedar. Able to navigate in but a foot of water, the *Chester* worked out of Kelso, her planking constantly being replaced due to the fact she literally sand-papered her bottom as she slid over the Cowlitz River sandbars. The photographer was another riverboatman, Captain Arthur Riggs.

Puget Sound Maritime Historical Society

Politofsky

The ungainly pioneer steamer *Politofsky* was built in 1866 of hand-hewn cedar at the Russian-American capital of Sitka. After Russia sold Alaska, they peddled the sidewheeler to the newly-formed Alaska Commercial Company — and learned about Yankee traders. The new owners promptly steamed the *Polly* to San Francisco, where they sold her copper boilers for $22,000. Re-boilered, the steamer passed into the hands of the Dexter Horton Company in 1879 and later jobbed around Puget Sound as a towboat for the Port Blakely Mill Company.

About her only eulogy came in 1896 from a Tacoma newspaper romanticist:

> *The boat now serves as a tug, but there was a time when it was put to other and more warlike uses … Thirty years ago she was in the service of the Czar of Russia and carried an armament of four guns. Fierce looking men in long coats paraded the deck, and at least once a day, before caviar sandwiches and tongue-biting vodka were passed around, the Greek priest prayed for the great Czar, and the crew never once dreamed that the day would come when their gallant little sidewheeler would be used in towing logs for an American sawmill, and carrying prunes, dried apples, flour, beans, pork, and other necessities of life to loggers, who probably do not know the White Czar and had no reverence for the great Russian empire.*

In 1897 the *Polly* returned to Alaska, a member of a comical armada of improbable Gold Rush vessels, led by the aging *Eliza Anderson*. The *Eliza Anderson* set the tone of the ill-fated hegira by ramming the clipper *Glory of the Seas* at Comox, B.C. (Earlier it had been discovered that she had no compass nor a sufficient amount of coal aboard.) In her wake came the tug *Richard Holyoke*, towing a smaller sternwheeler, the *W.K. Merwin*, and the sorry old *Politofsky*, now reduced to the role of a fuel barge.

The *Eliza Anderson* was abandoned by her angry passengers at Dutch Harbor and later broke up on the rocks. The *W. K. Merwin* and the remains of the *Polly* pounded to pieces on the beaches of Nome and St. Michael.

Seattle Historical Society

Ship Launching

Ship launchings became a social event at the turn of the century when yards like those of the Hall Bros. at Port Blakely were fashioning some of America's first lumber schooners. Here several generations gather on the deck of the newly-launched *H. K. Hall,* named in honor of one of the yard's founders, shown at center sporting a magnificent white beard. Between 1874, when Winslow, Isaac and Henry Hall brought their shipwright talents to Port Ludlow from Massachusetts, and 1903, the yard launched 108 sailing vessels. Of these, 31 were built at Port Ludlow, the remainder at the Hall Bros. yards on Bainbridge; first at Port Blakely, later at Eagle Harbor.

The five-masted *H. K. Hall* was 225 feet long and carried 1,500,000 board feet of lumber. During the year when she was launched, almost 10,000 seamen either shipped out or were discharged from ships in Puget Sound ports, most of them sailing vessels.

Earlier, the launching of the lumber schooner *Wildwood,* at that time the largest vessel built on the Pacific Coast, drew a crowd of 1,500 from Port Townsend, Olympia, Steilacoom, Port Gamble and Seattle, with the tug *Politofsky* arriving with a brass band. Unfortuantely for the planned collation aboard, the *Wildwood* wedged herself firmly in the mud after successfully sliding down the ways.

Seattle Historical Society

Lumber from Seattle

Well into the twentieth century, Puget Sound steamers were fueled by wood: cordwood consumed in their boilers and the timber that created their ports of call.

Scenes like the above of the *Stimson,* in 1910 became commonplace around the Sound. In 1872, a Washington Territory business directory noted there were "from 100 to 300 towns, (virtually all company-owned) in which no business but that of lumber is carried on." In a poetic burst not uncommon in business journals of the day, the writer continued:

> *Were it not for the heavy puffing of steam, the towns would seem to be Arcadian hamlets situated in some sheltered nook…*

Despite the presence of one of the Sound's first sawmills, Seattle was an importer of lumber. The town's most prominent mill owner, Henry Yesler had four mills between 1852 and 1859, all destroyed by fire. And when big mills across the Sound were processing up to 70,000 board feet of lumber daily, Yesler cut but 10,000 a day. Small wonder that an early geography book is said to have referred to Seattle as a lumber mill community "across the Sound from Port Madison."

Asahel Curtis, Washington State Historical Society

Loading at Port Blakely

The first exports of timber from Puget Sound consisted of a few spars Captain George Vancouver ordered installed on the top-sail yards of the *Discovery,* anchored off Bainbridge Island in 1792. "We only had to make our choice from among thousands of the finest spars the world produced," he wrote in his log. (Captain Vancouver also found use for spruce, making a beer which he described as "very excellent.")

The first shipments of Douglas fir from Puget Sound were loaded off Alki Point aboard the brig, *Leonesa,* in 1852, destined for San Francisco. In short order the towering tree with the chocolate brown bark began earning worldwide testimonials that would make a Weyerhaeuser ad man envious.

A French Navy report of the 1860s commended it for its "lightness, strength and absence of knots and other grave vices." Mare Island Navy officers found it "stronger than white oak." To the Board of Marine Underwriters in San Francisco, it proved "the finest material for docks in the world." From London to the Sandwich Islands, mansion woodwork gleamed with Douglas fir.

Pictured is the schooner, *Benecia,* loading at Port Blakely at the turn of the century.

Washington State Historical Society

Hall Bros. Shipyard

Turn of the century Port Blakely boomed with timber payrolls, including what was purported to be the world's largest sawmill (preceding pull-out pages), and the nearby Hall Bros. shipyard, shown here during the launching of the five-masted lumber schooner *H.K. Hall* on May 24, 1902. Another photograph showing the launching ceremonies, will be found on p. 77. Both were the works of Wilhelm Hester, Puget Sound's most active marine photographer.

Shamrock

Despite the challenge and weather of Washington's coast north of Long Beach (served by a fleet of Columbia River steamers), hardy vacationers flocked to hotels and summer cabins at Westport, Moclips, and Pacific Beach aboard doughty little sternwheelers like the *Harbor Belle* and *Harbor Queen* and the steamer *Fleetwood* docking at Westport and Cosmopolis.

Sternwheelers like the *Alliance* and *Dolphin* were sailing every week from Portland to Hoquiam, Aberdeen, Cosmopolis, North Cove, South Bend, Willapa and Bay Center. The steam launch *Jessie* would ferry you to South Aberdeen for a dime. Local yards were building sternwheelers like the *Montesano,* complete with "ladies and gents cabins, a dining room and five staterooms."

By 1908, popularity of Washington beaches and resorts led to daily runs between Portland and tiny South Bend on the Willapa River, requiring two steamers and a short train ride. Returning home, excursionists would board one of the Willapa Bay mail steamers, *Shamrock* (left) or *Reliable,* at South Bend, crossing to Nahcotta midpoint on the Long Beach Peninsula. Here trains would carry passengers to connecting OSN steamers docked at Ilwaco for the relaxing river ride back to Portland. Fare: $4.25.

In addition to carrying passengers, mail, and freight, the stubby steamers offered weekend cruises to view a wreck or whales. The most festive outing occurred on June, 1908, when the steamers rendezvoused for a viewing of the Great White Fleet as it passed off the coast.

Pacific County Historical Society

Olympia Dock

Olympia enjoyed a short-lived eminence as a port starting in 1850 when the brig, *Orbit,* sailed to San Francisco with a cargo of piling. The following year, Olympia became Puget Sound's first port of entry, issuing a coasting license for the brig, *George Emery.* The schooner *Mary Tyler* followed, becoming the first to trade on the Sound. In 1853, Olympia greeted the sidewheeler *Fairy,* the Sound's first American-owned steamer, which blew up in 1857.

The photograph, taken around 1910, shows Olympia's Percival Dock. To the left is the new tug, *Sandman.* Her gasoline engine was considered so revolutionary it was on display the previous year at the Alaska-Yukon-Pacific Exposition in Seattle. In the center, the launch *Lark,* one of the first in the growing fleet of Foss Launch & Tug at Tacoma, gets underway. Moored at the wharf are the mail boat *Mizpah* and the sternwheeler *Multnomah* which carried passengers and freight to Tacoma and Seattle.

Washington State Historical Society

Eliza Anderson

"No steamer went so slow or made money faster."

That accolade — or epithet — depending on whether you were a stockholder or a passenger, was richly earned by the *Eliza Anderson,* a Portland-built sidewheeler that arrived on Puget Sound in 1858. She quickly established links between Olympia, Seattle and Victoria and lesser satellites such as Steilacoom, Port Townsend and other stops.

One of the region's premier photographers, Asahel Curtis, has captured the *Eliza Anderson* docked near the location of today's Colman Dock in about 1888.

If the *Eliza Anderson* was slow (averaging nine knots), her owner's footwork was not; and for ten years she maintained a virtual monopoly on the route, earning up to $5,000 each voyage, in addition to a coveted $35,000-a-year mail contract. Despite challenges by vessels speedier and more luxurious, including the ex-Hudson River sidewheeler *Wilson G. Hunt,* the *Eliza Anderson* prevailed.

When faced with competition, her owners, skippers Tom, John and George Wright of Seattle, cut fares to as low as 50 cents round-trip between Sound ports and Victoria. When the competition withdrew, fares went back to $20 from Olympia to Victoria, and $10 from Seattle. This at a time when the steamer fare from Portland to San Francisco was $5. Cattle carried on the *Eliza Anderson* rode for $15 a head, sheep for $2.50 and all other freight, $5 to $10 a ton.

Freight charges were equally onerous. The *Eliza Anderson's* captain, D. B. Fitch, whom it was said made more money than the amply-rewarded owners, took advantage of the Sound's lack of banking facilities. Docking at Steilacoom, Port Madison, Port Gamble, Port Ludlow and Port Townsend, Fitch would scurry ashore to deal in sight drafts, cash checks and loan money. Not one to miss a cinch bet, Captain Fitch, who originally signed on as the *Eliza Anderson's* purser, also sold butter

and eggs in Victoria, doubling his investment. On the return trip, Fitch loaded up with Sandwich Island sugar, which he sold at premium prices in Seattle — tripling that investment.

Despite this unseemly pursuit of Mammon, he was a devout churchgoer and refused to sail on the Sabbath, waiting until one minute after midnight to depart from Olympia. He possessed a wicked sense of humor and gleefully enraged pro-British (and pro-Secessionist) residents of Victoria by playing *Yankee Doodle* and the *Star-Spangled Banner* on the *Eliza Anderson's* calliope during the holidays.

The *Eliza Anderson* managed to stay clear of customs violations despite her somewhat erratic behavior, perhaps as some said, because her owners prudently named her in honor of Alexander Caulfield Anderson, the first Collector of Customs at Victoria.

The clunky sidewheeler carried prospectors and adventurers during the Cassiar gold rush, then began her decline. She was laid up at dock side from 1877 to 1882, at one time resignedly sinking alongside her wharf. A few years later she was overhauled and returned to the Victoria run. But her passenger list attracted the attention of immigration officials and in 1885, she was seized at Port Townsend, charged with carrying contraband Chinese.

Cleared of what was regarded as a frame-up by her competitors, the *Eliza Anderson* made one last attempt at a comeback. In 1897, when the Klondike Gold Rush traffic welcomed any vessel that stayed afloat long enough to bribe a steamboat inspector, she was patched up and headed north, accompanied by four other discards. En route, after surviving a collision, she ran out of coal, forcing her passengers to help steal enough from a deserted cannery to make port at Kodiak. There, her passengers deserted her. A year later, the *Eliza Anderson* was driven ashore and broken up.

Paul Dorpat

Minnie M

The first Snohomish River passengers rode from Seattle to Mukilteo by steamer then completed their journey by Indian canoe. The first paddlewheel steamer, the *Topsy,* began operating from Snohnmish City in 1864. Traffic grew as the *Topsy* was joined by steamers named *Gazelle, Zephyr, Monte Carlo, Mikado, Gem* and others.

In 1891, J. D. Merideth built a stubby sternwheeler and named her *Minnie M* after his wife. The *Minnie M* drew but a foot of water, just enough to get her upstream from Monroe to clearings named Katherine, Daisy, Greyhound and Sultan. There, completion of her maiden voyage was saluted by a brass band.

The following year, a sidewheeler, the *Idaho,* later to become a floating hospital in Seattle, made a daily roundtrip to that city. In 1895, the *Clan McDonald* introduced lighted cabins. Of a Sunday, settlers chugged off on excursions to the San Juan Islands and way points like Lowell, where there was dancing on the wharf. In 1889, 300 villagers, accompanied by the Snohomish Coronet Band, boarded the *City of Denver* for a day-long outing to Port Orchard where they viewed the battleship *Iowa.* By 1892, the town counted nine docked steamers.

In 1902, 2,000 residents lined the banks of the Snohomish to view the launching at Berg's shipyard of the steamer *Garden City,* destined for the run to Everett. The band played, Miss Nellie Bergman swung the customary bottle of champagne, and the publisher of the local paper predicted Snohomish City would someday excel Seattle and Port Townsend as a shipping center. (His pet choler was the screeching whistle of a local steamer, the *Cascade,* and he once suggested, "Somebody ought to plug the thing up with the head of the man that blows it.")

Gov. Newell

There was hardly a touch of class to the *Gov. Newell.* Built in 1883 at Portland for the Shoalwater Bay Transportation Co., she jobbed around those waters until returning to the Columbia two years later.

What made the unimposing *Gov. Newell* a subject of conversation on the riverways was to be found in her pilot house. Here manning the wheel was Capt. Minnie Hill, at age 26 the first woman west of the Mississippi to hold captain's papers. She manned the helm while her husband Charles, also a captain, took charge in the engine room. The unique sharing of command started when Minnie, born in Albany, Ore. in 1863, began steamboating on the Columbia River with her husband, who won his skipper's license at age 24. She had few counterparts.

One of the best known early-day women captains, Dora Wells Troutman, could fill any steamer berth, including that of captain, purser or cook. After the mysterious disappearance of her husband, Capt. Daniel Troutman, in 1899, she took over the helm of the steamer *Dode.* Capt. Gertrude Wiman, also the wife of a steamer skipper, received her master's papers in 1907, and piloted the steamer *Verona,* famed for a key role in the so-called Everett IWW Massacre.

Like Capt. Minnie Hill, Capt. Della Walck, skipper of the tiny (55-foot) *Agnes,* running between Tacoma and Carr Inlet in 1911-12, shared command with her husband, Engineer John Walck. She was not only a tough competitor on the Sound, but a canny scavenger of fuel, pulling the *Agnes* up to log booms and prying off bark with a crowbar, or picking up floating slabs at mills.

Today, stimulated by tough Federal equal opportunity regulations, licensed women officers are commonplace on Sound tugs and ferries as well as deep sea vessels. In addition, the only Puget Sound ferry services in private operation are headed by women. They are the Port Angeles-to-Victoria car ferry, *Coho,* of the Black Ball Transport Co., whose president is Mrs. Lois Acheson of Seattle, and the fleet of 11 foot-passenger commuter launches connecting Port Orchard with Bremerton. The ferry firm, the Horluck Navigation Co., is headed by Mary Nearhoff Lieske and her brother. She has held skipper papers for more than 40 years.

Oregon Historical Society

Willie

The little *Willie* (67 feet long) took few days off. When she wasn't hauling freight and passengers between Olympia and Shelton, she packed families off for a Sunday outing. Built in 1883 at Seattle for jobbing along the Samish River near today's Bellingham, she was moved south in 1886 by her new owner, Captain Ed Gustafson, for service between Olympia and Shelton. In 1895, Captain Gustafson replaced her with a larger sternwheeler, the *City of Shelton.* The *Willie* finished her days on the Fraser.

Seattle Historical Society

Wooding Up

Until the development of steamer engines fueled by coal, and later oil, steam was generated by burning cordwood, consuming forests of timber and providing supplemental employment for cutters and those loading at "wooding up" stops like this one in the San Juan Islands.

In her book, *Island in the Sound,* Hazel Heckman estimated that Johnson's Landing near her home on Anderson Island dispatched more than 80,000 cords of wood for steamers during its 40 years of operation. Jacob Anthes, one of the founders of Langley and operator of its general store, estimated that between 1891 and 1893 his wood sales averaged 35 cords a day, employing seven teams and 25 woodchoppers. Most were paid between $2.50 and $3.00 a cord.

Sternwheelers were the biggest consumers, often burning up to five cords an hour. A woodyard on British Columbia's Skeena River at one time held a thousand cords—a pile four feet high, four feet wide and more than a mile long! On small steamers like the *Sophia,* which ran between Quartermaster Harbor and Tacoma, passengers were forced to crawl over piled cordwood to reach a tiny smoking room and ladies' cabin.

The rigors of loading cords of wood are illustrated in the photo at right of the sternwheeler *Nakusp* on Arrow Lake, B.C. When waters were stirred by gales and loading planks were covered with ice, loading often ended in a dunking, and occasionally, a drowning.

University of Washington Archives

British Columbia Archives

92

Alida One of Seattle's first holiday excursions was a free one — to Port Townsend aboard the newly completed sidewheeler, *Alida,* on Independence Day, 1870. The *Alida* is shown here at dockside that year with the University of Washington's lone building dominating the hillside above. The 115-foot steamer went on a mail run serving major communities from Olympia to Port Townsend and helped her new owners, a couple of wealthy Portlanders, Edwin and Louis Starr, become two of the Sound's most successful steamer operators.

Yesler Wharf Yesler Wharf, pictured sometime in the late 1800s, shows signs of steamer traffic, but little dockside activity. In the foreground can be seen the stack and wheelhouse of the *Teaser,* later to become the Arctic sealer, *Eva Marie.* Moored at Yesler Wharf, left to right, are the *Merwin,* owned by her skipper, W.K. Merwin; the sternwheeler *Zephyr* whose colorful master was Captain John (Hell-Roarin' Jack) Shroll; the former Columbia River sternwheeler, *Washington,* and the *City of Quincy,* built for service on the Lewis River. The time would be prior to 1896, when the latter vessel was dismantled.

The *Washington* and the *City of Quincy,* in addition to the steamers *Daisy* and *Nellie,* were owned by the Washington Steamboat Co., formed in 1880 to oppose the Oregon Railroad and Navigation Co., then making its bid on Puget Sound. The company was headed by Capt. D. B. Jackson, a New Hampshireman previously in charge of Puget Mill operations at Port Gamble (a great grandson is former Washington governor—now U.S. Senator—Dan Evans).

Seattle Public Library

95

George E. Starr

With remarkable clarity, this photo of the *George E. Starr* shows her clean lines and the walking beam then in vogue on riverboats of that period. The photo was taken August 12, 1879, near the foot of Columbia Street. In the background is the Washington Hotel, soon to receive one of its first guests, President Theodore Roosevelt, and soon to disappear, along with the hill, a victim of Seattle's first "regrade."

Built in Seattle in 1879, the *George E. Starr* left a long wake before being abandoned in 1911. Shortly after launching, the 154-foot sidewheeler gave Seattle its first glimpse of a U.S. President, Rutherford B. Hayes who, greeted by cannon, steam whistles and church bells, stood on the bow of the steamer lifting his hat as the *George E. Starr* approached the city. Later, she became a fixture on the Seattle-Victoria run for ten years. Following a single season on the Columbia River after the Oregon Railway & Navigation Company took her over, the *George E. Starr* returned to the Sound. Although she churned her way north as far as Skagway, she was best known on runs to Bellingham and Port Townsend.

Her new owners, Joshua Green's La Conner Trading and Transportation Company, found she was more suited to freight than passengers.

"We had a full load of canned salmon on her," Green once told a Seattle Rotary Club luncheon group, "and she was so slow that it cost us more to feed the passengers than the passage money amounted to."

The *George E. Starr* was retired in 1911, one of the last of her kind. Over the years she slowed down to the point she inspired this requiem:

> Paddle, paddle,
> George E. Starr,
> How we wonder
> where you are.
> Leaves Seattle at
> Half past ten,
> Gets to Bellingham
> God knows when!

Walking Beam

In 1822 inventor James Stevens designed a paddlewheel ferryboat with an engine featuring a beam, pivoted in the center above a vertical cylinder. This transmitted the motion of the piston down to the crankshaft by a long connecting rod. The "walking beam," as it became known, became as familiar a device as the locomotive drive wheel and, among the young, attracted similar attention. The walking beam engine became a power package that was to thrash the inland waters of America, including Puget Sound, where such popular carriers as the *George E. Starr, Olympian, North Pacific* and *Eliza Anderson* were powered by the "walking beam" engine.

Wilson G. Hunt

The *Wilson G. Hunt* was built in 1847 as an excursion boat for pleasure seekers headed for a gaudy New York amusement park called Coney Island.

Instead, three years later, answering the barkers of another carnival, she headed around Cape Horn to the Sacramento River. Here gold seekers were willing to pay up to $65 just for a six-hour ride from San Francisco to the bonanza sands around Sutter's Mill.

The owners never regretted the change of course, cleaning up almost a million dollars during the *Wilson G. Hunt's* first year on the Sacramento, before she headed north to Puget Sound.

In the years that followd she plied the waters of Puget Sound and hauled machinery and gold seekers up the Columbia and Fraser.

The appearance of the *Wilson G. Hunt* was marred by an awkward housing on her hurricane deck; a steeple-like frame encasing the piston rod and the connecting rod that turned her wheels. But here interiors were considered among the best of her day, and she set a trencherman's table.

The sidewheeler was broken up in 1890 after running out of Victoria for a period under the house flag of the Canadian Pacific Navigation Co., which William Irving had founded.

University of Washington Library

Early Seattle Harbor

Seattle's growing eminence as a trading port is somewhat fancifully illustrated in this drawing of the 1880s. While sailing vessels still dominate Elliott Bay, the steamers are making a bold entry, including a trio powered by the new, revolutionary walking beam engines. The artist seems to have waived all rules regulating the right of way in the harbor.

Paul Dorpat

Alaskan and Olympian While a few walking beam steamers continued to plod around the Sound until well into the 1900s, for most the turn of the century marked the end of the sidewheeler. Two of the more notable failures in this category are shown here in about 1888: a builder's drawing of the *Alaskan* and her running mate, the *Olympian*.

The steamers were built in 1883 at Wilmington, Delaware, for Henry Villard, who had taken the O.R. & N. into his short-lived empire that had included the Northern Pacific Railroad.

Both were lavishly appointed. But they were unable to survive a panic and the emergence of the more economical

propeller-driven steamers. The behemoths — they were 261 feet long and 73 feet in beam over the paddlewheels — were tried out on a variety of runs from the Columbia to Puget Sound and Alaska, always bucking a tide of red ink. Both died unhappily en route to new owners. The *Alaskan* sank off Cape Blanco in 1889 with a loss of 30 lives. In 1906, the *Olympian,* under tow, broke loose shortly after traversing the Strait of Magellan and was driven onto the rocks, where her bones are still visible.

Also pictured: one of the *Olympian's* early crews and a section of her dining room.

Paul Dorpat

Victorian

The beamy *Victorian* is shown here dwarfing the slender *Hassalo* at Seattle. The *Hassalo* was the third to bear that name. Built at Portland in 1899, she was best known for her speed and comfortable, leather-upholstered, Pullman-type seating.

University of Washington Library

North Pacific

The beam-engined *North Pacific,* winner in several classic steamer races, is pictured moored at Vashon Island in 1892 alongside another pioneer vessel, the *Lydia Thompson.*

University of Washington Library

Princess Louise

After losing a classic Victoria-Port Townsend race by three minutes in 1871, the walking beam sidewheeler *Olympia* earned nearly $50,000 in subsidies in an agreement under which her owners, Captain Duncan Finch and George Wright, agreed to stay out of Puget Sound.

She returned in 1878 and under ownership of the Hudson's Bay Company was renamed *Princess Louise*. She thus became the first in a long line of *Princess* vessels that, starting in 1903, were to serve Puget Sound, British Columbia and Alaska runs under the Canadian Pacific banner.

University of Washington Library

103

Str. VICTORIAN STARTING FOR WHITE HORSE SA

THE CANADIAN DEVELOPMENT CO'S DOCK.

LARSS & DU
PH
DAV

JULY 8TH. 1899.

42

Victorian

By 1899, men were still on the move along the waterfront of Dawson, Yukon Territory, already the largest Canadian city west of Winnipeg and not much smaller than Seattle or Tacoma. Here a jubilant boatload prepare to leave on the Yukon riverboat *Victorian* for Whitehorse, and thence to Skagway or Dyea and home. Within a year, rails of the White Pass & Yukon Ry. would reach Whitehorse from Skagway, thus ending the terrors of the Trail of '98.

Oregon Historical Society

Dode

The *Dode,* rebuilt in 1898 from an old Gold Rush schooner, was a wooden 99-footer that was tireless if not swift. She left Pier 3 on Tuesday. During the day she loaded and unloaded passengers and freight at Kingston, Port Gamble, Seabeck, Brinnon, Holly, Dewatto, Lilliwaup Falls, Hoodsport and Union City. The following day she returned over the same route.

University of Washington Library

Islander* and *Rosalie In the newly settled San Juan Islands crop movements became a life-support system to steamers like the *Rosalie,* shown docking at Friday Harbor in about 1910, and the *Islander,* debarking passengers at left. Settlers had broken ground on Decatur, Blakeley, Stuart, and Waldron Islands, all virtually deserted today but settled enough by 1900 to warrant post offices. Most island crops were grown on the bigger islands: Shaw, Lopez, Orcas and San Juan, cultivated by homesteaders from Ireland, Germany, Sweden, Norway, Denmark, England, Scotland and Canada. Others arrived fresh from the worked-out gold fields of California or the riffles of the Fraser.

Captains on vessels loading spars for Falmouth and Brest returned to come ashore and "swallow the anchor." Other island settlers were Civil War veterans and Midwest farmers beaming at the misty rains.

In 1900, Island County boasted its population had soared 40 percent during the past decade. Stripped of boosterism, that still meant a population of only 3,000. But the newcomers were prodigal producers.

Island apples became as popular as today's harvest from Yakima and Wenatchee, soon to begin bearing fruit and deny the islanders' dreams of becoming the "Apple Basket of America." Wagons rattled their way to island docks laden with fruits, dairy products, grains and beef. Islanders

raised more sheep than any other Western Washington farmers and San Juan mutton was featured in mainland butcher shops.

By the turn of the century, another bounty — along with the lime mined on San Juan Island — was making its way to market on the steamers. Drawn by the closeby migratory routes of salmon, fish traps, reef netters and boatsmen were bringing in a rich harvest. One Friday Harbor cannery alone packed 50,000 cases in a single year.

Vashon Island shipped berries, greenhouse tomatoes and cucumbers. Steamers stopped to load cases of eggs which were to win national blue ribbons.

On Whidbey Island, Langley and Coupeville docks creaked with movements of provender for Everett and Seattle, including potatoes grown by Chinese farmers and sacks of wheat harvested by Dutchmen who, until soils became depleted, harvested record-breaking yields of wheat (117 bushels per acre in 1892).

The San Juan Islanders became the first on the Sound and its ancillary waters to become wedded to the steamer. Most were landlubbers, but they relaxed aboard workhorses like the *Islander* at left and the *Rosalie,* shown docking at Friday Harbor in 1912.

Islanders had watched some of these being built by their skipper-owners on crude ways in a tideland clearing. To the islanders, the steamer was a truck, an ambulance, a school bus, a hearse and a bearer of mail and visitors. Best of all it was a social hall where, in the warmth of a cabin, coffee could be shared and loneliness melted as the blue-black shores of the islands flowed by.

Whatcom County Museum
University of Washington Library

Indianapolis

Built in Toledo in 1904, the 965-ton
steamer *Indianapolis* arrived in Seattle in
1906 via the Strait of Magellan, the first of
three Great Lakes steamers purchased by
the Puget Sound Navigation Company. Capable of 16 knots, the 180-foot steamer
became a familiar sight on runs to Port
Townsend, Victoria and Tacoma.

The Day of the Liner

In addition to spawning the automobiles and trucks that soon were to replace the Sound steamers, the early twentieth century also marked the dawn of the golden age of passenger ship travel.

In the decades to come, smart liners sailed from Seattle to British Columbia and Alaska ports, to Portland, San Francisco, Los Angeles, San Diego, the Orient, South America, the Caribbean, and the U.S. East Coast. They had faded from the scene by the mid-50s.

The last scheduled passenger ship to sail from Seattle was the *Denali* of the Alaska Steamship Company in 1954, ending more than 60 years of service to the Northland. On the occasion, the line's president, D.E. Skinner observed:

This is the end of an era. The days of leisurely passenger ships are gone — the airlines are here to stay. Most Alaskans can't waste time riding a ship.

(Not yet visible on the horizon was the cruise ship. In 1985, 14 passenger liners, among them some of the world's finest, cruised Alaskan waters from Vancouver, B.C. during the summer season.)

Pictured in around 1898 is a trio of passenger ships at Seattle, its skyline dominated by the newly-built Denny Hotel. Departing is the *City of Seattle,* a big loser on Puget Sound.

Upon her arrival on the Sound in 1890, a crowd of 20,000 had greeted the *City of Seattle* with band music, fireworks and boat whistles. The following year, accompanied by her running mate, the *City of Kingston,* and an armada of other Sound steamers, she carried President Harrison from Tacoma to Seattle. For a time, she worked the Seattle-Whatcom-Victoria run. But high costs and slackening in the economy sent her off to languish at dockside until the Gold Rush filled her staterooms.

Seen at dockside are two liners of the Pacific Coast Steamship Company: the *Umatilla* and the *City of Puebla.* Their usual run was from Seattle and other Puget Sound ports to California. Built in 1881 for the New York-Havana run, the *City of Puebla* set a record of 48½ hours from San Francisco to Victoria.

University of Washington Library

The Port of Seattle

Despite a deepening Depression, Seattle's waterfront in 1932 remained a busy hive of passenger and freight vessels of all sizes and configurations. At far left, four ships await cargo and passengers at what was then Pier 2, home of the Alaska Steamship Co. Just to the right is Colman Dock, where the auto ferry *Seattle* (formerly the graceful steamer *H.B. Kennedy*) is loading for Bremerton. Then in order are: the venerable fireboat *Snoqualmie*; a Mosquito Fleet steamer, possibly the *Hyak*; two break-bulk freighters of the Waterman Line, and at far right, a Skagit River sternwheeler.

The entire stretch of the waterfront shown in the photo is now known as The Gold Rush Waterfront, given over to restaurants, import shops, tour boat moorages, the Seattle Aquarium and other tourist attractions. Freight movements are largely by container ships that dock at huge terminals to the South. Seattle now vies with Oakland as the Pacific Coast's No. 1 container port, drawing carriers longer than any of the piers shown. Another changing aspect: of the vessels visible, including passenger liners and freighters, all were U.S.-built and manned.

Port of Seattle

The Finale

The *Telegraph* churns her way down Puget Sound in the '20s, her wake an epitath for the disappearing sternwheel steamer.

University of Washington Library

Trivial Pursuits and Other Steamer Getaways

Making a Getaway on Puget Sound

Long before America cranked up Henry Ford's "tin Lizzie" for family getaways, the steamers of Puget Sound were filling that role with great elan.

The steamer traffic peaked in 1910, when the so-called "mosquito fleet" became the family bus and freight wagon for settlers living along the shorelines of Puget Sound and its major rivers. As early as 1889, steamers, largely wheezing paddlewheelers, carried 892,000 passengers. This was at a time when Seattle's population was barely 43,000 and that of rival Tacoma, 36,000. For those living in these cities or in the smaller Sound hamlets, the steamer not only provided their day-to-day needs, but offered a welcome escape.

Most milltowns were company towns. Many were mere clearings, sited for their proximity to hillside forests and deep-water anchorages. Unlike the redwood "dogholes" of California's Mendocino Coast or the lumber ports along the Columbia, Puget Sound was shaped for commerce.

Samuel Wilkeson, a Northern Pacific Railway surveyor of 1864, wrote of these "wonderful waters" in his journal, recounting this appraisal offered by a Sag Harbor whaler:

A 74-gun ship can lie pretty much all over the Sound with her jib boom among the trees on the shore, six fathoms under her bows, and 20 fathoms under her stern.

A business directory of that period described the Puget Sound milltowns of 1872—none of them with a population of more than 2,000—as resembling Arcadian hamlets, "were it not for the heavy puffing of the steam."

Ashore however, the picture was less idyllic. Here a colorless monotony mingled the steam and mists. The high point overlooking the harbor and sawmill might house a few gabled manses for the millowner and his associates. Elsewhere, streets were but ruts leading to a straggle of workers' shacks and dormitories. Socializing was confined to the church, or possibly a meeting hall. The company town had no room for saloons or theaters.

The sawmills ranged between giants like those at Port Blakely, Port Gamble, Port Ludlow, Port Discovery, Utsalady and Tacoma, to small, scruffy gyppo mills, described by Norman Clark in his *Mill Town* as being "a series of rusty saws in leaky shacks, powered by belts from steam engines, locked in a dreary rhythm of overproduction and closedown."

All in all, Puget Sound communities well into the twentieth century were settings in which cabin fever flourished. Getting away from it all, even for a brief visit or an outing was dictated almost solely by the availability of steamer service. Roads were geared to logging, poking into a black forest for a few miles, then dwindling into Indian trails. The few crude roadways hacked out by volunteers made overland travel an ordeal. Listen to this plaint by an early traveller as recorded by Murray Morgan in *Puget's Sound:*

Whatever the season, I knew the next day's experience would be disagreeable. In summer the woods might well be on fire. If there was wind we would be required to help chop up fir trees that had fallen across the road. In winter, the ground was covered with mud and it was a rule of the road that all men had to get out and walk up and down steep hills.

Escape by small boat was possible of course, and Puget Sounders soon developed a proficiency for rowing, paddling and sailing, reminiscent of the Scandinavian fjords many could recall.

So the notes of the first steamer whistle floating across the Sound in the 1860's became a welcome serenade. They signalled the opening of escape lanes from towns blessed by forests in their backyards but cursed by the attendant mud, dust, fleas and loneliness.

Among the first to arrive were Columbia River sidewheelers, so broad in the beam they wallowed their paddlewheels out of the water during Puget Sound squalls. They were followed by shallow draft sternwheelers, able to nose into any bank for loading and unloading. Later the routes multiplied with the building of the sharp-nosed Mosquito Fleet steamers, their freight doors but a few feet above the waterline. Finally as times bettered following the turn of the century, the role of the steamer as romantic pleasure cruise vessels took on a new luster with the arrival of crack steel-hulled greyhounds imported from the Great Lakes, the East Coast and Scotland.

From the beginning it hardly mattered to the early-day recreationists where the steamer was headed. Getting there was most of the fun. Just stepping aboard made one buoyant. Pennants snapped. Everywhere brass and paintwork gleamed. On deck, the air was clean and, apart from the occasional belch from the steamer stack, free of the milltown's smoky pall — and the constant scream of the saws.

Once underway, even the pilot house had an open door for visitors. The exception was during thick fogs when the captain blew a short blast then leaned out the door, watch in hand, to count the interval when the echo returned. It was a sort of crude Scandinavian radar. But it affixed the steamer's position for the skippers, equipped as author Archie Binns put it, "with keen ears geared to rapidly calculating minds…like acrobats performing blindfolded on a high trapeze."

An early view of Port Blakely mill.
University of Washington Library

Rivalling the pilot house as a theater was the engine room, usually an open pit protected by a railing. From this gallery, passengers watched hypnotically as the gleaming pistons and rods plunged like aerobics running in place, the air filled with thumps and groans and the pleasant smell of hot lubricants. A few feet away, the open loading door would, on calm days introduce a counterpoint of hisses as the grey-green water flowed by.

Gliding along, usually at a speed no greater than a comfortable 14 knots, the steamer became a private club. The role of host was played by the skipper, who often turned the wheel over to the mate to go below and socialize or collect fares, sometimes making change from a streetcar motorman's change maker. The air of camaraderie seemingly was unaffected by the steamer's stingy wage scale: between $25 and $40 a month for deck hands — and no time off. Labor disputes were rare.

Recalls Wilbur Thompson of Poulsbo, who sailed on 19 Puget Sound steamers:

Wages were secondary. It was the boat that counted. It was our home.

If the steamers were erratic, their fares were cheap, a painful exception being the bold banditry of the *Eliza Anderson,* a pioneer in the sidewheeler fleet. During the 1860s when steamers were carrying passengers between Portland and San Francisco (the only seaway to go at that time) for $5, the *Eliza Anderson* was charging $20 for passage from Olympia to Victoria.

As populations increased, so did competition. During the 1880s, Washington's population quadrupled and that of neighboring British Columbia doubled. Almost a million tickets were sold to steamer riders during 1890. Within the next two decades that mark would be surpassed as Washington's population increased by 120 percent; one of the nation's highest rate growths.

With competition, fares became affordable to just about anyone — 50 cents on most runs. There was an abundance of free holiday pleasures. A typical early-day Fourth of July celebration at places like Seattle, Tacoma and Port Townsend would include rowboat, foot and horse races; band concerts and orations; a parade featuring a Grand Army of the Republic contingent, all concluding with fireworks and a grand ball. All but the beer was free.

(A decade or so later, holiday divertissements were more sophisticated — and expensive. During Fleet Week held during the Alaska-Yukon-Pacific Exposition of 1909, Seattle visitors had their choice of such fare as the New York Symphony at the Moore Theater, the San Francisco Opera Company in *Bohemian Girl* at the Grand, a musical comedy at the Star, or a burlesque at the Lyric. The accompanying parade, boat rides to warships, band concerts and fireworks were free.)

In addition, wily boosters in Seattle and Tacoma vied with a series of low-budget summer "expositions." Make-believe streets were whipped up of plaster of Paris, inspired by the glittering 1876 Centennial Exposition in Philadelphia and bearing such fanciful titles as the Seattle Mardi Gras and Midsummer Fest. In 1891, a Tacoma fete packed more than 2,000 Seattleites aboard the steamers *City of Seattle, Bailey Gatzert* and *Greyhound.* Hundreds were left behind and special trains were run for those unable to buy steamer tickets.

Excursionists from Seattle arrive at Poulsbo aboard the sternwheeler, State of Washington. *Docked at left are a couple of early day Mosquito Fleet steamers the* Norwood *and the* Dove, *flying a flag worthy of a liner.*
University of Washington Library

A marching unit of the Port Townsend Fire Department shown at the ready for a Fourth of July parade. The structure at the far right is one of the city's classiest hotels, The Olympic.
University of Washington Library

Hail—and Rain—to the Chiefs

Between late 1880 and 1903 Seattle gave new meaning to the term "whistle stop," welcoming three Presidents who arrived by steamer: Rutherford Hayes in 1880; Benjamin Harrison in 1891 and Theodore Roosevelt in 1903.

First to work the thinly populated Puget Sound hustings was President Hayes, a mediocre First Executive who like his successor, President Harrison, served but one term. He was ecstatically welcomed by lonesome Seattle.

The President, accompanied by his wife and son and a party that included General William Tecumseh Sherman and Secretary of War Alexander Ramsey, came from Olympia on the new steamer, *George E. Starr.* Off Alki Point they were met by the *Fanny Lake, Goliah, J.B. Libby, Success, Celilo, Oliver Wolcott, Blakely* and *Nellie.* All were decked in bunting as were six sailing ships in port. Bonfires were lit, and thousands of candles were placed in windows. One local writer estimated the President shook hands with 2,000 wellwishers at Squire's Opera House. A speech scheduled for the University of Washington grounds was rained out.

The entourage boarded the *George E. Starr* the following day for Port Blakely, where the big mill was shut down to provide mill workers with a view of their Republican President, and permit the ceremonial presentation of a slab of fir.

But there was no welcome mat at Port Madison. Here the sawmill superintendent was a Democrat. On his orders, the *George E. Starr* was not permitted to tie up at the mill dock, leaving the President of the United States fuming aboard while school children on the shore waved with non-partisan vigor.

Following the rebuff, the *George E. Starr* splashed on to Port Townsend, then returned the President and his party back to Seattle, safely in the camp of the Republicans.

119

Hail to the nation's President
Our city's guest today!
Ring, bells, roar, guns!
and voices cheer!

That bit of doggerel was inspired by the arrival in Seattle of President Benjamin Harrison, who as a lawyer, general, senator, and 23rd President of the United States inspired very little else.

Timing, apart from the incessant May rain, was propitious. True, business was off a tad, presaging arrival of the Panic of '93, but Seattle's population growth, as evidenced by the census of 1890, was up phenomenally.

Over lunch enroute to Seattle from Tacoma aboard the luxurious new *City of Seattle,* Seattle's Mayor Harry White boasted that Seattle's head count of 42,837 represented a twelve-fold growth in a decade. (He neglected to mention the fact that Tacoma, still 6,000 behind Seattle, had grown three times as fast.)

Downtown, the scars of the fire of 1889 had been erased by $10 million in new brick and stone buildings, now draped in bunting. One even housed a new library, with 7,000 books and separate reading rooms for men and women. Nearby, the University of Washington's sole building was crowded with 313 students and 11 instructors. The Legislature, generous then as now, had appropriated $25,000 for maintenance during the ensuing two years.

Accounts differ as to the size of the welcoming armada. Thomas W. Prosch, a historian of the period, counted 33 vessels. But it's obvious that just about everything afloat on that day turned out to greet the President.

Off Alki Point the *City of Seattle* had been joined by a welcoming armada. of more than a score of steamers headed by her running mate, the *City of Kingston* as well as by the *Bailey Gatzert,* the *T. J. Potter, Greyhound, Politofsky,* and others, including a scruffy freighter, the *Haytian Republic.* (The following year the latter made news when her owners were charged with importing opium and illegal Chinese immigrants. In 1897, she created

A National Guard unit forms ranks at First and Marion in Seattle in 1880 for parade duty.
University of Washington Library

120

worldwide headlines when under new ownership and name, the *Portland* arrived in Seattle with the first Klondike gold.)

As part of his Seattle tour, President Harrison took a cable car to the foot of Yesler Way. There his party boarded the tiny paddlewheeler, *Kirkland,* for a trip on Lake Washington, returning in the rain to the ferry slip at the foot of Madison Street.

President Harrison lost his cool but once. Looking out from his carriage on a sea of umbrellas unfurled in the continuous rain, the President, according to the *Tacoma Ledger,* growled:

It's an ugly day for a drive.

For royal welcomes to Seattle, The Day T.R. Arrived outshone them all. The date was May 23, 1903. The sun beamed. Mountains gleamed. Docks and streets were lined with throngs of unabashed flag wavers. Buildings, lamp posts, even the steamship bearing President Theodore Roosevelt and his party were wrapped in bunting. It was as if some super-patriotic Christo had been at work.

On that day Seattle was exactly 50 years old. Its population had passed 100,000. It was a confident, ebullient city. During its half-century, Seattle had already welcomed two presidents, but today was different. Rutherford Hayes and Benjamin Harrison hardly passed for heroic figures. But T.R. did. His arrival came only three years after the mustering out of the Rough Riders he had ridden to military and political victory. His administration had been bold and colorful; at times as dazzling as his toothy smile, corralling trusts, planting the seeds of a new land ethic called conservation and rattling the saber in Central America.

Just hours before his docking in Seattle he paused in Bremerton to pay tribute to the Navy Yard workers who had helped speed the battleship *Oregon* to victory in Santiago Bay. It was a race that convinced Roosevelt of the need for a canal across the Isthmus of Panama, even if it took a revolution to accommodate.

Roosevelt arrived in Seattle shortly after one p.m. aboard the *S.S. Spokane*. He had been up for seven hours in a day that began in Tacoma, where he was presented with a chair fashioned from the antlers of a Roosevelt elk. (This he accepted but declined the gift from Kalama of a bear cub that snapped at him when he petted it.)

En route to Seattle aboard the *Spokane*, he polished off a trencherman's lunch, dining from a menu that included oysters on the half shell, terrapin, chicken, turkey, ices and wines.

Off Alki Point, a barge sponsored by the Japanese Society, lobbed brilliant fireworks into the cloudless sky.

Entering Elliott Bay, the *Spokane*, nominally engaged in Alaska tourist traffic, passed between two lines of assembled vessels. In the van were the U.S. Revenue cutters *Grant, Manning, Perry* and *McCullough*; followed by the tugs *Holyoke, Sea Lion, Lorne, Tacoma, Tyee, Pioneer* and the press boat *Bahada*. Then came the Navy Yard tender *Pawtucket*, which earlier had carried the Secretary of the Navy to Bremerton, and the Alaska steamers *Queen, Humboldt, Senator* and *Roanoke*. Finally came vessels of the Mosquito Fleet, including the *Athlon* and the *Inland Flyer*.

Captain Norman Nicholson steamed the *Spokane* across the harbor at such a clip she outdistanced most of the welcoming armada, as well as the steamer carrying the press. President Roosevelt's scheduled arrival at Arlington Dock had drawn a densely-packed crowd that filled Railroad Avenue and adjoining vantage points.

With President McKinley's assassination fresh in mind, what passed for strict security was attempted, including the dispatching of five National Guard companies from Seattle, Everett and Whatcom, and the hiring of 20 extra police. All were swallowed up by the cheering crowds. (T.R. was shot in 1912 in Milwaukee, but he completed his scheduled speech before being taken to the hospital, where he quickly recovered.)

Roosevelt charmed Seattle enough to win the city's vote as a maverick Bull Moose presidential candidate in 1912. That was the year Seattle elected Progressives to Congress and the Socialist candidate for mayor received almost as many votes as the Republican candidate.

In his Tacoma, Bremerton, Seattle and Everett speeches, he stroked virtually everyone: veterans, the National Guard, the Seattle builders of the battleship *Nebraska*, children and workers. At Bremerton he won the hearts and votes of Navy Yard workers by assuring them:

> *You all did your part in winning them (the battles of Santiago and Manila) just as much as the men who actually fought.*

Now at Seattle he renewed a call for more arms. He tempered his militarism slightly by cautioning against "the spirit of arrogant disregard of those who are less well off." The loudest applause came when he warned:

> *We have passed the age in this country when we could afford to tolerate the man whose aim was to skin the country and get out.*

(T.R., whose Chief Forester, Gifford Pinchot, was to coin the term "conservation," delighted in the use of the "skin the country" description. On one occasion he elaborated on this theme by adding:

That man, that man whose idea of developing the country is to cut every stick of timber off of it, and leave a barren desert ... that man is a curse.)

A few days before his arrival on Puget Sound, President Roosevelt's conservationist zeal had been whetted when he hiked with naturalist John Muir along a Yosemite trail in a snowstorm. His enjoyment was honed by the discomfiture of National Park Service brass who, not anticipating the arrival of the Presidential party for another day, were out fishing when he did show up.

In Seattle, Roosevelt ended his day of bully speeches in late evening when he retired at the Washington Hotel. Minutes later his distraught secretary awakened him. Downstairs a late evening banquet crowd of 500 was anxiously awaiting his scheduled appearance. The President arose, dressed, and made his way to a balcony overlooking the banquet. There he apologized for being late, offered a few words of greeting, and returned to his bed.

The Hatching of the Mosquito Fleet

The patriotic fervor stirred all along Puget Sound by President Roosevelt's visit was fanned anew when on a May morning in 1908, the U.S. Atlantic fleet steamed out of the mists of the Strait of Juan de Fuca. It was a recruiting poster scene: 14 warships in a single line of battle, 400 yards apart moving at 12 knots past welcoming steamers en route to a celebratory Seattle. The big sternwheeler *Yosemite,* bore most of the University of Washington student body in a flag-waving welcome—young America saluting its entry into the wonderful world of imperialism.

Victoria, its tourist-wise merchants ever trying nobly to live up to its "little bit of England" billing, joined in this salute. Almost 20,000 excursionists rode the crack *Princess Victoria* and the newly-arrived Great Lakes steamer *Chippewa* during the four-day stay of the fleet.

There was plenty to celebrate. A deep depression that had begun with the panic of 1893 was ebbing, sluiced away by the Klondike Gold Rush and by a technological revolution that helped usher in a new day for rail and waterborne transportation.

Prime beneficiary of the gold rushes was, of course, Seattle. Canadian author Pierre Berton once described the Klondike Stampede as "in some ways the weirdest and most useless mass movement in history." But it made Seattle a city and Puget Sound's dominant port with more than 40 steamships in Alaska service docking at Seattle in 1900. Included was the *City of Seattle* bearing three tons of gold—treble the amount that touched off the stampede when first reported in 1898. Seattle now controlled 95 percent of the Territory's shipping and most of its commercial dealings.

(Seattle's *anschluss* dashed Tacoma's hopes of dominating Alaska trade.

(T.R. visit photos overleaf)

A Loud Whistle Stop for TR

Far left: *More than 30 steamers and tugs—and four U. S. Revenue Service cutters—escort the Alaska liner* Spokane *bearing President Theodore Roosevelt to a tumultous Seattle welcome on May 23, 1903.*

Top center: *Having outpaced her marine escort—and the press boat—the* Spokane *pulls into Arlington Dock in what the* Seattle Times *later described as "a blaze of bunting, a forest of flags, a mystic tangle of red, white and blue."*

Top right: *Doffing his silk hat, the President moves down the gangplank to be officially welcomed by Seattle Mayor Tom Hume. Despite the recent assassination of President McKinley, attempts to beef up security visibly failed.*

Lower right: *TR flashes his famous toothy grin for the benefit of the crowd of 50,000, the largest to assemble in a Washington city. The welcoming parade, shown passing through Pioneer Square, included 14 carriages, as well as contingents of the National Guard, police, Secret Service and Wagner's Band.*

Lower left: *This photo captures the size of the crowd, but not its stridency. Included was the sentimental welcome provided by a line of Philippine campaign veterans standing at attention, while the President executed a salute. "There was," vowed the* Times *reporter, "just the shadow of a tear at the eye of the President."*

University of Washington Library
Paul Dorpat

Inspecting arms — 1908. Gad! Could that be a swabbie sprawled in the foreground?

(Top of Page) One of the world's greatest assemblages of naval power, the Great White Fleet, moves out of the mists of the Strait of Juan de Fuca to enter Puget Sound in May 1908. At right, the visiting warships turn on their lights at sunset. Later, searchlight drills were part of the nightly show.

But 80 years later, Tacoma captured Sea-Land, Seattle's biggest shipper, including Alaska markets. It is now estimated that within the next 10 years 80 percent of the Puget Sound to Alaska seaborne trade, most of it containerized, will be moving through Tacoma.)

Even more widespread were the effects of the turn of the century explosion in technology.

Sawmill output shot up with adoption of milling machines, including band saws, first exhibited at the Philadelphia Exposition of 1876. In the woods, the first steam winches and logging locomotives were expanding the reach of the loggers' axes and crosscut saws. Coal mines in the Cascades were yielding mountains of coal, much of it to be exported over Seattle, Tacoma and Bellingham docks.

The huge cargo liners, *Minnesota* and *Dakota,* would not arrive on Puget Sound until 1905. But the Great Northern Railway's Jim Hill was already working for a seaway to link his rails with the Orient. On an August day in 1896,

The steamer T. C. Reed *once hauled loggers to places like Aberdeen and Montesano. Here she prepares to embark a load of visitors from the Great White Fleet warship* New Jersey, *her decks already jammed with onlookers. The* USS Nebraska *is at far right. More than a score of warships of the Great White Fleet visited Puget Sound in 1908 as part of a round-the-world "show the flag" mission.*

Seattle took a holiday to welcome the Nippon Yusen Kaisha freighter *Miike Maru,* the first steamship to join Seattle with Japan, brought there by Hill's persuasion. (Tacoma had established steamship runs to the Orient three years previously, a fact the welcoming speeches at Seattle overlooked.) The 3200-ton freighter, saluted by Wagner's First Regimental Band playing the *Miike Maru March,* sailed on her first return voyage to Japan with cargoes that included flour, lumber, and hundreds of "Made in U.S.A." bicycles. Trade to other world ports busied Seattle's docks as export shipments rose from $2.8 million in 1897 to $4 million in 1899, and imports shot up from $1.1 million in 1897 to $5.3 million in 1899.

Virtually every Puget Sound community shared in the technological upbeat. Seattle and Tacoma became the terminals for a web of rail lines over which rolled import-export freight as well as trans-continental passenger express trains. Bremerton welcomed the *USS Monterey,* first in a long line of warships to be overhauled at the Puget Sound Navy Yard. The Vashon Island hamlet at Dockton inherited a big drydock from Port Townsend, where shortly after 1900 a land speculation bubble burst, along with promises of a Peninsula railhead. At Port Blakely the Hall Bros. Shipyard, which had launched a hundred sailing ships before moving from Port Ludlow, was beginning to send down its ways steam-powered lumber carriers and sternwheelers for the Yukon and Tanana Rivers. The Moran yard in Seattle, soon to launch a battleship, was building a Navy torpedo boat and an armada of boats and barges for the Yukon. A dozen were completed in only six months, using an assembly line technique that was to make Seattle and Tacoma shipyards among the nation's most productive during two world wars.

Off on one of its boom-or-bust cycles, employment at Port Blakely's big sawmill passed one thousand. To show off its product to the world, the mill sawed out a giant timber — 44" x 44" and 144' long — and shipped it by rail to the World Columbian Exposition in Chicago. Perfection of a salmon cleaning machine, crudely termed "Iron Chink," and the adoption of gas engines that replaced sails and oars on fishing boats encouraged the development of canneries at Anacortes, Blaine, Bellingham, Everett, Poulsbo, Friday Harbor and Lopez Island; all to the benefit of steamer operators.

The new American dream of harnessing resources did not stop at water's edge. Within a few years after the dawn of the twentieth century, it was to send the Sound's clunky paddlewheelers off to the boneyard.

Replacing them were slim-hulled steamers poking into the remotest coves, leaving frothy wakes from the Strait of Juan de Fuca to Budd Inlet at the Sound's southern-most reach.

The Mosquito Fleet had arrived.

Most Puget Sound marine historians and steamer buffs agree on the origins of that indelible term — an unidentified Seattle newspaper reporter's observation:

> *At five o'clock in Seattle, the little commuter steamers scurry off to their destinations like a swarm of mosquitos.*

There is less general agreement on just how many vessels sailed under that mythical Mosquito Fleet burgee. Some put the figure into the hundreds,

Perfecting an assembly line technique, Seattle's Moran shipyard in 1898 built a dozen steamers for the Gold Rush duty on the Yukon River. One was lost en route north; the rest amortized their cost in but one season.

University of Washington Library

but include the larger steel-hulled steamers like the *Iroquois, Indianapolis, Olympia* and others.

Most, however, agree the term should apply only to that armada of small, wooden-hulled steamers that for more than 20 years plied the Sound's marine highways on runs of but a few hours. They carried farmers, loggers, fishermen, businessmen and, on weekends, crowds of those on a family outing.

The horizontal profile of a typical Mosquito Fleet steamer would show a narrow hull with a knife-sharp bow, the lines resembling those of a child's drawing: a horizontal line denoting a flat deck with two short vertical lines, slightly aslant, creating bow and stern. The main deck provided passenger facilities. Atop this was a pilot house, signal mast, lifeboats, and usually a single stack. The stack, which carried the line's trade mark—a black ball, a band of white, or some other device—was almost always black, although some owners laid on hues of blue, orange and yellow.

The steamer's lower deck housed engines, machinery, stacks of cordwood, (later fuel oil tanks), crew facilities and passenger seating. Most Mosquito Fleet vessels were short-haul day boats with no dining rooms. This permitted the main deck to be given over to a so-called promenade deck, an observation room, and a ladies' cabin. Seating ranged from uncomfortable, drafty, wooden benches to more elegant Pullman-type chairs, some of them upholstered in leather. Some of the later steel-hulled night boats, such as those serving Bellingham, Anacortes, and Port Townsend, provided attractive dining rooms and tiny staterooms, just large enough to accommodate two or three bunks in a double deck arrangement, a sink and a port hole.

Until the advent of coal-burning engines, and later those fueled by oil, propulsion was provided by burning cordwood, as it had since the arrival of the first steamer on Puget Sound, the *Beaver,* in 1836. And while the Mosquito Fleet steamers were more energy efficient than the plodding *Beaver*—which could devour up to 40 cords of wood in 24 hours—they, too, had prodigious appetites. The *Flyer,* equipped with engines that drew national attention, held

The Mosquito Fleet steamer profile is well illustrated in this 1913 scene at Tacoma, celebrating the completion of the 11th Street Bridge. In the foreground is the 112-foot Verona, *then the 140-foot* Nisqually, *soon to be taken off the Seattle-Tacoma run after 21 years of service, and the fleet* Flyer.

Oregon Historical Society

two cords of wood at a time in her big furnaces, and when running at top form could consume 24 cords in a day! By 1925, virtually all were converted to oil.

When scrapped in 1930, the *Flyer's* engines had set a reliability record that defied even the weather. One of her skippers, Captain Everett Coffin, (later to shepherd the world's fastest single-screw steamer, the *Tacoma*) recalled that during a record gale, a surveyor from Lloyd's of London "checked us from Alki to Robinson and found only a minute's difference in our running time." He added:

> *This was in the face of a gale that was throwing spray against the pilot house windows, something that does not happen very often to the Flyer.*

One of the Mosquito Fleet's key roles was that of serving as a farm-to-market highway for settlers. To farm women particularly it was a welcome role, one that introduced a measure of warmth and companionship into an often dreary rural setting. Like the fishing boats of Bergen, where the captain's wife brings ashore armloads of flowers to sell at the market shared by her husband and other fishermen, the Mosquito Fleet steamers serving farms on Bainbridge, Vashon and Whidbey Islands and other stops, furnished bright swatches of color on market day in Seattle. Here produce houses, and by 1906 the Pike Street Farmer's Market, provided a bazaar within walking distance of Colman Dock and Pier 3 where most steamers docked. Writes Murray Morgan, co-author of a recent book, *The Pike Street Market:*

> *When the boat whistled its approach, the farmers or their wives would gather on the dock, bringing chickens dressed and wrapped in cheesecloth; butter molded into rose patterns, wrapped in butterpaper, and packed in wooden boxes; eggs nestled in straw baskets; root vegetables in burlap sacks; milk in galvanized cans; crates of fruit; bundles of rhubarb.*

Another chronicler of Puget Sound folkways, veteran steamer skipper

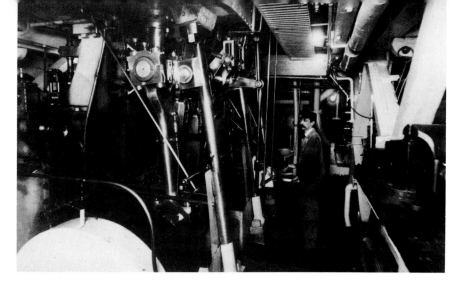

Engine room of the Flyer. *The engineer on duty is Harry Collier, later to become chairman of the board of Standard Oil Company.*

Captain Torger Birkland, has similar warm—if somewhat ungallant—recollections of the days when he was captain of the steamer *Hyak,* which brought farmers from Poulsbo and Bainbridge Island to Seattle on Saturday, the traditional market day. He recalls:

> *Everyone had a great time, with the hens cackling on their way to market and the women cackling on the way home, and the cabin filled with the aroma of Manning's fresh-ground coffee everybody brought home with them.*

Just getting on and off represented much of the challenge involved in early-day steamer travel. Early on, Seattle, Tacoma and Port Townsend provided the only facilities even remotely resembling a terminal. These consisted of but a cramped ticket office with a worn bench for waiting riders.

The first steamer riders at Seattle gathered in the Yesler Mill boiler room while awaiting departure. Later Pier 3, today better known as Ivars Acres of Clams Restaurant, housed a small waiting room. James Colman, a Scot engineer who ran the mill (and later played a prominent role in developing a railroad linking Seattle to the Renton coal fields), built the first in a series of terminals bearing his name.

The first Colman Dock, a rickety, shed-like facility sixty feet long, was built in 1882. It was replaced in 1886, destroyed in the 1889 Seattle fire, and rebuilt the following year. But comfort and convenience did not arrive until 1908. That year Colman erected his monument, a terminal 705 feet long, crowned with an Italianate clock tower and featuring a domed waiting room and 14 landing slips with gangways that could be raised and lowered while attendants bawled out arrivals and departures.

The mechanical gangways were no match for commuters, however. In 1912, a failure of the cog system plunged a score of passengers into Elliott Bay, drowning two. The *Argus* blamed passenger haste and impatience.

The dock with its landmark clock tower was replaced in 1936 by an unglamorous facility to which was affixed an art deco facade, a somewhat clumsy attempt to drag the Black Ball Line into the automobile age. The cramped terminal continued in use until 1965 when the State of Washington, which took over the Black Ball ferry system in 1951, demolished it and the adjoining Grand Trunk Pacific Dock, replacing them with today's Colman Dock. Through it each year pass ferry riders to Bainbridge Island and Bremerton, almost as heavy a traffic as that of the Seattle-Tacoma International Airport.

The early day steamer riders found even the first crude Colman Dock facility a blessing compared to those provided at many an isolated stop. Many

131

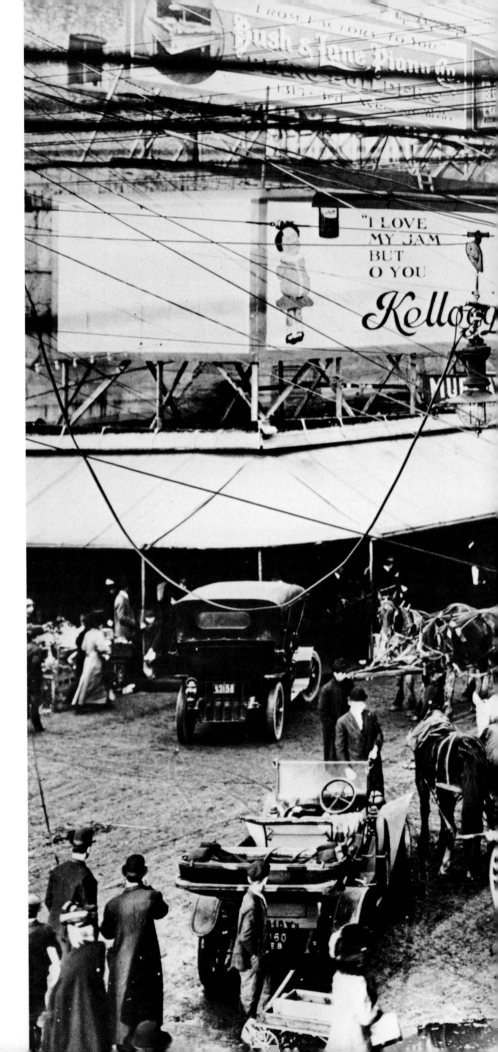

Seattle's Farmers' Market drew shopper throngs as well as farmers from cross-Sound points. The photo was taken about 1910.

Designed to accommodate up to 200,000 steamer riders monthly, a new Colman Dock was constructed in 1908. The facility, at the location of today's Colman Dock ferry terminal, was 705 feet long, boasted a domed waiting room, 14 gangways that could be raised and lowered mechanically, and a commodious freight area, served by a railroad spur and horse-drawn wagons.

Colman Dock, considered one of the country's best for that period, became one of the busiest. Steamers left Tacoma every two hours with fares as low as 35 cents. Other steamers departed daily for Port Townsend and Victoria, and there was service to Anacortes, Bellingham, Edmonds, Everett and San Juan Islands points.

All passengers were afoot, utilizing an elevated walkway within the terminal and another crossing Railroad Avenue to today's First Avenue.

The terminal saw heavy duty in 1908 with visitors attracted by the arrival of the Great White Fleet, the opening of the Alaska Yukon Pacific Exposition and the visit of President William Howard Taft, who departed from Colman Dock, Tacoma-bound on the yacht El Primero.

An addition to the present terminal, costing upwards of $20 million, has been designed for future construction.

Old Seattle Paperworks

of the steamer docks elsewhere were simply spindly walkways supported by untreated piling. Teredoes, time and tide soon whittled them down to what has been described as "thin, hour glass columns," that would vibrate menacingly when one ventured out on their rickety planks.

At many stops, usually signalled by a shout, a lantern, or simply a bit of arm waving, passengers were rowed out to meet the oncoming steamer. Archie Binns has captured the personal experience of such a paddlewheeler-boarding in his book, *Roaring Land:*

> *The distant, mellow whistle of the steamer leaving her dock called us back to the present and to the beach, where we scrambled into the boat. Father pushed off and rowed slowly toward the middle of the stream…. As steamer and boat drew toward each other, the gong clanged and the wheel thundered a few revolutions in reverse; another clang and the thunder ceased. Father unshipped his inside oar and each deck hand reached down with one foot, catching our bow and stern and holding the boat alongside while we scrambled on board and Father passed up the straw telescope and suit boxes, and took up the oars again. The deck hands shoved the boat away with the same feet which had welcomed it, and one of them sang out: "All clear, sir!" The gong clanged loudly near us; the engines sighed and the stern wheel thundered. Misty gray-green water, flecked with foam, went past the open doorway with a hissing sound; on the flood the boat faded astern and we were part of the big, rushing world of the steamer.*

By the turn of the century whistle stops gave way to docks, and steamers began maintaining a semblance of schedules. Most kept busy on a six-day week.

It was said that the reason the Mosquito Fleet steamers were seldom in drydock was that they never were motionless long enough for barnacles to collect. A look back at some typical runs seems to substantiate that claim.

The *Dode,* a wooden 99-footer that was tireless if not swift, left Pier 3 at Seattle on Tuesday. During the day, she loaded and unloaded passengers and freight from Kingston, Port Gamble, Seabeck, Brinnon, Holly, Dewatto, Lilliwaup Falls, Hoodsport, and Union City. The following day she returned over the same route.

The *Rosalie* on her Seattle run left Bellingham at 8:00 a.m. then stopped in Anacortes, Olga, Rosario, East Sound, Orcas, West Sound, Friday Harbor, Deer Harbor, Roche Harbor, Lopez, Argyle, Richardson, Smith's Island and Port Townsend, arriving (breathlessly) at Seattle at 6:00 p.m. Six hours later she retraced her steps.

The chunky *Perdita* and the *Lydia Thompson* followed a similar wake out of Seattle, providing thrice-weekly San Juan Island service, adding Bellingham and Port Townsend to their whistle stops.

Steamers linked Olympia with Steilacoom, Tacoma, Port Madison, Port Gamble, Port Ludlow, Port Townsend, Victoria and a score of whistle stops. The whistles echoed along the forested shores of Lake Crescent and Lake Whatcom. Steamers circled Vashon and Bainbridge Islands and called at tiny isles like Hartstene and Anderson. There were runs from Everett to Coupeville and up the Snohomish; from Langley to Anacortes, Renton to Leschi, Bothell to Madison Park and other stops on Lake Washington. Steamers butted out into the storm-thrashed Strait of Juan de Fuca to carry loggers and fishermen and stores to Neah Bay, Pyscht and Clallam Bay. Others penetrated river shallows. The entire Sound was a web of steamer routes.

Despite some grumbling, the little steamers became fondly regarded. Loud arguments ensued over the virtues and speed of the *Flyer, Hyak, Monticello, H. B. Kennedy, Burton, City of Everett* and other favorites.

While steamers by the score were logging millions of accident-free miles into the most remote reaches of Puget Sound and British Columbia, the runs were not without perils.

Accidents, usually groundings or collisions, were commonplace due largely to a lack of dependable charts and instruments. Positions during fogs were estimated by timing the whistle's echo. Some skippers and mates viewed their course through the bottom of a glass. Others, those on the competitive Seattle-Victoria run, were reluctant to sound the slow bell, regardless of visability.

Until the advent of lighthouses, warning buoys, charts and sophisticated navigation instruments, lack of visibility posed a constant threat. It was overcome only by the navigator's familiarity with the channel down which he periodically groped at night or during heavy fogs.

During night hours, the blackness would be punctuated only by the lantern light of some settler's cabin. Knowing the neighborhood became a matter of life and death.

The art of timing the steamer's echo to determine the presence of land went beyond a mere mathematical estimate, based on the fact that sound travels through salt air at the rate of 1,080 feet per second. (Navigators rounded this off at 1,000 feet). Experienced navigators not only could estimate how far they were from shore, but also could determine their position by the sound of the echo. This despite the fact a low coastline, a high bank, or a gravel beach all return a different sound. Another determinant was the length of the echo. A short echo denoted a narrow island or headland, for most of the whistle's sound continued on by on both sides. With only a few second's leeway, the navigators also had to decide whether the echo was bouncing from floating logs, buoys—or even a solid fog bank. As traffic increased, echo boards soon began dotting the Sound.

Human error took the heaviest toll of lives. The worst Puget Sound steamer disaster, that of the Puget Sound Navigation Company steamer *Clallam* in which 54 drowned, could have been largely averted if passengers had been kept aboard until rescue tugs arrived. All those who took to the lifeboats when the steamer was being battered by a January 1904 gale off Port Townsend died. Most of those remaining onboard survived. Even less explicable was the sinking in 1906 of the steamer *Dix*, rammed and sent to the bottom on a calm, clear night off Seattle's harbor shores. Thirty-seven drowned.

With a few other notable exceptions, loss of life from steamer mishaps was light. Minor mishaps even had comedic overtones. When the *Reliance* grounded off of Alki Point, passengers were rowed ashore and continued their journey by trolley. The grounding of the little *Sophia* is said to have occurred when the skipper's dog, trained to bark when he heard his master's craft approaching in a fog, was chased down the beach by an angry neighbor, the *Sophia* blindly following. Even the vaunted *Flyer* was accident-prone. In a multiple Elliott Bay hull-banger in 1903, the *Flyer* was rammed in a heavy fog by the steamer *Dode*, which was towing the *Bellingham*. On the rebound, the *Flyer* bashed into the German freighter, *Chili*. There were no injuries. In later years the *Flyer* rammed Colman Dock; collided with a tug off Dash Point and, in 1911, caught fire off Alki, surviving all incidents.

Since then, a succession of Colman Docks have been bashed by approaching steamers and ferries. The most spectacular was in 1912 when the Alaska line's *Alameda*, with the famed "Dynamite" Johnny O'Brien at the helm, tore through the end of the dock due to a confusion with engine room signals. The big steamer sliced off the the clock tower and crashed into the sternwheeler *Telegraph*, sending her to the bottom. The clock tower was replaced, the *Telegraph* was refloated, and the legend of Dynamite Johnny added a new chapter.

On balance, the steamers were an uncommonly safe mode of transportation during an era when the seas had only begun to yield their supremacy.

Marine historian Gordon Newell in his book, *S O S North Pacific*, runs an inventory of vessels claimed along that hazardous littoral. But he also reminds us that the safety record, rather than the disaster toll "is the most remarkable thing about the Puget Sound Mosquito Fleet." He writes:

The little ships carried their millions of people to and from a hundred harbors along the shores of the inland sea. They carried them somewhat slower than the modern automobile, but they carried them safely. Puget Sound steamboats could probably boast of a lower death rate than any other transportation system in modern history; but this is an age of Progress and they are all gone now.

A rowboat completes the journey of two passengers from the Capital City.
University of Washington Library

The Path to Victoria: Steamers Last Stand

The Rosalie *nears her dock at Friday Harbor in the early 1900s. Hotel at left has been restored as a tourist facility.*
University of Washington Library

The demise of the Mosquito Fleet marked the end of a class of steamers that could trace its lineage back to New England. It was a cocky breed of wooden-hulled vessels, simple and cheap to build and operate. (The long-lived *Flyer* and *Athlon* cost around $4,000 each.) Skipper-owned, they spent their days hauling farmers, loggers and fishermen and, on weekends, families on bargain outings. As America began its love affair with the automobile, the auto ferry, contempuously described by Mosquito Fleet skippers as "double-ended chicken coops on a raft," gradually took their places.

But another steamer fleet, as regal as the Mosquito Fleet was plebian, continued to flourish. Flying the proud house flag of the Canadian Pacific Railway, it carried millions of passengers in luxury until well into the 1940s, creating a marine highway connecting Seattle, Victoria and Vancouver.

At the outset it was a route best known for its financial reefs. After the monopoly of the *Eliza Anderson* was at last broken, the runs between Puget Sound points and Victoria began attracting a polygot assembly of steamers. Some were creaking wooden-hulled vessels of little distinction, and as it turned out, minimal safety. But the lure of the international run, one plied since the arrival of the *Beaver* in 1843 to help found Fort Victoria, was irresistable. Even before 1900, it was drawing some of the Pacific's finest passenger vessels, virtually all of them soon sinking under a load of debt.

The roll call included the O. R. & N.'s *Olympian* and *Alaskan*, the last of the leviathan sidewheelers. They arrived just as the boom tide was subsiding, sweeping the big paddlewheelers to anguished ends. Both became fatalities while seeking more profitable runs; the *Alaskan* sinking off Cape Blanco in 1889 and the *Olympian* pounding to pieces on the rocks off the Strait of Magellan in 1906.

In 1890, a crowd of nearly 30,000 jammed Seattle's waterfront to welcome the showy *City of Seattle,* flying the house flag of the newly organized Washington and Alaska Steamship Co. Among officers of the enterprise, forerunner of the dominant Alaska Line, was its general manager, Charles E. Peabody, soon to move into the Victoria sea lanes with his own trio of crack steamers.

Following arrival of the *City of Seattle* came a sister, the *City of Kingston,* arriving at Port Townsend on Feb. 17, 1890, sixty-one days out of New York. The first riders of the two steel-hulled vessels marvelled at the grand staircases and carpeted staterooms with brass bedsteads and wash basins of pink marble. They dined enthusiastically from an elaborate menu. But the mammoths proved too expensive to feed. The *City of Seattle* was withdrawn from service and languished at dockside until rescued by the Gold Rush. The *City of Kingston* continued to lose money on the Victoria run until she sank in a collision at Tacoma in 1899.

Early in the 1900s as a newly minted affluence began creating a market for luxury holidays, Victoria merchants began demanding improved steamship service to Seattle. The demands became clamorous following the 1904 sinking of the Puget Sound Navigation Company's wooden steamer *Clallam,* en route to Victoria from Port Townsend.

It didn't take long for one of the world's savviest merchants of travel to fill the need. On Jan. 20, 1904, twelve days after the *Clallam* tragedy, the *Princess Beatrice,* newest steamer of the Canadian Pacific Railway, sailed for Seattle, the key link on what was to become the Triangle Route joining Seattle, Victoria and Vancouver. Despite the apparent haste of the *Princess Beatrice's* entry, the plans had been long forming.

By 1896, the Canadian Pacific Railway had spanned Canada, clawing its way over the Rockies and reaching tidewater at Vancouver. Here white-hulled *Empress* liners were to race across the North Pacific to Japan and China. Along its newly-laid trans-Canada tracks, the CPR built a series of unmatched luxury hotels, geared to the smart traveler of the newborn twentieth century. Two more hotels, the *Empress* and another at Vancouver, were being readied for construction, and the firm was testing the potential of the Inside Passage steamer lanes to southeastern Alaska.

The *Beatrice* with a capacity of but 350 passengers was powered by a 1,300-horsepower engine and soon proved inadequate to meet traffic demands. The CPR responded decisively, ushering in a golden age of steamers with the first in a series of compact liners, the *Princess Victoria.* With a length of 300 feet, she was twice the size of her predecessor, eye-catching with a gleaming white hull of steel and three buff-colored stacks topped with a black band. Built in Scotland at the yard that was to launch the Cunard liners that ruled the Atlantic, she was the forerunner of a fleet virtually unmatched for workmanship and appointments.

In addition to offering more speed—the *Princess Victoria* could top 22 knots—the CPR liner provided superior dining rooms, accommodations and service.

Assignment of the regal *Princess Victoria* to the international run burnished the visitor appeal of Victoria, with its boast of being "a bit of Old England." The sobriquet was not all booster puffery. The one-time Fraser River gold rush tent city had been replaced by one that was storybook Victorian; a place of misty beauty and a climate that was Canada's mildest (as were its property and income taxes). In this setting, Victoria bloomed. Writing of the city's transplants, with their baggage of old-school ties, eccentricities and treasured memories, Canadian historian Bruce Hutchinson said:

> *Thus it was that while there was much that was England in Victoria it was never a bit of Olde England. It was colonial England done over in memory of an England that quite probably never existed.*

Victoria, artifices and all, became an irresistible draw for visitors. Streets were alive with handsome equipage, horses clip-clopping down avenues lined with Garry oak, lilacs, dogwood and mansions.

Even back in 1880, with a population of but 20,000, the city boasted a hostelry, the Driard, that was, according to British officers on recuperative leave, equal to the Raffles at Singapore. Along the seashore, near today's Outer Wharfs, the Hotel Dalles offered a bathing pavilion, a ladies' dining

Elliott Bay at the peak of the Mosquito Fleet's eminence. Steamer at left is the Kulshan. *Visable at dockside are the* Monticello, Flyer, Tacoma *and* H. B. Kennedy. *The year is 1913, immediately before completion of the Smith Tower.*

Joe Poon

room with private entrance, and a rooftop promenade that included an observation tower manned by a porter who awakened guests when he saw their ship rounding Race Rocks. A *New York Sun* reporter visiting in 1880 termed Victoria "the quaintest town in North America… where residents were more idle than visitors." A St. Paul magazine writer found it "almost funerally quiet," a silence not unwelcome in a city where city hall clocks stopped striking between 10:30 p.m. and 7:30 a.m.

(The run the liners were to ply, Seattle-Victoria-Vancouver, survived for more than 40 years as the Triangle Route. It was one that would captivate generations: a waterway serene and scenic, fought over with savage rate wars and extravagent investments in elegant steamers.

The main contenders in this battle for route supremacy were the enormously wealthy Canadian Pacific Railway and an upstart from across the border, the newly-formed Puget Sound Navigation Company. For almost five years from that April day when the *Princess Victoria* glided into Victoria's inner harbor, the Canadian Pacific and the newly-minted Puget Sound Navigation Company slugged it out with races and rate wars that tumbled fares down to as low as 25 cents between Seattle and Victoria. But even with the introduction of its Great Lakes imports, *Chippewa, Indianapolis* and *Iroquois,* P. S.N. lasted but a few rounds as a major contender.

In 1908, with the Alaska Yukon Pacific Exposition due to open in Seattle the following year, the Northern Pacific Railway interceded and arranged a truce. The rate war was over. Puget Sound Navigation Company continued to provide occasional summertime excursions to Victoria or Vancouver for another 30 years, but the Princess steamers of the CPR ruled the Triangle Route.

Aside from summertime excursions offered by Puget Sound Navigation Company vessels, including the *Kalakala,* an old "streamlined" auto ferry dangerously unsuited for the cross-Strait run, the only real competition offered the Canadian Pacific came from its rail rival, the Grand Trunk Pacific.

The GTP made its entry in 1910 with a pair of built-in-England liners, the *Prince Rupert* and *Prince George,* each capable of carrying 1500 passengers with stateroom accommodations for 220. In addition to connecting Seattle, Victoria and Vancouver, the 3372-ton triple-stacked liners made a stop at the railway's terminus, Prince Rupert. But with only weekly service, the GTP proved little threat to the Canadian Pacific.

In 1930, the Government-owned railway made a final bid, placing in Triangle service the Birkenhead-built *Prince Henry, Prince David* and *Prince Robert.* Weighing in at 6,892 tons each, they were the largest steamers to ply Puget Sound and Northern coastal waters. Despite their smart appointments and 24-knot speed, they proved to be heavy losers. In September 1931 after but two seasons, they were retired, leaving the CPR in sole possession of the Triangle, its glitter already dimmed by a rising Depression.)

By 1909, Victoria had taken a new polish. In 1908, less than five years after the *Princess Victoria's* first sailing, the CPR added another luxury liner, the 4,000-ton *Princess Charlotte,* to the Triangle Route and threw open the doors of its magnificent hotel, The Empress, designed by London architect Francis Mawson Rattenbury (who later was slain in England by his young chauffeur, said to be his wife's lover).

From upper floor rooms looking seaward, visitors would soon see the arrival from the Orient of the great Empress-class liners. Along the Inner Harbour causeway, fashioned to look like a chunk of the Thames Embankment, Rattenbury designed another set piece, the British Columbia Legislative Building. Police were issued Bobby helmets. The Empress and the adjoining Crystal Gardens featured afternoon teas and lawn bowling. Evenings at The Empress featured dancing—but no cocktails (guest Winston Churchill was able to get his libation of Scotch only by agreeing to have it poured from a concealing teapot). With all this quaintness, much of it contrived, Victoria's popularity soared. By the mid-Thirties, before effects of the Depression became acute, Victoria's noted artist Emily Carr was to complain that the visitors pouring off the steamers "look at us … as if we had been dust-covered antiques."

By then the popularity of Canadian Pacific steamers, operating over routes that stretched from Skagway to Seattle, were at their peak. In 1938, the *Princess* liners carried 878,000 passengers, requiring, during peak months, a total of 1,200 crew members, more than half of them in the steward's department. Impressive as it might be, the passenger total represented virtually no increase over the previous year. The number of cars carried, awkwardly

The venerable sidewheeler, North Pacific, *heads for dockside in Seattle as the lavishly-appointed* City of Kingston *heads out.*
University of Washington Library

loaded through side ports, doubled. The storm signals had been raised.

The role of the steamer as a carrier of automobiles in Puget Sound waters began when some goggle-eyed motorist paid to have his Apperson loaded as deck cargo aboard a sternwheeler. With the development of paved roads, stimulated by the movement of workers to the Sound's war industries, the auto ferries quickly began supplanting the Mosquito Fleet.

The ferry run from Seattle to Bremerton paved the way for what in ensuing decades would become the Sound's most popular holiday trail: a ferry ride to Bremerton, a drive along Hood Canal to Anacortes, thence via auto ferry to Victoria. Institution of car ferry service between Victoria and Vancouver eventually made it possible to return to the U.S. via Highway 99 with its spectacular Chuckanut Drive—a Grand Tour for car-happy America.

The starchy Canadian Pacific, encrusted in the barnacles of tradition, moved gingerly into this new world. Concerned by the traffic pouring off the auto ferries *Mount Vernon* and *City of Angeles* which linked Anacortes with Sidney, the CPR ordered its first—and only—car ferry.

In 1923, it launched the *Motor Princess,* built in slightly more than three months at Esquimalt, B.C., and capable of carrying 600 passengers and 45 cars on an experimental run between Sidney, near Victoria, and Bellingham. The run was moderately popular, but after three years the CPR abandoned the auto ferry concept on Puget Sound, turning that growing market over to Puget Sound Navigation Company, which, early on, saw its future linked to highway traffic. As late as 1949 when the CPR ordered the last of its elegant packet liners, the *Princess Marguerite* and *Princess Patricia,* they included provisions for but 45 automobiles. Their decor, heavy on the brasswork and panelling, with furnishings more correct than comfortable, were not unlike the first installed on the *Princess Victoria* in 1903 and subsequently on the *Princesses Charlotte, Margaret, Kathleen,* and *Elizabeth.* As Mosquito Fleet steamers began heading for the boneyard in the 1930s, the *Princess Elizabeth* continued to offer such amenities as "clothes pressing, light tailoring or shoe shining while you sleep," with attentive stewards to adjust windows, turn up the heat, provide extra bed clothes or serve tea or coffee and toast in staterooms for 25 cents.

But the niceties could not compete with the lure of an outing in the family automobile, trembling impatiently on the car deck of the auto ferry while the family munched hot dogs and unfolded a new chart to the future—the road map. While the *Princesses* would outlive the Mosquito Fleet, their days, too, were numbered.

On September 15, 1975, the *Princess Marguerite* blew Seattle a kiss and headed for Victoria on the last CPR run over the Triangle Route. From the 1904 debut on the *Princess Victoria,* until the CPR rang Finished With Engines on Puget Sound, a total of 23 CPR steamers had coursed that international sea lane and others in British Columbia and Alaska. Today's replacement cost would exceed a half-billion dollars. (The venerable *Princess Marguerite* with faded regality continues the ever-popular summertime Seattle-Victoria run, heavily subsidized by the British Columbia government.)

The Princess Victoria *underway. She was built in Scotland, but due to the shipyard strike, arrived in Victoria in 1903 with her upperworks uncompleted. Her smart staterooms, dining room and other passenger facilities were completed at a Vancouver yard. Even before she was completely outfitted, the* Princess Victoria *was in demand as an excursion vessel, making the first run to Seattle with a boatload of the Native Sons of British Columbia.*

Provincial Archives

The Reign of Victoria

Discovery of gold on the Fraser River gave Victoria a brief taste of being a rowdy boomtown, zooming from a hamlet of a few hundred farmers and traders to a tent city of thousands. Its population by 1858 had reached 5,000, but by that time respectability was catching up with the island community, described by author Alfred Wassington as a "home of a few, quiet, gentlemanly behaved individuals … secluded as it was from the whole world."

That unruffled pace in a setting of tranquil beauty quickly made Victoria attractive to visitors from Seattle, Tacoma, Olympia, Port Townsend and other Sound communities.

First to appear on the historic run in 1854 was the 97-foot wooden steamer, Major Tompkins, known, and not always affectionately, as "Pumpkins." The diminutive steamer, launched in 1847 at Philadelphia, wove a leisurely course, starting at Olympia and meandering down the Sound with stops at Steilacoom, Seattle, Dungeness, Penn Cove, Whatcom, San Juan and finally, Victoria.

The Major Tompkins was followed by the Eliza Anderson, who prospered until her monopoly was broken. She was followed by a succession of steamers, some of them the Coast's finest. The competition reached its peak in 1871 with a dramatic winner take-all race. It occurred after a

couple of wily Portland merchants, Edwin and Louis Starr, financed a crack new steamer, the North Pacific, and in the midst of a furious rate war, challenged the rival Olympia, operated by Captain D. B. Finch, former master of the Eliza Anderson. The North Pacific won the lackluster but decisive race between Victoria and Port Townsend. The defeated Olympia retired to California, paid a monthly subsidy to remain out of competition. She made a comeback after seven years when the Hudson's Bay Company bought her and returned her to British Columbia where she was refitted and renamed Princess Louise, the first of a long line of steamers to carry that royal designation.

Prior to the turn of the century, service between Seattle and Victoria drew such elegant steamers as the Islander, Olympian, City of Seattle and others. But it was not until a growth in population and prosperity attracted the Canadian Pacific Railway, the Grand Trunk Pacific (Canadian National), and Puget Sound Navigation Company to the run that first class service was provided on a year-round schedule. The Triangle Route, as it became known, had arrived. It survived to become the oldest inland sea route on the Pacific Coast.

The explosive growth of steamships serving the inland waterways of Puget Sound, British Columbia and Alaska is captured in

this photograph, taken in Victoria's splendid Inner Harbour in around 1912. From left to right are the Princess Alice, Princess Beatrice, Otter and Princess Victoria. On the right at the Grand Trunk Dock are the Prince George and Prince Rupert. In the distance, the City of Nanaimo departs.

British Columbia Archives

Cut off from mainland British Columbia, and denied its dream of a cross-channel railroad bridge, Victoria over the years has been served by a variety of marine transport, ranging from wallowing sidewheelers to compact liners of the Canadian Pacific and Canadian National railroads.

In 1923 the CPR launched its first auto ferry, the 165-foot wooden-hulled Motor Princess, *putting her in service between Victoria and Bellingham, later re-routing her to a crossing between the mainland just south of Vancouver and Sidney, about 20 miles from Victoria.*

Sidney today continues to be the principal auto ferry terminus for Victoria, served by B.C. Ferries from the Vancouver area and Washington State Ferries originating at Anacortes.

Year-around auto ferry service direct to Victoria proper is provided by Black Ball Transport's 5360-ton Coho (lower), *designed by Nickum & Spaulding of Seattle and launched in 1959 by Puget Sound Bridge and Drydock Co. The* Coho *shuttles between Victoria and Port Angeles, with a capacity of 108 cars, in addition to trucks and 500 passengers and is one of the few ferries remaining in private ownership.*

The Coho *is shown gliding past the last of the CPR "Princess" fleet, the* Princess Marguerite, *which continues to be a summertime favorite on day-long excursions from Seattle.*

At center, the newly reconditioned Klickitat *is pictured on the Washington State Ferries run between Anacortes and Sidney, near Victoria, via the San Juan islands. She was built in Oakland more than 50 years ago for San Francisco Bay Area ferry service and remodelled in 1984 — at a cost four times that of building her.*

B.C. Archives   Washington State Ferries   Jim Faber

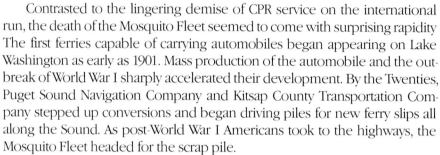

Contrasted to the lingering demise of CPR service on the international run, the death of the Mosquito Fleet seemed to come with surprising rapidity. The first ferries capable of carrying automobiles began appearing on Lake Washington as early as 1901. Mass production of the automobile and the outbreak of World War I sharply accelerated their development. By the Twenties, Puget Sound Navigation Company and Kitsap County Transportation Company stepped up conversions and began driving piles for new ferry slips all along the Sound. As post-World War I Americans took to the highways, the Mosquito Fleet headed for the scrap pile.

Their death was not unmourned. For more than half a century, the steamboats had enjoyed a symbiotic relationship with the communities they made possible all around the Sound. Now ribbons of concrete were ending that mutual dependency.

Some steamers like the *Flyer* were burned for the metals in their hulls and hearts. Others rubbed rusting shoulders in Lake Washington boneyards. The *Reliance, Bremerton* (ex-*Kitsap*) and *Dart* were destroyed by fire while awaiting execution. Stripped of her engine, the *F. G. Reeve* rotted away in the San Juans as did the *Hyak* on a Duwamish River mudflat. Not far away, wreckers' torches sliced up the *Tacoma, Winslow* and other steel greyhounds.

By the end of the 1920s, fewer than a dozen Mosquito Fleet steamers remained.

Marine historian Gordon Newell in his *Ships of the Inland Sea*, provides an eloquent obituary:

Suddenly, in the mid-1930s the people of Puget Sound found that their Mosquito Fleet was gone. It surprised them and made them a little sad, for the darting white steamers, weaving their foamy patterns on the blue water against the eternal background of evergreen shores and shining mountains, had, it seemed, always been there. They had been a part of the peculiar charm and magic of their lovely inland sea. The small white ships disappeared so gradually that they were hardly missed by the people who used to ride on them. Only when they were gone did they begin to look over the quiet reaches of the Sound and feel that something fine and exciting was suddenly missing.

The little ships of the inland sea are only a poignant memory now in the minds of the generations old enough to look backward sometimes, and sigh a little over the glories of the past .... The little ships had much of humanity in them. Few of them had great adventures, for they had their humble, daily tasks to do in their own small world ... from Flattery to Olympia. They worked hard and well, making many friends. They seldom hurt anyone. They managed to retain their particular sort of jaunty, wind-swept beauty until the end. Those are the qualities of good people as well as good ships. Perhaps that is why people of the Pacific Northwest remember them in the way that good friends are remembered.

The Mosquito Fleet has been scrapped, replaced by the popular auto ferry, and with it, the holiday line-up at Colman Dock. Sic transit.
University of Washington Library

145

Scaramento River Paddlewheelers

The role of the steamer as a pleasure boat on the Pacific Coast began on the Sacramento River. Here the love of the plush attracted some of the period's best—and worst—steamers; those able to survive passage around the Horn and the equally lethal operational hazards then prevalent. Despite all the gilding, 19th century paddlewheel travel was risky. On the Mississippi, the average life expectancy of pre-Civil War steamers was five years. By 1850, 1,070 riverboats had been lost with a loss of life of 4,180.

The finest steamers to enter the Gold Rush trade were East Coast sidewheelers, such as the *Senator* and the *New World*, pictured lower right at San Francisco's Cunningham Wharf in 1856.

Passage on the Sacramento was more serene, but not without fatalities. The sidewheeler *Yosemite,* pictured (far right) docked at Sacamento in 1879 after an extensive refit, was one of the most popular steamers running between San Francisco and Sacramento. This despite the fact that in 1865 her boilers had blown up during a race, killing 55.

Popularity of the Sacramento River paddlewheelers—the coast's original "love boats" — lasted until the late 40s when the sternwheelers *Delta Queen* and *Delta King* retired. (The *Delta Queen* continues to thrash her way upriver, now operating as a Mississsippi excursion boat.)

Early on, the Sacramento riverboat popularity was matched by that of steamers departing from the burgeoning San Francisco Ferry Terminal (shown upper right in 1886) for such cross-Bay points as Sausalito, Oakland, Alameda, Berkeley, Vallejo and others.

National Maritime Museum, San Francisco

Bancroft Library, University of California

The *General Frisbie*

Despite the stern mein of the couple in the foreground, one of the Bay Area's most popular steamers for an outing was the *General Frisbie,* later known to Puget Sounders as the *Commander.* She is pictured here (lower right) at Vallejo in about 1905, ready for a one-hour and forty-five-minute run to San Francisco and other East Bay stops. The 183-foot *General Frisbie* was a tribute to Puget Sound woods and shipbuilding skills, remaining in service for about half a century.

Launched in New Whatcom (later a part of Bellingham) in 1900 for the Monticello Steamship Company of San Francisco, she was loaded with lumber and towed to San Francisco where a 1,000 h.p. engine was installed. The wooden-hulled steamer not only remained popular with California travellers for almost 30 years but also lived to return to Puget Sound in 1929. There, converted to diesel engines and renamed *Commander,* she went into service on the Seattle-Bremerton run under the banner of the newly-formed Union Ferry Company, a joint venture of the Kitsap County Transportation Company and Puget Sound Freight Lines.

Bancroft Library, University of California

UP THE COLUMBIA

THE GRANDEST RIVER TRIP IN AMERICA

The River Queen

The "Grandest River Trip in America," boasted posters from the Regulator Line, which featured Sunday excursions on the Columbia. The line flourished briefly, competing heartily with the O.R.& N. and featured the *Bailey Gatzert, Regulator* and *Dalles City.*

Of all sternwheelers, the *Bailey Gatzert* was considered the grandest, boasting cabins and other passenger facilities with decor selected and in some cases fashioned by Harnett, a prominent British artist of the day. From the day of her sideway launching at Ballard in 1890 when she hit the water with steam up, the *Bailey Gatzert* was a fast and impatient boat, easily winning the "golden broom" (an ordinary broom, gilded, fastened to the pilot house after a race indicating a clean sweep) over all competitors until the *T. J. Potter* arrived on Puget Sound from the Columbia and took it down. Shortly after, the *Bailey Gatzert,* which wallowed miserably in rough seas, was re-assigned to the Columbia River. Long after Columbia River commercial traffic had ebbed, she continued to ply her way to the ocean or to the Cascade Locks on excursions. In 1905 during the Lewis and Clark Exposition at Portland, she made two trips daily, with a fare of $1.50. An ode, the *Bailey Gatzert March,* was featured during the event.

The dramatic racing photograph (lower right), from the Joe Williamson Collection, shows the *Bailey Gatzert's* arch rival, the *Charles R. Spencer,* being overtaken on the Columbia just below Vancouver. Such races occurred daily on the Portland-Astoria run, with the *Bailey* usually winning.

150

The excursions featured in the accompanying photographs show the *Bailey,* berthed next to the *Dalles City,* departing Portland on an Independence Day excursion in 1913 (left). An accompanying photo at left shows that even after being tamed by the opening of the locks, the run required keen skill to traverse the rock-studded rapids.

Again, photographed moored alongside the *Dalles City,* the *Bailey Gatzert* is shown (right) in what could be viewed as a tryout role as an auto ferry, foreshadowed by the presence of two touring cars on her front deck. The proud sternwheeler became the first to regularly carry automobiles to the Olympic Peninsula in 1918 when she was purchased by Puget Sound Navigation Company and returned to Puget Sound for the Seattle-Bremerton run. In 1920, she was sponsored out (widened) to accommodate 30 cars, being retired from service in 1926. Her five-toned "chime" whistle is often exhibited at Seattle's Museum of History and Industry.

Oregon Historical Society

Columbia River Maritime Museum

Skamania County Historical Society

Joe Williamson Collection

151

Bailey Gatzert *(continued)*

The *Bailey Gatzert* pauses at Cascade Locks in 1915.
Columbia River Maritime Museum

The *Bailey's* few Columbia River stops were informal ones.
Columbia River Maritime Museum

T. J. Potter

The *T. J. Potter* heads down the Columbia in the early 1900s with a crowd of excursionists (who unaccountably seem to be all male). Riverboat purists scoffed at the new pilot house, installed during the *T. J. Potter's* 1901 refit, terming it a "white elephant's howdah." The remodelling also cut several knots from the *T. J. Potter's* speed, eliminating her as one of the river's top speed queens. The travel poster depicts the *T. J. Potter* prior to her refit, which included dressing up the dining room (upper right) and its impressive menu (both shown).

Photo of the crew, from the collection of Captain W.R. Eckhart, is from 1901, headed by Captain Al Gray, second from left.

The remains of the once-proud riverboat, scrapped in 1902, are shown on the beach near Astoria.

Oregon Historical Society

The *Georgiana*

Columbia River boat builders were unexcelled in construction of paddlewheel steamers. And, while they launched such crack propeller-driven vessels as the *Flyer,* these slim-hulled steamers proved to be more suited to Puget Sound waters than to the Columbia.

An exception was the slim-hulled *Georgiana,* a late-comer on the Portland-Astoria run. She was launched at Portland in 1914 from the Joseph Supple Shipyard, builders of the *Flyer* and other river speedsters. Maintained like a yacht, her twin stacks and gleaming white wooden hull made her a pleasing picture on the river.

But, as popularity of the ocean-beach excursions waned in the early 1930s, the *Georgiana* depended more and more on freight hauls along the lower Columbia. In 1936, she was withdrawn from service. After an unsuccessful try as an excursion boat running to Bonneville Dam, she was beached and abandoned.

Columbia River Maritime Museum

Black Prince

A frame of life in the slow track is provided in this photograph of the sternwheeler *Black Prince* in the early 1900's. Locale of the outing is not known, but quite likely is somewhere along Puget Sound near the mouth of the Skagit River. The *Black Prince* was built at Everett in 1901 for a rail line that was more impressive in its title than it was in actual performance—the Skagit and Snohomish, Puget Sound and Baker River Railroad. The *Prince* paddled around the Sound until the 20's, when she became a towboat. Upperworks for a time served as a clubroom for the Everett Yacht Club in the 30's.

(Just who is that hussy in the wheelhouse—and the lonely lady sitting on the lifeboat?)

Seattle Public Library

City of Seattle

"The ferry dock?"

"It's straight ahead, ma'am — and watch out for the teams and the trains."

Getting to the city's first ferry, the *City of Seattle,* posed a few problems as illustrated by the turn of the century view at left looking down Seattle's Marion Street. At its intersection at Western Avenue, with its rows of fruit and vegetable wholesalers, it was one of the city's busiest intersections.

After navigating a course around the stacked crates and dodging the handtrucks, ferry riders crossed Railroad Avenue, its planked surfaces a maze of railroad tracks, spurs, freight wagons and horse droppings.

Allen Beach, a Bainbridge Island old-timer, marvelled in his book, *Bainbridge Landings:*

> How a woman with a flock of children, all loaded with bundles, was ever able to cross this myriad of dangerous confusion in time to catch a departing boat, was truly a miracle.

The *City of Seattle* was bereft of amenities, but became popular with commuters as well as holiday excursionists, shown boarding the ferry at Seattle, (lower left) and debarking at West Seattle (lower right).

The 121-foot *City of Seattle* has few peers in longevity, and now serves as an office-residence at a San Francisco Bay Area marina. Built in Portland in 1888 of Douglas fir, she became the first ferry to make her way up the coast to Puget Sound, powered by a coal-burning engine generating no more than 270 horsepower.

A running mate was added in 1907, a red-and-white sidewheeler, the *West Seattle,* (upper right) built in Tacoma to carry up to a thousand commuters fleeing downtown Scattle for the bosky dells of West Seattle. Shortly after her maiden voyage, the *West Seattle* bashed into the Seattle ferry dock, thereby establishing a long and, as yet, unbroken precedent.

Owners of the ferries, the West Seattle Land & Improvement Company, attracted a steady flow of early-day commuters, who were offered a connection with a cable car that twisted its way to the top of the bluff above Admiralty Head. But with the flowering of suburbia came streetcars. The ferries — and cable cars — were soon running in the red.

In 1913, the West Seattle Land & Improvement Company, faced with mounting losses, established another precedent, turning over the cross-bay run of the *West Seattle* to a public agency — the Port of Seattle.

That same year, the *City of Seattle* was towed south to run between Martinez and Benecia near the estuary of the Sacramento River. Despite her age, she was drafted in 1944 and assigned to the Mare Island Navy Yard where she became the *YFB54*. Following the war she donned civvies again as the *Magdalena* of the Mare Island Ferry Company. Later converted to diesel, she had a brief fling as a paddlewheel yacht before finally being raised on pilings at a Sausalito marina. There, clad in yellow, she serves as the residence and office for the proprietor of the Yellow Ferry Harbor — and awaits her 100th birthday in 1988.

Capital City

A Seattle photographer Richard Wittelsy, captures the pleasant flavor of a 1900 Sunday outing aboard a Sound steamer as the sternwheeler *Capital City* backs out from her Seattle dock for Tacoma and Olympia. Despite the habit the oil-fired steamers had of spewing out clouds of resinous smoke, the wearing of hats apparently was *de rigueur*—even for the children.

The Nome gold rush had just started at the time, and boys and girls manning the *Capital City's* railings could fantasize on the days when the sternwheeler carried prospectors to Dawson during the earlier Klondike stampede that began at these same Seattle docks. She was the *Dalton* then, built with three other steamers at Port Blakely for the Canadian Pacific Railway, then planning a so-called All-Canadian route to the Klondike via the Stikine River which debouched at Wrangel. But the tenuous land-water route had little appeal and the *Dalton* and her companions were assigned to the Yukon. After a few months under the flag of the White Pass & Yukon Railroad, the *Dalton* was sold to the veteran Puget Sound steamboat firm, S. Willey Navigation Co., which put her on the Seattle-Tacoma-Olympia run.

The *Capital City* had her day of drama, too. In 1902 she was struck by the freighter *Trader* off Dash Point and was holed below the waterline. Her skipper, Capt. Mike Edwards, signalled Full Ahead and headed the *Capital City* for the nearby beach. Her engineer, Robert Scott, remained at the throttle in waist-deep water until the steamer was successfully beached.

Paul Dorpat

Fairhaven

Beach wear in the early 1900s was anything but informal as evidenced by passengers debarking at Alki Beach from the old (1889) sternwheeler *Fairhaven,* a veteran of Joshua Green's La Conner Trading and Transportation Company, later operating under the Puget Sound Navigation Company banner.

Joe Williamson

Camano

It cost but a dime to ride the *Camano* to Alki Point. Built in 1906 at Coupeville, the 88-foot steamer provided more thrills than the Luna Park roller coaster. In 1912 she was sunk at dockside in Seattle when rammed by the steamer *Sioux,* which also dispatched the 75-foot launch *Island Flyer* to the bottom after a mix-up in control signals sent the steel-hulled steamer at half-speed ahead instead of half-speed astern. There were no injuries, but four died when the *Camano* collided in a fog with the tug *Magic* and sank off Bainbridge Island in 1917.

University of Washington Library

Luna Park

By today's standards, Luna Park on Duwamish Head didn't provide much in the way of thrill rides, featuring the Figure Eight Roller Coaster (in foreground), the Chute the Chutes Water Slide, the Giant Swing, Canal of Venice, Natatorium, Dance Palace, and of course, a Merry-Go-Round (under the onion dome). For a time in the early 1900s, the Duwamish Head resort also boasted the longest bar in town. Under the permissive policies of Mayor Hi Gill it soon produced a rash of muckraking stories from the *Seattle Post-Intelligencer* which righteously opposed Gill not so much for his lack of moral probity but that he was supported by the *Seattle Times.* One *P-I* story had a contemporary ring, observing that "the Sunday night dances at Luna Park...girls hardly 14 years old, mere children in appearance, mingled with the older, more dissipated patrons and sat in dark corners drinking beer, smoking cigarettes and singing."

Shortly after, Mayor Gill was recalled (only to be reelected two years later as Seattle's electorate completed another of its own figure eight rides) and the bar closed. Luna Park closed in 1913, its Natatorium surviving until torched by an arsonist in 1931.

Washington State Library

163

Picnics

Soon after the North Pacific's first steamboat, the *Beaver,* arrived in 1835, her owners, the Hudson's Bay Company, were hosts for the region's first steamer excursion. The trip aboard the inelegant sidewheeler included a stop along the banks of the Willamette, where lunch hampers were broken out for the guests which included Company men and their ladies from Fort Vancouver.

The day was not without its sobering moments. The year was to see an historic meeting at the Oregon Territory settlement of Champoeg. Here the settlers vowed that regardless of future boundary decisions, Oregon was to be part of the United States. Reflecting this newly minted spirit, one of the passengers, the Reverend Samuel Parker wrote:

> *The gaiety which prevailed was often suspended while we conversed for coming days when with civilized men, all the rapid improvements in the arts of life should be introduced over this new world, and when cities and villages shall spring up on the west, as they are springing up on the east of the great mountains, and a new empire be added to the kingdoms of the earth.*

The first such outing on Puget Sound, at least the first to be recorded, was a Fourth of July picnic held by the crew of the Wilkes Expedition's *Vincennes* near Fort Nisqually in 1841. Because Independence Day fell on the Sabbath, the picnic was held the following day. It appears to have been a success. The *Vincennes* log book tells us there were extra servings of "old rum," noting the temperature reached an estimated 120 degrees, an all time high — at least for the chronicler.

From that day on, a clambake and a picnic lunch spread on driftwood logs became a familiar scene just about anywhere available by Puget Sound steamers.

Alki Drive-in

Not everyone came to Alki Beach by steamer as indicated by this 1912 Asahel Curtis photo.

University of Washington Library

164

It's a Breeze

Summer excursionists, including a few sailors, emerge from a summer excursion aboard the *Hyak*.

Paul Dorpat

Wetback

What's a Puget Sound cookout without one prudent soul who brings an umbrella?

University of Washington Library

Fun Boat

History doesn't record exactly what these happy Husky fans are waiting to cheer.

University of Washington Library

166

Rental Dugout

Long after the "Canoe Express" no longer carried passengers to Puget Sound points, Indians found a ready market for customers among the younger generation.

University of Washington Library

Salmon Beach

Salmon Beach just south of Tacoma was a summertime destination for passenger launches, including those of the fledgling Foss Launch & Tug Company.

Washington State Library

Keep Clam

That's not a Maypole but a bed of steaming clams this group is ringing as Henry hurries back for more film.

Regatta

Two paddlewheel steamers and
an assortment of smaller steamers and
launches carry the spectators for this
regatta of canoes and sailboats
at Tacoma.

Oregon Historical Society

USS Washington   One of the most popular warships drawing throngs to Seattle during the 1908 visit of the Great White Fleet was the *USS Washingon,* captured here with a telescopic lens by photographer Asahel Curtis.

Repesenting a new class of warships — the armored cruiser — the 14,500-ton *Washington* bristled with arms, including four ten-inch, 16 six-inch and 23 3-inch guns. The 502-foot cruiser was but a year old when she dropped anchor in Elliot Bay with her crew of 861. Her launching, with the Navy's newly-honed skill for targeting appropriations, featured Helen Stewart Wilson, daughter of Washington's U.S. Senator, John Wilson.

In addition to her Seattle call, the *Washingon* visited Bremerton, Port Townsend and Port Angeles during the tour of the Great White Fleet.

The cruiser had an undistinguished career, "showing the flag" during rebellions in Cuba, the Dominican Republic, and Haiti. Renamed the *USS Seattle,* she underwent a submarine alert during World War I convoy duty, but sailed off the scrapyard in 1946 without having ever fired a shot in anger or error.

President Wilson Visit

Not until 1919 did Fleet Week match the drama of the Great White Fleet's visit. It was climaxed by the appearance of President Woodrow Wilson and while he was greeted by crowds basking in the victory of World War I, he carried with him the baggage of controversy. Purpose of his cross-country junket was to whip up sentiment for the Versailles Peace Treaty and the League of Nations, both of which the Senate later rejected. Less than two weeks after his Seattle visit, President Wilson suffered a stroke, from which he never fully recovered. In the photo, the Presidential party moves north on Second Ave. near Madison St.

Seattle Public Library

Anchors Aweigh

Our storybook war, that with Spain in 1898, gave America a new roster of heroes, born in the storming of San Juan Hill and in the fiery Navy victories at Manila and on Santiago Bay. In the peace that followed, the United States emerged as a leading Navy power, an eminence Puget Sound communities soon discovered could be both entertaining and remunerative. Warships ranging in size from slender torpedo boats to battleships were assigned to Puget Sound communities for visits. A PR-conscious War Department rolled out the Navy grey carpet. In Seattle, landing floats were moored at downtown docks and scores of Navy launches were assigned duty shuttling visitors to and from the anchored warships. At night the dreadnaughts, as they were heralded following launching of the *H.M.S. Dreadnought* in 1908, were outlined by electric lights festooning hulls and upperworks.

Between Fleet Weeks, the Puget Sound Navy Yard at Bremerton became a visitor target. When the *U.S.S. Iowa* arrived for an overhaul in 1901, as many as 6,000 excursionists daily crowded aboard six steamers pressed into Seattle-Bremerton service, with more docking from Tacoma.

(Competition was even keener for patronage of the battleship's crew heading to Seattle on liberty and one savvy skipper proved that not polishing the brass had its own reward.

Virtually all of the steamer owners were captains or ex-captains. So out of deference to rank, they charged no fares for the *Iowa's* officers. The canny skipper of the Sound steamer *Pilgrim* was the sole exception. He charged the Navy officers full fare. The result was predictable, and for the *Pilgrim's* skipper, profitable. The affronted officers of the *Iowa* boycotted the *Pilgrim,* which each trip filled up with sailors who could reel aboard from liberty with no apprehensions.)

The Navy responded by giving visitors free rein. When the battleship *Oregon* returned in 1913, welcoming crowds were permitted to line the drydock walls while the historic warship entered for her refit.

Following World War II, visitors were barred from the Navy Yard except on rare special events. But thousands each week rode the ferry to Bremerton for a chance to stroll the decks of the historic *U.S.S. Missouri.* In 1984 the *Big Mo* was drafted and left her Bremerton moorings for good. Today a low-key Fleet Week continues to be observed in Seattle and a few other Sound ports.

Battleship Parade

Rounding Magnolia Bluff into Elliott Bay, the Pacific Fleet moves into Seattle's harbor in September 1919. Leading the parade of battleships is the *USS New York,* followed by the *Texas, Wyoming, Idaho* and *Mississippi.*

Launching

A float at the foot of Seattle's Washington St. awaits the discharge of sailors, officers and visitors. Launches like the one just pulling out also carried visitors, but gigs such as the one at center were strickly for officers. Battleship in the background is the *USS Oregon.* Time is September 14, 1919.

USS Oregon

Competing in popularity with Fleet Week visits of warships was the opportunity to watch dockings at the Puget Sound Navy Yard. Here visitors are given free rein, lining the dry dock to welcome the historic *USS Oregon* at Bremerton in 1913. The

Oregon had been refitted at Bremerton immediately prior to her dash around the Horn in 1898 to join other U. S. Navy units at Santiago de Cuba near Havana, scene of the final defeat of the Spanish navy during the Spanish-American War.

Washington State Historical Society

Sightseers

Fleet Week continued to be a major Puget Sound event all during the Thirties. During other months, the Seattle-Bremerton ferry run carried sightseers to the Puget Sound Navy Yard at Bremerton. A favorite for many was the *Kalakala,* shown here passing down Battleship Row in Seattle's harbor. While opinions vary on identification of the warships, most agree they are, left to right, *Nevada, California* and *Maryland.* (Others favored *Arizona, Maryland* and *Tennessee,* and a couple opted for *Oklahoma, Tennessee* and *West Virginia.*

University of Washington Library

H. B. Kennedy at Colman Dock

The surprising success of 1909's Alaska Yukon Pacific Exposition fostered a "what do we do for an encore?" mood, particularly among the city's hoteliers and merchants. The answer was found in creation of an annual summertime festival, the Potlatch. Here, the crowds lining Colman Dock are awaiting the appearance of a flying machine over Elliott Bay, one of the highlights of the 1911 Golden Potlatch (named to commemorate the arrival of the gold ship *Portland* in 1898). The flyover, in a Curtiss bi-plane, came off as scheduled, moments after this photo was taken. After that, crowds boarded the *H. B. Kennedy* (left), the *Athlon* (right), and other Mosquito Fleet steamers for a naval parade.

Frank Maslan

Potlatch

Seattle's summertime frolic, the Potlatch, draws a crowd to the waterfront to cheer a reenactment of the arrival of the 1898 Gold Rush ship, *Portland*. The crowd — and a dray loaded with kegs of beer — is massed near Colman Dock. To the north is the waterfront fire station and beyond it Pier 3, terminal for a score of Mosquito Fleet steamers. The year is 1912.

Paul Dorpat

Yosemite

The big (283-foot) steamer *Yosemite* was a crowd pleaser among Sacramento River Gold Rush sports. Later she was a hit on Canada's Fraser River. In 1906 she took on the role of a rather gamey excursion boat following acquisition by the Puget Sound Excursion Line, formed in anticipation of Alaskan Yukon Pacific Exposition crowds. A dancing floor was installed, Wagner's band hired, and the *Yosemite* was off to view the arrival of the Great White Fleet, provide moonlight dancing or fill the lower deck with fans of boxing matches. She is pictured here loaded with members of the Georgetown Volunteer Fire Department, all of them Rainier brewery workers.

The accompanying photo shows the *Yosemite* following a spectacular ship-wreck on July 9, 1909, after the big sternwheeler, loaded with more than a thousand AYP excursionists, was caught in the eddies of a turning tide near Bremerton. Her back was broken as she swept onto Orchard Rocks at full speed. All aboard were saved but the steamer was a total loss.

A hearing attributed the wreck to negligence of the captain and engineer. But newspapers hinted darkly at scandal, insinuating her errant course was determined more by provisions of an insurance policy than it was charts. McCurdy's authoritative *Marine History of the Pacific Northwest* simply states that "it is widely believed the *Yosemite* was deliberately wrecked for her insurance."

University of Washington Library

Puget Sound Maritime Historical Society

Colman Dock

Colman Dock in the early 1920s, before ascendancy of the auto ferry. The overhead ramp at left housed offices and led to a waiting room and gangways. Note the gangway at right for the steamer *Chippewa* displays the star-diamond insignia of Puget Sound navigation Company, later to become identified by the familiar black ball.

Joe Williamson Coll.

Railroad Avenue

James Colman, a Scot engineer who operated Yesler Mill among a multitude of other activities, built his first dock in 1882. It was destroyed by the Seattle Fire of 1889. In 1890 he built his spartan terminal on Railroad Avenue.

This splintered thoroughfare, built of planking atop piling, was a constant source of embarrassment for Seattle boosters. During the Depression when maintenance funds dried up, the planking became so rotten it gave way under the weight of trucks. The City Council tried to help by officially renaming Railroad Avenue, dubbing it, with a bit of Camelot artifice, "Cosmos Quay." Fortunately, cooler heads prevailed until the strand was finally named Alaskan Way.

University of Washington Library

Whatcom

The San Juan Islands were among the Sound's earliest excursion destinations, with frequent service from Seattle, Anacortes and Bellingham Bay points. The *Whatcom,* shown here, was built in Everett in 1901 for the Thompson Steamboat Company and went into service between Seattle, Port Townsend and Victoria. The following year, Thompson sold out to the newly-formed Puget Sound Navigation Company under whose banner the *Majestic,* renamed *Whatcom,* was busied on a variety of runs, including a voyage to Alaska in 1904 and excursions to the San Juan Islands. In 1921, Puget Sound Navigation Company converted the *Whatcom* into the auto ferry, *City of Bremerton.*

Whatcom Museum

Flyer

The trade magazine *Railway and Marine News* in 1908 termed her "the most remarkable steamer in the world." Scaling off the exaggeration, the slender-hulled *Flyer* was indeed one for the record book.

The *Flyer* was built in Portland of Douglas fir by Capt. U. B. Scott, a Midwest transplant with a unique savvy for extracting the maximum speed from a steamboat. His Columbia River sternwheeler *Telephone* was a consistent winner in races between Portland and Astoria. Later he designed the aptly named propellor, *Fleetwood,* again winning the broom for speed. In 1898 the steamer made a record run from Tacoma to Seattle rushing a fire engine to join the battle against the Great Fire.

So finely drawn were the lines of the knife-nosed *Flyer* that when launched in 1891, sans equipment, she rolled over. The hull was then sponsoned out; in other words a second hull was wrapped around the original. This second hull was improperly sealed, allowing tons of water to enter and remain sloshing around inside the hulls. Despite this handicap, the *Flyer* emerged fleet and dependable; a skinny upstart outrunning just about everything moving on Puget Sound.

Along with speed the *Flyer* became as dependable as the tides. "Citizens of Seattle," vowed the *Railway and Marine News,* "used the *Flyer* whistle instead of clocks." At the time of the magazine's accolade, the 170-foot *Flyer* had voyaged the equivalent of 51 times around the world, largely on the Seattle-Tacoma route (running time: 1 hour, 40 minutes), carrying more than three million passengers.

Unlike any of her sisters, the Flyer boasted a dining room. Entertainment was provided by a viewing of her flashing engine, with its symphony of thuds and hisses seasoned with the smell of steam and hot oil. The triple-expansion engine, a duplicate of one designed for J. P. Morgan's *Corsair,* was capable of 2,000 horsepower, but due to boiler limitations never operated at more than 1,200. Despite a cruising speed of 16 knots, the *Flyer* created no more wake than a Mallard.

University of Washington Library

Flyer *(continued)*

The *Flyer* logged her share of mishaps, including a fire, a collision, and a couple of docking accidents. One occurred in 1905 when her flamboyant skipper, Capt. E. D. Coffin, was following his usual tactic of approaching Colman Dock at full speed, then signalling Full Astern. On this occasion a throttle pin broke and the *Flyer* plowed through a moored oyster barge. Her only involvement in a fatality occurred in 1912 when a Colman Dock gangway collapsed, dropping 60 passengers into Elliott Bay, drowning two.

The cocky little steamer was no match however, for the growing popularity of the auto ferry. On June 12, 1929, she was towed to Richmond Beach near Seattle and burned for her metal. Her obituary was provided by a *Tacoma Ledger* reporter:

> *"Once the speediest of all passenger ships on Puget Sound, the steamer* Washington, *the former* Flyer, *went to an inglorious end on a burning funeral pyre at Richmond Beach yesterday afternoon while hundreds of onlookers watched the flames eat the heart out of the venerable Sound greyhound."*

University of Washington Library

Joe Williamson

Christmas Dinner 1901

Str. FLYER — WM. WILLIAMSON, MASTER

OYSTERS
Eastern Raw   Olympia Cocktail

POTTAGES
Mock Turtle   Chicken   Okra   Oyster

FISH
Broiled Trout   Baked Halibut—Tartar Sauce

RELISHES
Bleached Celery   Young Onions   Radishes   Queen Olives   Dill Pickles

BOILED
Ham and Champagne Sauce   Chicken—Wine Sauce

ENTREES
Chicken Gibletts Saute on Toast   Macaroni and Cheese
Olympia Oyster Patties   Chicken Fricassee—Green Peas
Punch Cardinal   Pineapple Fritters   Brandy Sauce

SALADS
Lobster En Mayonnaise   Shrimp and Chicken
ORLEANS   DURKEES

ROASTS
Turkey—Chestnut Dressing and Cranberry Sauce   Chicken
Goose—Sage Dressing   Pork and Apple Sauce

VEGETABLES
Mashed and Brown Sweet Potatoes   French Peas En Cream
Asparagus, Cream Gravy on Toast   Stewed Winslow's Sweet Corn

PASTRY
Home-Made Mince   Cranberry   Green Apple   Lemon Cream
Huckleberry   English Plum Pudding—Hard and Brandy Sauce

DESSERT
Strawberry Ice Cream   Sliced Bananas and Cream   Lady Fingers
Macaroones   Christmas Cake   Walnut Cake   Fancy Assorted Cakes
MASON & BISHOP'S Bon Mange
Orange Marmalade   Strawberry Preserves   Crackers   Swiss Cheese

FRUITS
Oranges   Bananas   Apples   Grapes   Asst. Nuts   Salted Almonds
Pro Finis
Cafe au Noire.   Pousa Cafe
Green or Black Tea   Coffee   Milk   Zinfandel

W. ROFENO, STEWARD

LOWMAN & HANFORD STATIONERY & PRINTING CO.

Flyer *(continued)*

This "night" shot of the *Flyer* was taken at
5:15 in the afternoon. The lighted windows are the pen work of photographer
Asahel Curtis.

University of Washington Library

Volume VI. No. 48	**THE**	Price 5c at all News Stands.

SEATTLE MAIL AND HERALD

A CRITICAL JOURNAL OF THE NORTHWEST.

SEATTLE, WASHINGTON   OCTOBER 10, 1903

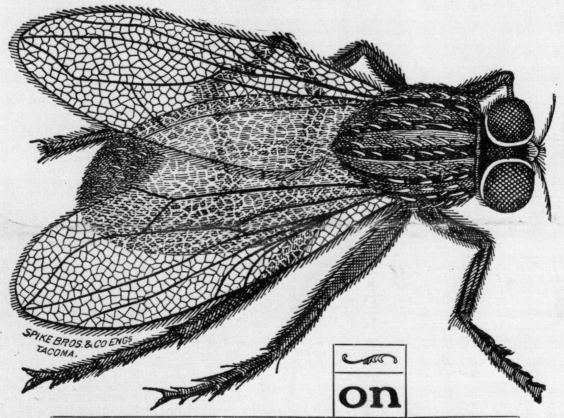

Seattle-Tacoma Route

SPIKE BROS. & CO ENGS.
TACOMA.

on THE FLYER

"Fly on the Flyer" is a household expression in Seattle, and it refers particularly to the steamer Flyer, which has year after year for over a decade furnished transportation between Seattle and Tacoma.

The Flyer is far and away the superior of any local boat; if not, indeed, of any small boat on the Pacific, in the matter of speed and equipment, and she holds the enviable record of traveling more miles in a given year than any boat in the world. The Flyer is a distance annihilator, and furthermore, the schedule is absolutely reliable.

This world beater makes four round trips daily between Seattle and Tacoma on "railroad time." One can always tell the minute when the Flyer will speed out from behind Alki Point on her return from Tacoma; her exits and entrances may be likened to the laws of the Medes and Persians.

For a few days last spring the Flyer was laid off for repairs, and during a certain day a worthy physician rang up the Flyer office and calling Mr. Seeley, the Manager, inquired in an aggrevated tone what was the matter with the Flyer.

He was told that the boat had been laid off a few days for repairs.

"Well," said he, "for more than five years I and my wife have been getting up by that 6:45 whistle of yours. This morning it did not blow, and you've made me more than an hour late to my patients."

This Seattle stand-by is owned and operated by the Columbia River and Puget Sound Navigation Co., of which Mr. Uri Seeley is local manager.

TIME CARD--In Effect October 3, 1903

LEAVE SEATTLE...........7:30, 11:15 a. m.; 2:45, 6:15 p. m.
LEAVE TACOMA...........9:25 a. m.; 1:00, 4:30, 8:00 p. m.

Table Service Unsurpassed

Fridays—"Flyer" or "Athlon"

LEAVE SEATTLE...........7:30 a. m.; 12:00 m.; 6:15 p. m.
LEAVE TACOMA...........9:25 a. m.; 3:00, 8:00 p. m.

Seattle Telephone Main 176 Seattle Flyer Dock.   Tacoma Telephone Main 211, Tacoma N. P. Ry. Dock

The Doomed Clallam

"Women and children first!"

That hoary rule of the sea became a dirge on the night of January 8, 1904, aboard the storm-tossed Puget Sound Navigation Company steamer, *Clallam*. The 168-foot wooden vessel had left Port Townsend in the face of storm warnings, bound for Victoria. She was sighted briefly the following morning, drifting helplessly, badly battered by a gale. As rising waters put out the fires and stilled the pumps, Captain George Roberts ordered the women and children into the lifeboats. They were quickly engulfed by the seas. All 44 who had taken to the boats died.

Shortly after 10 a.m., the tug *Richard Holyoke* got a line aboard the stricken steamer, now wallowing midway between San Juan and Smith Islands, a few miles from Victoria. Just before noon, the *Clallam* rolled over and sank. The 36 passengers and crew aboard were all saved by the *Richard Holyoke* and the tug *Sea Lion*.

A board of inquiry suspended the licenses of Captain Roberts and Chief Engineer Scott de Launcey.

Historical Society of Seattle and King County

The *Dix*

The steamer *Dix,* built for the short haul commuter and pleasure run to Alki Point, was working a relief run to Port Blakely on the night of November 18, 1906, when Captain Percy Lermond turned the helm over to his mate, Charles Dennison, and went below to collect fares from the 60 passengers aboard. The night was clear, the waters glassy calm. Off Alki Point, Captain Lermond paused from collecting fares in the ladies cabin as he heard the mate signal for a stop.

"Just as I got on deck, on the starboard side," Captain Lermond said later that night at Port Blakely, "I saw the bow of a vessel loom up. Almost instantly she struck us… and heeled the *Dix* over like a top."

The vessel was a three-masted steam schooner, the *Jeanie,* laden with a shipment of iron ore. Mate Dennison, who had sighted the schooner earlier, inexplicably failed to steer out of a collision course. Minutes later the *Dix* sank, stern first, many of her passengers trapped inside.

Later Captain Lermond recalled clinging to the railing as the *Dix* sank:

> *The sight fascinated me by its horror. Lights were still burning and I could see people inside of the cabin. The expressions on the faces were of indescribable despair…. There were cries, prayers and groans from men and women, and the wail of a child and the shouts of those who were fighting desperately to gain the deck.*

Captain Lermond and 37 others were picked out of the chill waters. Thirty-five people drowned, the Port Blakely Mill shutting down briefly in their memory.

University of Washington Library

Boats at Pier 3 At the peak of Puget Sound steamer traffic, Pier 3, the Galbraith Dock (now the Sound's best-known seafood restaurant, Ivar's) was known as the Mosquito Fleet dock.

Vessels shown in this 1912 photo by Asahel Curtis include the Vashon Island-Olympia *Magnolia* at far left, which has been loading grain and other cargo, including an old Dodge touring car visible on the lower deck; the 1903-vintage *Florence K,* which ran to Eagle Harbor, and the *Mohawk* (ex-*Indian Flyer*) which has been loading passengers for Bainbridge Island points.

Identity of the large steamer in the fore-

ground is not known. Lifeboats indicate her port of registry was Portland, Maine.

Note the paddlewheel steamers at far left docked at Pier 4, terminus for passengers and freight service to Poulsbo and Liberty Bay points.

The two tallest buildings on the 1912 skyline were the Bon Marche at far left, and the Savoy Hotel, center.

Marguerite

The *Marguerite* served the mills and residents of Lake Whatcom near Bellingham, including providing outings such as this. In 1907 she ran on the rocks during a winter fog, sinking by the stern. Passengers and crew were rescued by the tiny steam launch *Elsinore,* formerly operating on Lake Washington as part of Capt. John Anderson's fleet.

Whatcom Museum

City of Angels

The *City of Angels* in the San Juans. The
128-foot steamer, built in 1906 in San Pedro
as the *City of Long Beach*, first entered
Puget Sound service in 1913 for the Port
Angeles Transportation Co., later being acquired by Puget Sound Navigation Co.

University of Washington Library

East Sound House

Early on, the San Juan Islands became a favorite of vacationers. But it took a bit of determination — and time — just to get there. At the turn of the century, those heading for the favorite isle, Orcas, went by steamers like the paddlewheeler, *State of Washington,* to Anacortes. There they boarded a smaller steamer for the island. Service was also provided from Whatcom, and via the *Lydia Thompson* direct from Seattle.

Favorite hostelries included the East Sound House shown here with its verandah rocking chairs at the ready. An early reviewer outlined other attractions:

Hammocks and rustic seats are found in many a secluded spot, silently weaving a web of enchantment to entrance (sic) the mind and lull the heart to happy rest. Out upon the beach, salt water bathing can be enjoyed during the languid summer afternoons, while at evening clam bakes with bonfires and singing, charm with wild delight.

San Juan County Album, University of Washington Library Collection

197

The Road to Flanders

In 1914, the regal Princess liners became troop transports, at first ferrying soldiers from Vancouver Island training camps to Vancouver, and the long road to France. Here the *Princess Victoria* debarks from Victoria.

One of the CPR wartime fatalities was the newly-launched *Princess Irene,* commandeered by the British Navy before she ever reached Victoria where she was to enter service on the Triangle Route. In 1915 in Sheerness Harbour, England, she blew up, killing 274 crewmen and 74 shipyard workers. There was one survivor.

British Columbia Archives

Sicamous

The beautifully crafted sternwheelers of Okanogan Lake in British Columbia offered a royal excursion. Here the *Sicamous* is pictured arriving at Summerland in 1919, bearing the Prince of Wales, who was visiting the Okanogan Country on his cross-Canada tour. In 1951, the vessel was towed to Penticton to become a historical exhibit.

British Columbia Archives

Iroquois, Indianapolis and Chippewa

In 1906 and 1907, the newly launched Puget Sound Navigation Company made a bold bid to meet the challenge of the Canadian Pacific Line's entry into Puget Sound, purchasing three smartly-appointed steamers from the Great Lakes: the *Indianapolis, Chippewa* and *Iroquois*. First to be delivered, in 1906, was the *Indianapolis,* which made an uneventful 51-day passage on her 15,000 mile route from the Great Lakes to Puget Sound. She is pictured (upper left) docked under a five-cent cigar billboard at Chicago, from where she sailed daily to Michigan City.

The next to put out for the long voyage to a new home, the *Chippewa,* (lower left) found transiting the Strait of Magellan was as horrendous as legend would have it. The engine room log of the 1111-ton steamer, equipped with four coal-fired boilers, railed not at bad weather, but at the quality of the workmanship provided by workmen who fitted the *Chippewa* out for her baptism in the deep sea. Wrote Chief Engineer C. F. Bishop, who had nursed the *Indianapolis* through her delivery, too:

> *Bulkheads stove in ... fire broke out ... running lights shorted out ... boiler gaskets blew out ... pumps sprung leaks ... also steam lines ... boat seems to be hoodooed ... if we had some of the whelps here who drove the pipe fittings in Hoboken it would be all we could ask.*

After more than a week went by, Captain Charles McClure soberly observed:

> *Nothing but eternal vigilance and good seamanship and luck will ever take this ship out of here. Nine days today since we entered Magellan Strait and I hope it will be 900 years before I enter it again. Give me the open sea.*

A few days later the *Chippewa* succeeded in fighting her way through the worst of the Horn's waters. On a calm May day in 1907, after 79 days at sea, she passed up Puget Sound.

Despite Engineer Bishop's angry fulminations, the workmanship on the *Chippewa* proved excellent. While never proving to be much of a threat to the classier CPR steamers on the international runs, the *Chippewa* remained on Sound duty for many years (upper right). In 1926, still propelled by her original steam engines, she was converted into the largest auto ferry operating on Puget Sound (right center), hauling 2,000 passengers and 90 cars on the Seattle-Bremerton run.

(The *Indianapolis* suffered a similar fate. In 1933, after 27 years in service, she was converted into an auto ferry, her bow bobbed and rounded off and a turntable installed to facilitate movement of the 33

cars she carried. She was scrapped in 1939.)

All three steamers (*Iroquois, Chippewa* and *Indianapolis*) quickly shed their white livery, adopting the conventional black hulls and white deckhouses of Puget Sound Navigation Co. The upper left photo shows the *Indianapolis* in her Great Lakes colors. At lower right she enters Tacoma harbor with repaint.

The *Chippewa* and *Iroquois* are shown here in their trappings as excursion vessels operated by the Arnold Transportation Company of Mackinac Island. The *Chippewa* entered this service in 1900, followed the next year by the *Iroquois.* Both were sold in 1906 to the Puget Sound Day Line, a subsidiary of Puget Sound Navigation Company.

Delivery of the third Great Lakes trio, the *Iroquois,* (following pages) was completed without incident. On her run up the coast from Chile to California, she was under sail to conserve coal. She was returned to the Great Lakes — this time through the Panama Canal — in 1920. It was an unprofitable venture that lasted for seven years before the *Iroquois* came back to Puget Sound. Like her companions, she was patterned after a cross-Channel packet and carried but limited overnight accommodations. In 1927 she was extensively remodelled into a night boat, including bridal suites, furnished for some baffling — and frustrating — reason with twin beds. The refit also provided the *Iroquois* with a profile of monumental ugliness. Despite these shortcomings, and the fact she was a wretched sea boat, crossing the Strait of Juan de Fuca, the *Iroquois,* with radio speakers beating out jazz tunes for those gyrating on her newly laid dance floor, proved to be highly popular. In 1951, her upper decks were removed, steam engine replaced, and the *Iroquois* worked as a freight carrier until converted to an Alaska fish packing plant in 1969.

B.C. Provincial Archives

University of Washington Library

Iroquois

The smart lines of the *Iroquois* virtually disappeared when she was remodeled into a night boat in 1927 (left). She was to undergo two more refits during her 83 year career, being converted into a Puget Sound freight carrier in 1952 for Black Ball Transport, mainly carrying paper products from Port Angeles and Port Townsend. In 1973 the pride of the Great Lakes became a crab processor at Akutan, Alaska. In 1984, she was towed to sea and sunk by an explosive charge.

Chippewa and *Iroquois*

The *Chippewa* (left) and the *Iroquois* docked at Port Townsend's Union Wharf.

P.M.Richardson

368

Princess Marguerite

The first *Princess Marguerite,* built in 1925 at the famed John Brown Shipyard at Clydebank, Scotland, together with a sister ship, the *Princess Kathleen.* A proud three-stacker, she carried 1500 passengers, provided 136 staterooms, space for 30 automobiles, and had a top speed of 22 knots. In 1942 she was torpedoed in the Mediterranean and sank with a loss of 55 lives. The *Princess Kathleen* also on troop carrying duty, survived the war. The *Princess Adelaide* is to the rear.

British Columbia Archives

205

Princess Kathleen

The dining room of the *Princess Kathleen* represented the finest in traditional British dining room fare and facilities: crisp white napery, heavy silverware, spotless glassware and a menu that was uninspired but dependable. The *Princess Kathleen's* dining room seated 168. One of the larger CPR liners, she had a capacity of 1500 passengers, with stateroom accommodations for 136. Below decks she accommodated 30 cars. Built in Scotland, she had a top speed of 22 knots.

As in the case of her running mate, the *Princess Marguerite,* the *Princess Kathleen* was not named for any member of the British Royal family. Both vessels honored the daughter of Lord Thomas Shaugnessy, one time CPR president.

Pictured at upper right is a deluxe stateroom aboard the *Princess Kathleen.*

British Columbia Archives

Princess Louise Stateroom

An economy stateroom on the *Princess Louise*. Unlike most of her regal companions on CPR runs, the *Princess Louise* was built in a North Vancouver shipyard, launched in 1921. The single-stacked 4000-tonner was the largest in the fleet at the time of the launch, serving on runs to Alaska, with occasional assignments on the Triangle Route. Her accomodations ranged from Spartan two berth cabins such as the one illustrated, to suites with eiderdown comforters. She continued in service until the 1960s.

British Columbia Archives

Victoria Ferry

The CPR auto ferry *Motor Princess* loading
at Tsawwassen for her run to Victoria.

Prince Rupert

The Canadian Pacific's fine liners on runs to Puget Sound, British Columbia ports and those in Southeastern Alaska were matched in appointments only by those of the Government-operated railroad, the Grand Trunk Pacific. Pictured in this (broken) glass plate photo is the *Prince Rupert* which arrived in 1910 from the shipyards of Swan, Hunter and Wigrams in England. The *Prince Rupert,* in tandem service with a sister (or brother) ship, the *Prince George,* was 306 feet long, lavishly equipped with accommodations for 1500 day passengers and 220 staterooms. Because of the necessity to make stops at the line's railhead at Prince Rupert, the liner's operated on an awkward weekly schedule between Seattle, Victoria and Prince Rupert, with calls at Stewart at the southern tip of Southeastern Alaska.

The entry of the Grand Trunk Pacific did little to lessen the dominance of the CPR, particularly on the Triangle Route. In 1930, on the cusp of the Depression, the Grand Trunk, by then known more conveniently as the Canadian national, made a last bid for traffic on the Triangle Route, entering the new *Prince David* on the run along with the *Prince Robert.* But the timing as bad and the *Princes* were exiled from the run in 1931.

Vancouver Public Library, British Columbia Archives

City of Victoria

The *City of Victoria* was the last in a wavering line of luxury vessels entered by U.S. shipping interests to compete with the CPR on the Puget Sound-Victoria run. The 293-foot steamer carried 600 passengers, including 167 in staterooms of glitzy gold and white. It provided room for 60 automobiles, a broad-view observation salon and an acceptable dining room (both pictured). But despite these offerings, and a round trip fare of but $3.50, the *City of Victoria* was but another loser.

Built in 1893 as the *Alabama* (above) of the Baltimore Steam Packet Co., she was billed as the Queen of the Chesapeake, capable of 19-plus knots. She was purchased in 1928 by the short-lived Edmonds-Victoria Ferry Company, organized by a foursome of shipping heavies: D. E. Skinner, H. F. Alexander, Herbert Fleishacker and Henry Seaborn. The following year, 1929, she was handed off to the Independent Ferry Company, headed by two captains, John L. Anderson, whose steamers had dominated Lake Washington and J. Howard Payne. They kept her afloat for another year and then the *City of Victoria* became another Depression fatality. She later served as an air base construction barracks at Sitka in World War II and in 1948 was burned for scrap at Edmonds, not far from where she had sailed so proudly 20 years earlier.

Lower right: (The only explanation for the toney crowd pictured seated in the observation room — seemingly unaware of the fact the steamer is still at dockside — is that it was posed by an advertising agency — who neglected to assign a photo retoucher to the product.)

University of Washington Library

Travel in Luxury Between Seattle and Victoria on the Palatial Auto Ferry Steamship

City of Victoria

The City of Victoria, largest, finest, fastest American steamship on Puget Sound, has all the travel accommodations and luxuries that you enjoy on a big passenger ship.

You can drive your automobile on and off the ship with ease. The deck used for parking is commodious.

You will be glad of your choice, if you take the City of Victoria on trips to Vancouver Island or when making the Seattle-Victoria-Vancouver circuit with your car.

Two Round Trips Daily
Leave EDMONDS 8 A. M.
Leave VICTORIA 1 P. M.
Leave EDMONDS 6 P. M.
Leave VICTORIA 1 A. M.
STEAMER STAGES leave Central Stage Terminal, Eighth and Stewart, Seattle, 7 A. M., connecting with morning boat, and 5 P. M. connecting with evening boat. Stops en route between Seattle and Edmonds to pick up passengers.
PASSENGERS
$2 one way; $3.50 round trip, Including Stage Fare.
AUTOMOBILES
$3.50 one way; $6 round trip, including driver.

SHORT   AUTO FERRY ROUTE

Operated by Independent Ferry Company
J. L. ANDERSON, Pres. J. HOWARD PAYNE, V. Pres. and Mgr.
TICKET OFFICES, 414 University St. MAin 7123 and MAin 3039
Central Stage Terminal, Eighth and Stewart. ELiot 1401

210

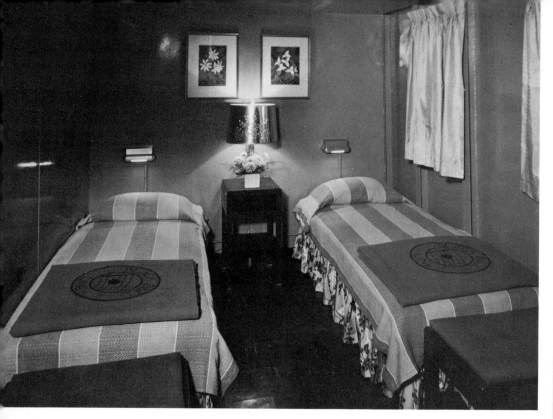

The Chinook   The *Chinook* didn't quite live up to the boast of her designer, William Francis Gibbs of the prestigious New York marine architectual firm of Gibbs and Cox. Gibbs dubbed her "the *Queen Elizabeth* of the Inland Seas." The $2 million vessel was launched April 22, 1947 at Todd Seattle Shipyard with Mrs. Alexander Peabody acting as sponsor.

Her 100 staterooms (upper left) and her three public lounges (lower left) were lavishly outfitted by Frederick & Nelson of Seattle.

212

of Puget Sound "M.V. Chinook"

Johnston

The 328-foot *Chinook* had a capacity for 1200 passengers and 100 cars, operating first on the Port Angeles-Victoria run. In 1955, as one of the last vessels operated by Captain Peabody following the sale of Puget Sound Navigation Company to the State of Washington, she was assigned to the Horseshoe Bay-Nanaimo route under the Black Ball Ferries Ltd. flag.

Captain Peabody sold the *Chinook* and four other ferries in 1961 to the British Columbia provincial government for $6,700,000. Joshua Green, once a major stockholder in the company, wryly observed:

"It was a sad but profitable funeral."

Loren Smith

Victoria Harbour

The above scene captures the busy mood of Victoria's Inner Harbour during the ebbing days of the smart ships of the late Forties. Midstream the Black Ball Line's new $2 million *Chinook* is heading for Port Angeles, about to pass by the inbound CPR steamer, *Princess Kathleen,* operating on the more popular Triangle Route. A companion on that run, the *Princess Charlotte,* is shown at the CPR dock. The *Princess Alice* is on the terminal's landward side. Further down the harbor, the *Princess Adelaide* is docked.

The *Alice* and the *Adelaide* were testimonies to the indestructability of the Scot-built steamers. Both served on CPR runs from 1912 until 1949, when they were sold to Greek interests and continued cruising the Aegean until 1966 and 1968 when they were scrapped.

William Thorniley Coll., Courtesy George Bayless

214

Princess Marguerite II

Sole survivor (as of 1985) of the fabulous Canadian Pacific fleet of the *Princess*—class steamers, the *Princess Marguerite* had few rivals for speed and durability. (Shown framed by the Empress Hotel turrets in 1984.)

The *Princess Marguerite,* operated by the British Columbia government, made her last sailing for the Canadian Pacific in 1975, ending 70 years of CPR service on the inland waters of Puget Sound. The *Princess Patricia,* her companion on the Triangle Route (earlier known as the Tri-City Route), remained in service on seasonal Alaska excursions until 1981.

Jim Faber

BOTHELL,
WASH.

May Blossom

The marine highway to Bothell and Sammamish Slough way points was a pastoral one, as evidenced by this shot of the excursion steamer *May Blossom*.

Puget Sound Maritime Historical Society

The Look-Alikes

Like the tiny *May Blossom* on the preceding page, the *City of Bothell* was a familiar sight on Lake Washington and the Sammamish Slough around the turn of the century.

At left, a look-alike from Maine, the *Sabino,* illustrates how the shape of the Puget Sound steamers was influenced by New England boat designers, who carried the plans West in their memories. The *Sabino* was built for coastal service in Maine in 1908. Today, powered by her original compound engine, she hauls excursionists out of Mystic Seaport in Connecticut and shares honors with Puget Sound's *Virginia V* as one of America's oldest wooden-hulled steamers.

In contrast with the piles of detailed plans and specifications required for today's ferries, vessels of the Mosquito Fleet took to water without a single blueprint. (This was not true of the larger steel-hulled steamers such as the *Tacoma, Sol Duc, Kulshan, Sioux,* and *Potlatch*).

It is now generally accepted that the configuration of the Mosquito Fleet steamers was carried westward in the memories of New Englanders drawn here to build and run sawmills, and an immediate by-product, schooners, for the timber trade. So many of these were from Maine that a familiar amendment to the shout of "man overboard!" alongside a Sound lumber dock was, "If he's not from Maine, throw him back!"

Phil Spaulding, the dean of Puget Sound naval architects, is among those who see the Maine influence in the Mosquito Fleet. As shipyards began springing up, they attracted steamboat entrepreneurs, many of them captains who knew what they wanted. Says Spaulding:

> *They'd come into one of those little yards and sit down with the owner and tell him, "I need a boat about 125 feet long, something like the old so-and-so!" Maybe he'd hand over a crude*

sketch. There was a handshake — and work started. That was it.

Larry Glosten, another prominent Seattle naval architect whose firm has designed tugs, ferries and a wide variety of specialized research vessels, is another who sees in the Mosquito Fleet designs a Maine connection. He says:

They were products of carpenters who would whittle away until they had a satisfactory configuration. Then they'd build another, four or five feet long, and saw it up into sections, haul it up to the mould loft, and expand it.

Early Puget Sound and Lake Washington shipyards were about as elaborate as those of a blacksmith shop. There was a shed housing the band saw which would cut out the frames and other timbers. Another served as a warehouse and office. Nearby was the shipway, usually uncovered.

Above the warehouse was the most important element in the design of the new steamer — the mould loft. Virtually empty of equipment, the loft's outstanding characteristic was a broad, smooth floor, well lighted by deep windows, lamps and, later, electricity. Here the loftsmen determined the shape of thing to come. Some were carpenters, more at home building sawmills than steamers; others included Scandina-vian shipwrights drawn here by reports that yards were to be established on Puget Sound for maintaining a large fleet of whaling vessels. (Only one such yard, located between Kirkland and Yarrow Point, materialized.)

Launching of the *Fortuna*

The launching in 1906 of the trim steamer *Fortuna* on Lake Washington marked the high water mark in the fortunes of Seattle's lake steamers. While there was limited service on Lake Union until development of street car lines, most plied Lake Washington. From the main terminus at Leschi, steamers crossed the lake to Mercer Island, Newport (where a roadway to Snoqualmie Pass was to create the lake's first auto ferry crossing), Renton, Bothell and other hamlets. Small steamers even pushed their way up Sammamish Slough to Lake Sammamish, one designed with a hinged stack to permit passing under low bridges.

Following a consolidation in 1906, most of the lake steamers were operated by Captain John Anderson, a visionary boatbuilder and operator. By 1909, when the Alaska Yukon Pacific Exposition drew visitors by the thousands, he had assembled 14 steamers — two of them converted yachts — under his Lake Washington Steamboat Company burgee. By 1916, competition from the publicly-owned lake ferries and newly opened highway routes had idled all but three of them.

The *Fortuna* was designed and built by the Swedish-born Anderson, who ran away to sea at age 14. He went to work on the lake steamer, *C. C. Calkins* soon after his arrival at Seattle in 1888. He moved up the ladder to fireman and then purser before becoming a captain.

Like all steamers of her day, the *Fortuna* was built without recourse to blueprints. Captain Anderson even designed the *Fortuna's* boilers, which he patented, and made the engine a showpiece with rods of polished steel and the entire housing encased in nickel-plated sheet metal. "The four-cylinder, 550-horsepower engine," recounts Captain Bob Matson, a nephew of Captain Anderson and an early deckhand on the lake steamer, *Dawn,* "ran as smoothly as a sewing machine."

The *Fortuna* became Captain Anderson's favorite in the steamboat fleet. But he continued to direct his talents to her yacht-like working mates, their polished nameboards celebrating Greek mythology with names like *Xanthus, Atalanta, Aquilo*

(continued overleaf)

221

and *Cyrene*. Altogether, Captain Matson recalls, the Anderson Steamboat Company provided more than 50 stops along the shores of Lake Washington. The steamers were speedy, capable of upwards of 16 knots when required, and they were equally tireless. The tiny *Dawn,* for example, made a dozen stops around the circumference of Mercer Island before returning to Leschi, where after a pause, the route was repeated.

The *Fortuna* lost her girlish figure in 1915 when she was converted into a stubby auto ferry with a capacity for 15 autos. In 1928, obsolete and worn out, she was scrapped.

One of Mercer Island's early day stops brought guests to an ornate and short-lived resort hotel, the C. C. Calkins, served by the steamer that provided Captain Anderson with his first job in the U.S. The hotel, turreted and gabled, had 75 rooms, four cottages and a greenhouse for grow-ing dining room flowers. It was spread over 25 manicured acres, "graced by the notes of tinkling fountains." Despite these and other inducements of "culinary as well as sylvan attractions," the C. C. Calkins flourished as a resort hotel for but two seasons and burned in 1904.

No such problems beset the resort own-ers at Leschi, start of most lake crossings and headquarters for the Anderson Steam-boat Company. The completion in 1888 of a cable car line placed Leschi only a three mile ride from Pioneer Square, a giddy trip over a wooden trestle not unlike a roller coaster. By the early 1900s the lakeside resort became the Pacific North-west's most popular resort — 40,000 were drawn there on the Fourth of July, 1908. Other resort developments followed at Madrona and Madison Park beaches and steamers shuttled between them with dime fares.

Most of their divertissements were old fashioned family fun: swimming, picnick-ing, canoeing, fishing and gawking at caged sea lions and other inmates of a small zoo. But there were racier offerings, too — vaudeville shows, dancing in cavern-ous pavilions and drinking in taverns. One Leschi hotel, recalled a cable car conduc-tor, served sandwiches to "occupants of rooms which were only occupied for an hour or so."

When competition from cross-lake ferries operated by King County and the Port of Seattle drastically curtailed steamer reve-nues, Anderson became the first to offer water tours through the Lake Washington Ship Canal into Seattle's harbor, a popular excursion he continued on the Mosquito Fleet steamer, *Sightseer,* (ex-*Vashona*) until 1935.

Joe Williamson Collection

Cyrene

Launched in 1891 for Lake Washington
excursions, the yacht-like *Cyrene* was
remodeled in 1909 for Alaska Yukon
Pacific Exposition sightseers

University of Washington Library

L. T. Haas

The *L. T. Haas* was built in 1902 for the Leschi Park-Meydenbauer Bay run of the Interlaken Steamboat Company. She later was acquired by Captain Anderson when he consolidated his Anderson Steamboat Company with Interlaken. The *L. T. Haas* was destroyed by fire in 1909.

Leschi Landing

Leschi was headquarters for the
Anderson Steamboat Company soon to
dominate steamboat traffic on Lake
Washington. Preparing to debark is the
Cyrene, pictured in 1908.

University of Washington Library

Deception Pass Ferry

One of Henry Ford's "flivvers" of the 1920s awaits arrival of an early auto ferry at a landing serving the Deception Pass crossing. It was made on a barge lashed to a motor launch.

Leschi (overleaf)

Holiday use of the auto ferry hadn't caught on in 1914, as evidenced by this Memorial Day photo of the *Leschi* ready to depart from Bellevue for Leschi in Seattle.

Paul Dorpat

Ferry *Mercer* on Lake Washington

Before the joys of driving over the floating bridges were discovered, this is how one travelled to Seattle from Bellevue, Kirkland, Newport and Mercer Island. Here on a misty day in 1928 the ferry *Mercer* and the sidewheeler *Leschi* await docking.

The *Mercer* was built in 1916 on Vashon Island and was operated on Lake Washington by King County. Following completion of the first Lake Washington Floating Bridge, she ran between San Pedro and Terminal Island as the *Islander*.

The *Leschi* was the last Lake Washington ferry, serving the Medina-Kirkland-Leschi route even after completion of the first floating bridge. Built in 1913, she was for a time operated by the Port of Seattle, the first such publicly-owned ferry.

Asahel Curtis Photo

Boeing Ferry

During the Depression, when Boeing Airplane Co., was grounded due to lack of orders, the company dabbled in building furniture, launched a few sailboats, then won a contract to build a ferry at Vancouver, B.C. The 130-foot diesel-powered craft carried 30 cars and a few hundred passengers. Inelegantly christened *North Vancouver No. 4,* she went into service in 1931, running across Burrard Inlet from Vancouver to North Vancouver. According to her skipper, Capt. William Sprackin, she "handled like a yacht." She remained in service for 30 years on the commuter run. Her cost: $46,135.

Vancouver Library

54577
ASAHEL CURTIS

Last Port of Call

Awaiting their turn under the wrecker's torch, three Puget Sound Navigation Company veterans are moored in Lake Washington. In the foreground is the *Kulshan,* built in 1910 for the Seattle-Bellingham run by the Moran yard, using Port Townsend steel. Next is the popular *Tacoma* (see prologue) and beyond her, the *City of Victoria,* built in 1893 as the *Alabama,* the queen of Chesapeake Bay runs.

Joe Williamson Collection

Epilogue:

The Course Ahead

At Tacoma, an unnamed apprentice deck hand poses at the wheel of the schooner Dimsdale *built at the Charles J. Pepper yard in Londonderry.*

Hester Collection, University of Washington Library

The Course Ahead

A lot of water has passed under the bridge since that day in 1913 when Captain Everett Coffin eased the *Tacoma* into Colman Dock for the last time and signalled "Finished with Engines."

In the years to follow, the steamers of Puget Sound one by one were reduced to scrap and on all but the most remote lakes and rivers the thrash of the paddlewheeler was stilled.

Today almost two and one-half million people reside along the Puget Sound littoral that once was the breeding ground for the Mosquito Fleet. Ninety percent live along the Sound's eastern shore, a megalopolis stretching from Olympia to Everett. They seem to spend much of each weekend escaping by ferry to the less populated western shores.

Like the steamers of the Mosquito Fleet, the ferries of Puget Sound are as indigenous as its rainfall. Usually locally designed and built, they are manned by Puget Sounders, some of whom recall when grandfather or grandmother crewed on the Mosquito Fleet. The ferries serve a market largely local. Of the 18 million passenger fares collected each year, less than 10 percent come from tourists, although ferries rank among the state's four most popular visitor attractions (a fact not lost on management, which raises fares during each tourist season). The 22-ferry fleet, America's largest, is state-operated. The State purchased the ferry system in 1951 from Puget Sound Navigation Company, ending more than a half century of operation. The takeover followed a tumultous period after World War II, during which peacetime inflation forced up demands for fare increases and wage hikes. This in turn led to costly work stopages, first by ferry unions and later by Puget Sound Navigation Company management, insisting on a new fare structure.

For once the ferry riders united—for state ownership. The politicians, sensing an acceptably populist issue (and the emergence of a brand new bureaucracy), fell in line. Finally, on June 11, 1951, the Black Ball Line hauled down its colors. Washington State Ferries was born. Ferry riders have been complaining ever since.

They anguish over every fare increase. They fret over lineups and other delays. They fume at scheduling changes. They criticize the system's management, its ticket takers, washrooms and hamburger buns. Only grudgingly they concede WSF has an outstanding safety record: no fatalities during more than 35 years of operation.

Puget Sound ferry riders are anarchistic: no one has yet welded them into a consumer's lobby. Yet for decades they have closed ranks to beat back every proposal to replace the ferries with bridges. To date, plans for six cross-Sound spans, all of which would provide significant savings in time and money, have been shelved, probably for good. One of the islands sited for a bridge connection with Seattle was Bainbridge. It takes two ferries, each with a capacity of a thousand passengers and more than a hundred cars, running virtually around the clock, to haul commuters and pleasure seekers on this run. Fares are high and terminal lineups are, well, terminal. Yet a few years ago when Charles Prahl, then head of the State Highway Department, was presented

The ferry continues to be an all-weather favorite for Puget Sounders.

Jim Faber

a gift at a ferry boat dedication, he opened it to find a chunk of concrete and a note:

"This is a sea anchor to throw the cross-Sound bridge plans overboard at a spot of your choosing."

Puget Sound, as Murray Morgan reminds us in his Foreword, is indeed a moat. For most of us, this moat, this blessed Sound, has created a delightful separation of state. The islanders, and those tucked away in the more untouched Olympic Peninsula backwaters, continue to live in their own version of bucolia, accepting the surge of weekend and summertime visitors. No where in America, in fact in few places worldwide, does the scene mellow so rapidly as it does after half hour ferry crossings to islands like Vashon, Bainbridge and Whidbey or the lengthier routes to the San Juan Islands. Here and there, developers have established a beachhead. Puget Sound pollution is a growing threat. The protective mantle of second growth evergreen forests is nearing maturity, and before this century's end will fall to the lumberman. But today most west side highways provide a jump into another time frame, limned by the serrated peaks of the Olympic Mountain range, one of America's few remaining terrains a mapmaker can label unexplored.

Repelling invaders is a costly exercise, one that becomes increasingly vexing as state revenues shrink. Ferry fares finance only 62 percent of Washington State Ferries operational expenses. The rest comes from state funds. Capital costs continue to escalate: a 100-car ferry now costs several million dollars, in 1980 dollars. Just to remodel three former San Francisco Bay ferries, bought by Puget Sound Navigation Company in 1940, is costing $18 million. They cost $500,000 each to build back in 1927.

There's more. With heavy traffic increases anticipated between now and the year 2000 (up 85 percent by one estimate) Washington State Ferries estimates it will require $223 million for terminal construction and improvements. But the item that dramatizes the big coming change in Puget Sound transportation is one that calls for spending $20 million on five new ferries. Each will carry 300 passengers—and no cars.

Not since the launching of the *Tacoma* and her running mates has a carfree ferry been built for Puget Sound service. We're out to re-invent the Mosquito Fleet. It's a move that will require some blueprint time by marine architects. For agreeing on a design acceptable to a mixed bag of constituents

The younger generation finds the same attractions on Puget Sound as did their grandfathers. Pictured is the landing at Steilacoom of the Pierce County ferry, Islander.

Jim Faber

At top, an earlier family member gets a paint touch-up. In the engine room photo above, Engineer David Hogan adjusts a lubricator on the Virginia V's *81-year-old steam engine.*

that includes the Coast Guard, the Inland Boatmen's Union, ferry riders and beach property owners measuring the wake, is a problem never faced by Mosquito Fleet operators.

The Mosquito Fleet steamers were workhorses, many continuing their plodding way until dropping dead in their traces many years later. Built in crude open boatyards by carpenters working without lines and offsets, they were marvels of durability and simplicity of design.

A classic example of those virtues has sent a whooping whistle echoing down Sound inlets for more than 50 years: the wooden-hulled *Virginia V,* sole survivor of the Mosquito Fleet. Now operated and maintained by a preservation foundation, the *Virginia V* is the handiwork of a Vashon Island boatyard owner, Matt Anderson. No blueprints, no stacks of specifications, hardly more than a handshake to cement the deal. The *Virginia's* owner, Captain Nels Christensen, knew what he wanted: a steamer like his outworn *Virginia III* and *Virginia IV,* third and fourth in a line of Christensen-manned steamers.

Framed by a beached cedar log, the Virginia V *pauses for a salmon bake luncheon at Kiana Lodge on Agate Pass during a summertime excursion run from Seattle.*

Jim Faber

Captain Don Moss and son Ted on an excursion run in the Virginia V's *original wheel house.*

Jim Faber

Virtually every night after placing his order, Captain Christensen would row over from his home at nearby Lisabeula to Anderson's Maplewood yard. Together the men would discuss the shape of things to come on the morrow. After the skipper left, Anderson would work up some drawings by lantern and take them up to the mold loft. The next day, shipwrights would use the plans to fashion pattern boards and then cut out timbers which, when bolted together, created the frame, engine beds, deck and skin, bent to the shape of the frames by being soaked in a steambox.

The last of the famed Puget Sound Mosquito Fleet, the 61-year old steamer continues to carry excursionists to various Sound nooks, powered by a steam engine built in 1904. Christened in 1922 with spring water from the island home of the steamer's skipper-owner, the venerable vessel has been spared the fate of her compatriots through efforts of the Virginia V Foundation. The non-profit group conducts annual drives for funds, donated labor and materials to keep the *Virginia* operating and continue her restoration.

Following her launching in 1922 on Vashon Island, the steamer operated for 17 years between Seattle and Tacoma on a seven-day a week schedule, carrying more than eight million passengers without a single fatality. Unlike the express steamer *Tacoma* the *Virginia* had a leisurely pace, cruising at 12 knots and making 13 stops along Vashon Island's West Passage between the two major cities. At most docks, she picked up families of farmers taking baskets of eggs, berries and produce to market. Later she operated on numerous excursion runs throughout Puget Sound and briefly on the Columbia River.

Today from May to October the *Virginia* offers a series of scenic day cruises out of Seattle. Aboard, excursionists stake out claims for space in the steamer's observation lounge, crowd lower deck benches that arc around the stern or lean out lowered windows only a few feet above the hissing Sound. On the pilot house deck, lovers snuggled up in the lee of the stack are impervious to the whoop of the steam whistle.

The real steamer buffs line the railing looking down into the engine room housing the triple expansion steam reciprocating engine, built in 1904 and

239

Today's foot passenger ferries have little resemblance to their Mosquito Fleet counterparts. An exception is the City of San Francisco *(lower left), designed by Nickum & Spaulding of Seattle and built by Nichols Bros. on Whidbey Island for dinner excursions on San Francisco Bay.*

The same yard is building seven Australian-designed catamarans, like the Klondike *(upper left) now in Yukon River tour service.*

The innovative Sea Bus, Burrard Beaver *(below), and her sister vessel have carried so many millions on runs linking Vancouver and West Vancouver that need for another cross-channel bridge has been eased. They make their run in 10 minutes and can load and unload 400 passengers in about one minute.*

Nichols Bros.
Nickum & Spaulding
Sea Bus

transferred from the *Virginia IV* in 1922. Here the chief engineer mans the oil can, eyes the brass-bound gauges and answers bell signals from the pilot house, keeping an alert eye on the dock or shore through an outboard window only a few feet away. Occasionally he fills a small copper tank from which oil slowly flows into nine copper tubes. These end in a cotton wick, which when contacted by an ascending piston, bathes it in a squirt of oil. Sharing the two-level engine room is a fireman responsible for controlling the oil cocks, pumps and auxiliary steam engine generating power for lights.

The wheeze and gasp of the engine, embellished by the smell of hot oil and the constant ballet of smoothly plunging parts (like robots running in place) makes the engine room the *Virginia's* center stage, rivalled only by the passing tableau of water, islands and mountains and the activities of the captain and mate in the pilot house—also open to view.

It is questionable whether the foot passenger ferry of tomorrow will have much resemblance to yesterday's steamer, but the possibility is there, as we shall see. Meantime it's a buyer's market with Puget Sound yards ready to adopt new design concepts to win the $20 million passenger-only contract.

For several years officials of Washington State Ferries and its parent, the State Department of Transportation, have been familiarized with a wide range of passenger vessels, including such exotics as the hovercraft (an unlikely choice due to its high noise level), the hydrofoil, and Vancouver's innovative Sea Bus.

Boeing's hydrofoil, once a favored contender, has been scratched, the

aerospace company having abandoned its entry into the field of marine transportation. One new concept which has been well received abroad, is a passenger-carrying catamaran, licensed in Australia and now being built and successfully marketed on Puget Sound.

A footnote here will bring *Steamer's Wake* full circle. I jotted it down a few years ago during an interview with Ed Hagemann of the naval architectural firm of Nickum & Spaulding in Seattle. Betting on the future, the firm which has designed ferries for runs on Puget Sound, San Francisco Bay, British Columbia and Alaska, had been assessing the traffic potential of the passenger-only ferry and how best to shape it to those needs.

Hagemann concluded the interview by saying:

"After looking at a lot of concepts, you know what I think the look of that ferry should be?"

He tossed over a drawing. It showed a twin-stacked passenger boat in Elliott Bay, framed by Seattle's skyscraper skyline of today. The vessel looked familiar.

"Exactly," Hagemann said with a grin. *"It's the* Tacoma. *With a couple of diesels and a few modifications, you could have an 800 passenger ferry capable of 25 knots and low operating costs. They'd love it!"*

Drawing by D.R. Johnson

242

Appendix:

Racing, Gold, Fires, and Other Dramas

Racing

The Last Steamer Race (upper left)

The last two passenger steamers built on Puget Sound, the *Virginia V,* right, and the *Sightseer,* (ex-*Vashona*) churn their way to the finish line during a National Maritime Day race in 1948. The *Virginia V* won.

Joe Williamson Collection

Whitehorse Rapids Bound

Steamer racing prevailed from the Yukon to the Sacramento. Here the Canadian Development Co. sternwheeler *Columbian* is being outpaced by the Yukon Flyer Line *Eldorado,* racing from Dawson to Whitehorse Rapids on July 4, 1899.

University of Washington Library

Final Contest for the Sternwheelers

August of 1950 saw the Sound's surviving sternwheelers pitted in a race on Lake Washington. Winner was the Army Corps of Engineer's snagboat, the *W.T. Preston,* shown edging out the *Skagit Chief,* center, and the *Skagit Belle,* both of the Skagit River Navigation & Trading Co. The *Preston* now serves as a maritime museum at Anacortes

Puget Sound Maritime Historical Society

The River Runners

Until the coming of the railroads, a series of rock-strewn rapids divided the navigable Columbia into the Lower River, stretching from the Pacific to the Cascades, upriver from Vancouver; the Middle River from the Cascades to The Dalles, and the Upper River, from Celilo to Priest Rapids and Asotin.

As demands for upriver freight soared with the discovery of gold in Idaho, small sternwheelers were built along the Upper and Middle Rivers. A few others fought their way upstream through the rapids at high water. Promoters controlling the portages laid down crude narrow gauge rail lines and began charging all the traffic would bear.

This brigandage continued until 1881 when the OR&N completed laying track along the south bank of the Columbia all the way to Portland, thus sounding a knell for upriver steamers.

To return them downstream to more profitable waters, the rapids at the Cascades had to be run, a contest more challenging than any race. There were plenty of volunteers among river captains and passengers alike.

Among the first to churn its way through this roaring gut was the *R. R. Thompson* with Captain Thomas McNulty at the helm. With engines idling, Captain McNulty took the sternwheeler through the rapids in exactly six minutes and 40 seconds—a downstream run at a clip of almost 60 miles an hour!

Soon to follow in running the rapids was the *Hassalo,* an event that drew thousands of excursionists from Portland and The Dalles to line the banks of the Cascades (pictured). With the veteran Captain James Troup, river-born and river-raised, at the helm, the *Hassalo* was swept downstream in seven minutes flat.

Puget Sound Maritime Historical Society

Cargoes of Gold and Misery

There was no easy road to riches during the Klondike Gold Rush.

The few overland routes to the Yukon Territory existed mainly in the heads of self-annointed guides. Many led only to the grave. From the outset, most of the movement was by water. The most popular route led up the Inside Passage to the Southeastern Alaska ports of Dyea and Skagway, hastily spawned on the mudflats. Here, two miserable trails and an equally pitiless river route snaked their way to Dawson City on the Yukon. Another popular steamship route led across the Bering Sea to the old Russian outpost of St. Michael. St. Michael, frozen in for nine months of the year, offered hastily-patched connections with Dawson, 1,800 miles up the Yukon.

Within a year Seattle became the Klondike's main gateway. In March of 1897, the port logged 18 Alaska ship arrivals and departures. A year later, there were 173. During the height of the stampede as many as 20,000 adventurers sailed north in a single month. They boarded a polyglot fleet that included sailing vessels, steam schooners, Long Island and Catalina excursion craft, tugs and barges, and the 180-foot steam yacht, *Cutch,* built for the Maharajah of Cutch. (One tug from the Columbia River, the *Wallowa,* was beached near Skagway, but survived to live a colorful life and today is the museum tug, *Arthur Foss,* based at Seattle.) Old Puget Sound steamers headed north with hardly a cursory inspection, and in the instance of the venerable *Eliza Anderson,* without a compass. Later the *Eliza* ended up on the beach near Nome, but she was followed by more Sound favorites: *George E. Starr, Rosalie, Idaho, Victorian, North Pacific* and others.

The steamers were joined by freight and passenger ships drawn from the world's oceans: scores of freight and passenger ships, usually sailing criminally overcrowded. An old coal carrier, the *Willamette,* packed 800 passengers aboard, along with 300 horses. The improvised dining room seated only 75. There were a dozen sittings each meal, with appetites whetted by carcasses of beef hanging from the saloon bulkheads

and occasional trickles of horse urine, mixed with coal dust, seeping down from stalls on the deck above. Passengers, numbering more than a hundred, who boarded the tiny *Al-KI* found they were sharing space with 900 sheep, 65 head of cattle and 30 horses. Among the few that could qualify as first class was the *City of Seattle,* (end sheets) which had been a financial flop on Puget Sound but starred in Alaska. Two years after her first run to Skagway in 1898, she returned to Seattle with three tons of Klondike gold, part of $22 million in dust and bullion unloaded that year at Seattle by 45 steamers, including those serving the strike on the Nome beaches.

Accidents were commonplace during the anything-goes stampede of 1898. That year saw 34 wrecks, mostly of smaller vessels, but including a fire and grounding of the steamer *Clara Nevada.* The disaster claimed more than a hundred lives. It led *The Seattle Times'* choleric Colonel Alden Blethen to lead a charge against the federal steamboat inspectors (part of a Democratic administration the publisher attacked regularly). He wrote:

> *Those fellows should be arrested and given a fair trial … and decorate the end of an elevated rope.*

The most popular alternative to the Inside Passage was an all-water route terminating at St. Michael, frozen solid from September until June. It was termed "The Rich Man's Route," a cruelly inaccurate description despite the fact it eliminated toiling over the Chilkoot or White Pass out of Dyea or Skagway. Instead, there was a 1600 mile passage from Seattle to St. Michael over one of the world's coldest and stormiest seas. Debarking, passengers transferred to river boats that made an 80 mile open sea run to the mouth of the Yukon. Up to a month was required to push 1,700 miles upriver to Fortymile, then on to Dawson City, weather permitting. During the winter of 1897-98, 2,500 gold seekers lived as wretched captives aboard sternwheelers trapped in the river ice, some of them reaching Dawson only after a freezing hike out.

Summertime brought little relief. Steamer windows were closed to prevent entry of mosquitos and blackflies, trapping heat from the boilers, their fires consuming as much as two cords an hour as the craft toiled upriver. After a 19-day run to Dawson, one debarking survivor described his transportation as "a flat-bottomed, wood-burning stew pan." With a diet consisting primarily of salt pork, molding potatoes and smoked bacon, a stew would have been welcomed.

(A more celebrated boiler room was that aboard the sternwheeler *Alice May,* frozen in Lake Lebarge in 1900. It served as an improvised crematorium when the freeze-up made burial impossible, leading an inspired Whitehorse bank clerk, Robert Service, to pen his first celebrated epic poem, "The Cremation of Sam McGee.")

With all their hazards and discomforts, the riverboats were, as were those on the Sacramento, Columbia and Fraser, bigger bonanzas than those discovered ashore. Typical was the sternwheeler *Leah* which, on her maiden upriver run to Dawson City, amortized her entire cost — and that of an accompanying barge — and ended up with a $41,000 net profit.

The profits stirred shipway innovations. Adapting techniques perfected by the English in providing riverboats to serve their colonial outposts, sternwheelers were built in U.S. and Canadian yards, then shipped to places like Vancouver, Unalaska and St. Michael for assembly.

But it took a young self-trained Seattle machinist, Robert Moran, to perfect the assembly-line technique that permitted building a dozen 176-foot Yukon River sternwheelers at once, reviving an old Mississippi saw, "built by the mile and cut apart in proper lengths."

(Moran two years previously had been a steamer deck hand, then fired on Stikeen and Fraser riverboats before opening his machine shop in Seattle. It was the start of a shipbuilding career climaxed in 1904 by the launching of the battleship *Nebraska.*)

He assembled a work force of 2,100 men, an impressive number for that day, and in slightly over five months, completed his pre-fab riverboats.

The Yukon River armada sailed in 1898 from Roche Harbor on San Juan Island. All but one of the dozen sternwheelers survived the hazardous voyage to St. Michael, the *Western Star* being wrecked in Shelikoff Straits with no loss of life. The 400-ton riverboats proved to be gold mines, each filling their capacity of 24 passengers in staterooms, with more than 200 sleeping and eating on deck. The first trip into Dawson paid off the costs of the entire fleet.

Moran and his brothers defended their high fares and freight rates, stressing that the 11 vessels loaded with foodstuffs and other sorely needed supplies, including cases of whiskey, "eliminated much suffering in the country."

A U.S. Department of Labor bulletin issued in 1898 estimated that 40,000 reached Dawson during the year that began on July 25, 1897. Few struck it rich. Another 20,000 didn't make it. Thousands died or were crippled by scurvy, frostbite and snow blindness.

On the steamers heading north in 1897, a heartening clipping passed hand to hand. From the July 21, 1897, issue of the *San Francisco Chronicle* it read in part:

> *Two million dollars taken from the Klondike region in less than five months, and a hundred times that amount awaiting those who can handle a pick and shovel tells the story of the most marvellous placer digging the world has ever seen.*

SS *Ohio* leaving for Gold Rush

Unlike many of her compatriots, the *S.S. Ohio* of the White Star Line, was well equipped for her runs to Alaska during the Nome Gold Rush. When launched in 1873 she was the largest liner built in the U.S. (360 feet) and was capable of 13 knots. She is pictured departing for Nome in the early 1900's.

Paul Dorpat

Grand Truck Dock Fire

The Grand Trunk Dock wasn't Seattle's busiest. Neighboring Colman Dock, terminus for most of Puget Sound's Mosquito Fleet, earned that honor. But the Canadian pier had more style; its commodious panelled waiting rooms not only serving those waiting for Sound and Victoria-Vancouver steamers but periodically packed with travellers boarding liners for San Francisco ($15 first class) or tourists heading for Alaska ($60 for an eight-day tour). On July 30, 1914, a spark from a burning cigar or cigarette met a pile of sawdust and, in less than two hours, the 600-foot pier and its 130-foot tower were destroyed by a fire that took four lives.

The blaze caused $10,000 damage to Colman Dock, not including the loss of numerous souvenir items looted from the Ye Olde Curiosity Shoppe. No vessels were damaged, although the Sound steamer *Athlon* and the Coast liner, *Admiral Farragut,* were at dockside. They left hastily as the fire spread rapidly, fed by creosote soaking the four-year-old wooden dock and fanned further by the explosion of a fire truck trapped on the dock.

The engineer aboard the *Athlon* first noticed the fire shortly after 3 p.m. on the hot summer afternoon. Engine Co. No.5 quickly responded, driving onto the dock. They were quickly engulfed in flames.

Post-Intelligencer reporter Frank (Slim) Lynch reported:

> *They said they were just standing there — and the very air about them seemed to turn to flame.*

Four firemen lost their lives in the fire.

Pictured in action is the fireboat *Snoqualmie* which teamed up with the *Duwamish* (not shown). The Revenue Cutter *Unalga* also participated and was credited with saving Colman Dock tower.

Joe Williamson Coll.

The Warm Air Flight of the Flying Bird

It's doubtful if any Puget Sound passenger craft of the future will receive the attention and affection accorded the *Kalakala.*

On her trial run in 1935 the Black Ball Line ferry was powered by a 3000 hp diesel, but she was propelled into world prominence by the inspired hype of the line's talented publicist, William Thorniley. Under his ministrations the *Kalakala,* built atop the scorched hull of a hard-luck San Francisco Bay ferry, emerged as the "World's First Streamlined Ferry." Photos showing the vessel's teardrop configuration were widely distributed, framed by the Seattle skyline. The world's press, already enamoured with the spread of Art Deco and other examples of modernism in design, gave them wide and enthusiastic use. The *Kalakala* became the region's most popular postcard and soon was adopted as Seattle's symbol. It was more than 30 years before the magic finally ebbed, and the Flying Bird was towed off to Alaska, there to squat in the mud as a fish processing plant.

The *Kalakala* was a triumph of showmanship over steamship. Although she proved seaworthy on her usual Seattle-Bremerton run, some questioned PSN's decision to run her from Port Angeles to Victoria across the Strait of Juan de Fuca, carrying but two small workboats and no lifeboats.

While the idea for her 276-foot long tear-shaped superstructure has been attributed by some to Boeing, it actually was a brainstorm of one of America's top avant-garde industrial designers, Norman Bel Geddes.

George Nickum, co-founder of Nickum & Spaulding, who have designed more ferries than any other North American firm of naval architects, as well as a myriad of other craft (46 different types during World War II) recalled the fact recently:

> *The conceptual design for the* Kalakala *was the work of Norman Bel Geddes. Bull Schmidt (brother of a U.W. prexy) did the working drawing but actually Cap Peabody designed the thing as it went up. He would walk around selecting the placing of stanchions and making changes that were more cosmetic than practical; done for their architectural effect rather than structural. The framing, for instance, was horrible. That's why the damn thing vibrated so badly. Around three years later, Cap asked us to do a structural analysis but he resisted making most of the changes we suggested.*

Asked about the curved combing on the upper deck that prevented the skipper from seeing the dock except by looking through a porthole (pictured) while landing, he said, "That was a Bel Geddes design and Cap wouldn't change it."

The configuration of the *Kalakala* is similar to that of an ocean liner designed by Bel Geddes in 1932 — but never built. it would have been a monster, but a smooth one, 1808 feet long, weighing in at 70,000 tons and capable of carrying 2000 passengers and a crew of 900. Wrote its designer:

> *The entire superstructure is streamlined. Every air pocket of any kind whatsoever has been eliminated. All projections have either been eliminated or enclosed within the streamlined shell. The single protrusion is the navigator's bridge and this is cantilevered and similar in shape to a monoplane wing, consequently offering a minimum of resistance to the air. The smokestacks are a radical departure in appearance. They are oval on the inside, but on the outside, due to the streamlining, they dissolve into the mass form of the ship almost to the point of disappearing.*

Bel Geddes, famed for his stage sets, went on to design everything from World Fair buildings to toasters, radios and gas ranges. But he never built another dream boat like the *Kalakala.*

(left)

The *Kalakala* was powered by a 3000-horsepower Bush-Sulzer diesel which gave her a top speed of 18 knots, although she normally cruised at around 15.

George Bayless

(right)

This stylized poster drawing of the *Kalakala* was in keeping with the campaign to make her part of the Streamlined Age.

George Bayless

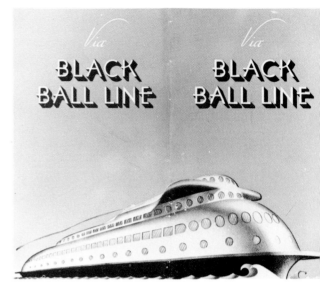

(left)

The *Kalakala's* upper deck portholes were dandy for sightseers, but posed a problem to navigators during docking.

Don Normark

(right)

The *Kalakala* was built on the burned out hull of the crack San Francisco Bay ferry, *Peralta,* launched in 1927 with a capacity of 2000 passengers. Five died in a freak accident in 1928, when swept from the *Peralta's* lower deck while underway. She was destroyed by fire in 1933 and towed to Seattle to be converted into her star role.

Bancroft Library, University of California

(right)

The *Kalakala's* coffee shop. Her bill of fare was popular on the 55 minute Seattle-Bremerton run, with such favorites as ham and eggs (and coffee) for 55 cents, hamburgers for 15 cents and sirloin steak, potatoes, toast and coffee for 75 cents.

Black Ball Collection and Washington State Ferries

(left)

When built, the 256-foot *Kalakala* could carry 1500 passengers and 115 cars (reduced to 65 as autos fattened).

Joe Williamson Collection

(right)

What is it? seems to be the question these sailors are puzzling over as the *Kalakala* passes.

Don Normark

Who Coined the Term "Mosquito Fleet?"

For more than a half century the term "Mosquito Fleet" has been applied to the hundreds of steamers that plied Puget Sound starting at the turn of the century.

Where did that description originate?

The accepted version is that an early-day newspaper writer, in describing Seattle's harbor wrote:

> *At five o'clock in Seattle, the little commuter steamers scurry off to their destinations like a swarm of mosquitos.*

I have used the phrase many times in writing of Seattle and its steamers, and never did it ring true. The evocation of a swarm of mosquitos simply would not fit the scene of a dozen steamers backing out of Colman Dock and the adjoining Pier 2. More puzzling was the fact that no writer or historian has been able to locate the Seattle newspaper in which that term allegedly was first used.

Where then did the term originate?

I am convinced it was first applied to the waterfront scene by Midwesterners or Southerners familiar with Mississippi River steamboat traffic. I erect this theory on thin piling. My conviction stems from a single source: the book *Steamboats on the Western Rivers,* published in 1949. Considered by many to be the definitive volume on early steamboats, the book was published by Harvard University in cooperation with the Committee on Research in Economic History of the Social Science Research Council, the American Historical Association and the American Council of Learned Societies.

In it, authors Louis and Beatrice Jones Hunter describe a shallow-draft Mississippi River steamboat, built in the late eighteen fifties to carry freight and passengers, drawing but 16 inches. They write:

> *This success in building steamboats of very light draft extended to the navigable seasons on the trunk lines of the river system until there were not many days during the average year in which the small sternwheelers, described somewhat contemptuously as "the mosquito fleet," were unable to operate, although little cargo could be taken and at times they carried passengers only.*

While my efforts to further substantiate this theory have been unproductive, I firmly believe that at some point back at the turn of the century someone familiar with these Mississippi River craft looked out at Seattle's rush-hour steamer traffic and mused to his companions:

> *Why, back home we had boats about that size. We called it our mosquito fleet.*

And the term caught on.

Painting by Michael Spakowsky

252

Flotsam

Ship Gender
Feminine — Italy, United States
Masculine — France
Neuter — Germany
Feminine-Masculine — Spain
Feminine-Neuter — England

The earliest known ship name, according to Don H. Kennedy's *Ship Names* (published for Mariners Museum by University Press of Virginia) was *Pride of Two Lands*. It was given to a 167-foot cedarwood Egyptian vessel in the time of Sneferu, about 2,680 BC.

Black Ball Line

Toast and Coffee	20c
Hot Cakes and Coffee	25c
Side Order Ham or Bacon	25c
Eggs, Toast and Coffee	40c
Ham and Eggs, and Coffee	55c
Bacon and Eggs, and Coffee	55c
Omelet, Plain	40c
Cereals with Cream	20c
Toast, Marmalade and Coffee	25c
Sliced Orange	25c
Grape Fruit (Chilled)	20c
Doughnuts and Coffee	20c
Butterhorn and Coffee	20c
Pie and Coffee	15c
Coffee or Tea	5c
Chocolate	15c
Milk	10c
Soup	15c

STEAKS

T-Bone Steak with Potatoes and Toast	85c
Sirloin Steak with Potatoes and Toast	75c
Club Steak with Potatoes and Toast	60c
Pounded Steak with Potatoes and Toast	50c
Hamburger Steak with Potatoes and Toast	40c

SALADS

Lettuce, with Choice of Dressing	25c
Sliced Tomatoes	20c
Lettuce and Tomato Salad	30c
Combination Salad	35c

Black Ball Line

SANDWICHES

Ham	15c	Peanut Butter	15c
Fried Ham	20c	Ham and Egg	30c
Hamburger	15c	Lettuce and Tomato	20c
Tuna Fish	20c	Chicken	45c
Cheese	15c	Sardine	20c
Toasted Cheese	25c	Hot Beef with Potatoes	40c
Club House	60c	Baked Ham	20c
Cold Beef or Pork	20c	Fried Egg	15c
Egg Salad	15c	Minced Ham	15c

ICE COLD BEER, BOTTLE, 20c

FOUNTAIN SPECIALS

Ice Cream	10c
Fruit Sundae	20c
Fruit Nut Sundae	25c
Ice Cream Soda	20c
Milk Shake, any Flavor	20c
Malted Milk	25c
Malted Milk with Egg	30c
Soda Pop	10c
Near Beer	20c
Ginger Ale	35c
Bromo Seltzer	10c
Green River	10c
Coca Cola	10c
Root Beer	10c
Orange Crush	10c
Soda Water, Assorted Flavors	10c
Tomato Juice	15c
Fresh Lemonade	20c
Ice Cold Bottle Beer	20c

CIGARS — CIGARETTES — CHEWING GUM
CANDY — PLAYING CARDS

A hamburger for 15 cents, sirloin steak .75, ham and eggs .55 — and coffee a nickel. Just a few menu items from the ferry Kalakala *in the 30's.* Washington State Ferries

---

Crews on a typical Mosquito Fleet steamer usually numbered six or seven: captain, mate, the chief engineer and his assistant, deckhands, engine room helpers and a crew cook. The skippers and chief engineers were paid up to $100 a month. At the bottom of the scale, deckhands and oilers received around $40. Hours were long, time off with pay, unknown. It was not until the settlement of the 1934 coastwide waterfront strike that captains and engineers were given one day off a week.

Port Angeles never drew the number of elegant steamers that began serving the Victoria run following the turn of the century, but it was home for one memorable sternwheeler, the *Dispatch*. Recalls an early day passenger:

> *Eventually we stopped at Old Dungeness. Captain Morgan left the boat to go up and have a sociable drink and a game of poker. The game lasted all night and meantime the tide went out leaving the ferry [sic] slowly tilting over on one side. Mother stowed us all away in bunks for the night. However, the tide returned in the morning and righted the boat and so did Captain Morgan. He tooted the whistle and we pulled out for Port Angeles.*

The era of steamboats on the West Coast began in March of 1836 when the Hudson Bay Company's *Beaver* arrived, and ended in 1957 when the *Moyie* was retired from service. In the interim, over three hundred boats had travelled the 572,000 square miles of British Columbia and Yukon Territory.

Dr Peter Charlebois, *Sternwheelers and Sidewheelers*

Steamers, like the City of Seattle, *were the Seattle-Everett Freeway of the 20's. Fare to Edmonds was .50, to Everett, .75.* University of Washington Library

Maps
and Index

Puget Sound

Puget Sound is one of this region's most commonly used geographical place names. Yet, its principal boundary can be found on few, if any, maps and few of us are precise on the Sound's limits.

Most of us know the tale of how Captain George Vancouver bestowed the name of honor of Lieutenant Peter Puget, applying it to the waters south of the Tacoma Narrows. In his log he wrote:

> *Thus by our joint efforts we have completely explored every turning point of the extensive inlet (Admiralty Inlet) and to commemorate Mr. Puget's exertions, the south extremity of it I have named Puget Sound.*

Since that day Puget Sound has inexorably crept north, halting only after engulfing the San Juan Islands. The Sound's first expansionary push was guided in the 1860s, as were many land grabs of that period, by the Northern Pacific Railroad. The Northern Pacific, having obtained a charter to build a railroad west, from the Midwest to Puget Sound, discovered to its chagrin that Captain Vancouver's original description eliminated consideration of Seattle, Everett, Bellingham and Port Townsend as termini. Lots were at stake, the NP land speculators warned Congress. Their lobbying tactics were rewarded in March 1869. Congress passed a resolution stating in part that "the term Puget Sound as used here and in the act incorporating said Company, is hereby construed to mean all waters connected with the Strait of Juan de Fuca and within the territory of the United States."

The State Supreme Court in 1896 upheld the designation. There were a few sporadic attempts to broaden the Sound's bounds. In 1913, a Clallam County Superior Court judge held, in a case involving State fishing laws, that the Strait of Juan de Fuca is part of Puget Sound. Even today, the U. S. Coast Guard includes the Strait in defining its Puget Sound Vessel Traffic System.

Most authorities, however, rule out de Fuca's estuary. The authoritative Washington Writers Project (WPA) *Guide to Washington* embraces the San Juan Islands, but leaves the Sound's eastern boundary undefined. States the WPA guide:

> *Puget Sound, for which the Puget Basin is the trough, is 80 miles long, 8 miles at the broadest point, and has depths of 900 feet: a body of water flanked by forested bluffs and low dikelands, with extensive bays, inlets and passages between the 300 islands that lie within its shores. Of these, the 172 inhabitable islands of the San Juan group and Whidbey Island, second largest in continental United States, are most noteworthy.*

The University of Washington Department of Oceanography is more precise. The Sound's northern limits it holds are:

> *South of an imaginary line between Port Townsend and Fort Ebey, west of Whidbey Island and those waters south of Deception Pass and east of Whidbey Island.*

The Sound, the University's summary states: has a length of 125 miles with an average width of 5.25 miles; an area of 1018 square miles, and a shoreline of 1157 nautical miles. Its average depth is 205 feet; its deepest point, 938 feet, mid-channel east of Point Jefferson just south of Kingston.

Puget Sound has a mean average temperature of 50 degrees. Its highest wind velocities, other than those generated by sailing windbags describing the Big Blow, was 61 mph, recorded at Tacoma in December 1940. Chances for summer sunshine are 60—64 percent. Chances of winter sunshine: less than 20 percent.

If you think Eagle Harbor, Fox Island, Partridge Point, Agate Pass and Port Orchard were named by nature-loving voyagers, you're wrong. Eagle Harbor was named by the Wilkes Expedition of 1841 for Henry Eagle, a Navy lieutenant. Agate Pass was named by Wilkes for the expedition's artist, Alfred Agate. He named Fox Island after his surgeon. Port Orchard, a

name given by Captain George Vancouver to an inlet near Bremerton (and later applied to the Kitsap County seat) honored H. M. Orchard, the clerk of Vancouver's ship *Discovery.* Captain Vancouver named Partridge Point after a family friend. On the other hand, Captain Vancouver named the Gulf of Georgia to honor King George III, thus easing the workload of cartographers and navigators but stealing away the poetic designation given the waterway by the Spanish explorer, Eliza: Gran Canal de Nuestra Senora del Rosario La Marina.

PUGET SOUND

> Length—125 statute miles
> Average Width—5.25 miles
> Area—1,018 square miles
> Shoreline—1,157 nautical miles
> Average Depth—205 feet
> Deepest Point—938 feet, mid-channel east of Point Jefferson, just south of Kingston
> Northern Limits—South of an imaginary line between Port Townsend and Fort Eby, west of Whidbey Island and those waters south of Deception Pass and east of Whidbey Island

University of Washington, Department of Oceanography

PUGET SOUND CLIMATE

Mean Average Temperature—50 degrees
Highest Wind Velocities—61 m.p.h., Tacoma, December, 1940*
Chance of Summer Sunshine—64 percent
Chance of Winter Sunshine—Approximately 20 percent

*The Coast Guard reported winds reaching 88 mph off the West Point light station in 1962, considerably higher than the 61 mph reached during the big blow of 1940. Gusts as high as 100 mph have been reported at Hood Canal, and 160 mph at the Naselle radar station in Pacific County (not on Puget Sound).

Maps by Helen Sherman

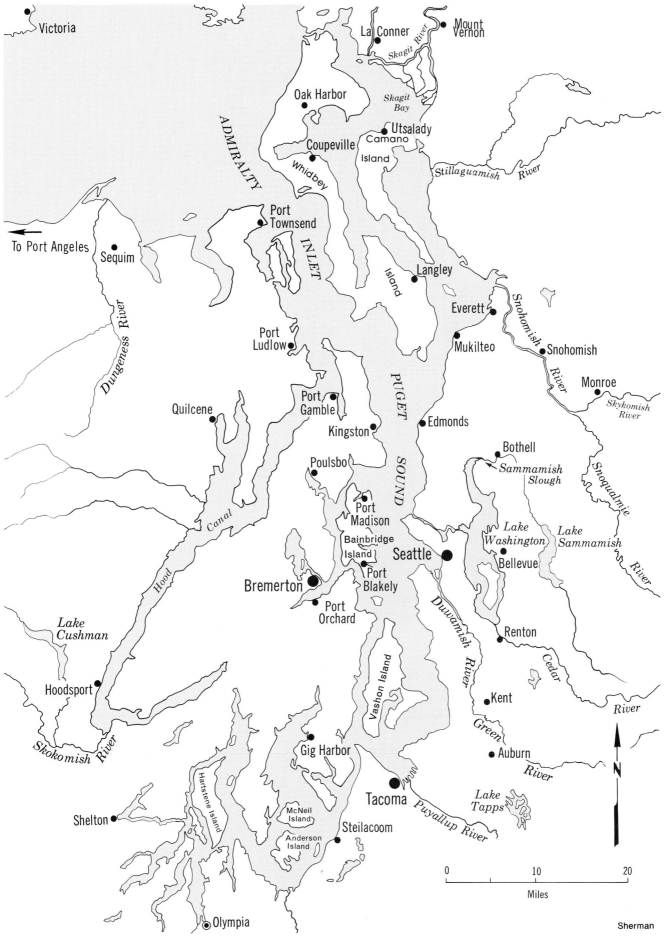

Victoria

La Conner

Mount Vernon

Skagit River

Oak Harbor

Skagit Bay

Utsalady

Camano
Island

Coupeville

Stillaguamish River

ADMIRALTY

Whidbey

Port
Townsend

INLET

To Port Angeles

Sequim

Island

Langley

Everett

Snohomish River

Snohomish

Dungeness River

Port
Ludlow

Mukilteo

Monroe

Skykomish River

PUGET

Quilcene

Port
Gamble

Edmonds

Bothell

Kingston

Sammamish Slough

SOUND

Poulsbo

Snoqualmie

Hood Canal

Port
Madison

Lake Washington

Lake Sammamish

Bainbridge
Island

Seattle

Bellevue

River

Bremerton

Port
Blakely

Lake Cushman

Port
Orchard

Duwamish River

Renton

Cedar River

Hoodsport

Vashon Island

Kent

Skokomish River

Green River

Gig Harbor

Auburn

River

Hartstene Island

Tacoma

Lake Tapps

Shelton

McNeil
Island

Steilacoom

Puyallup River

Anderson
Island

N

0   10   20

Miles

Olympia

Sherman

257

Rivers of Timber and Gold

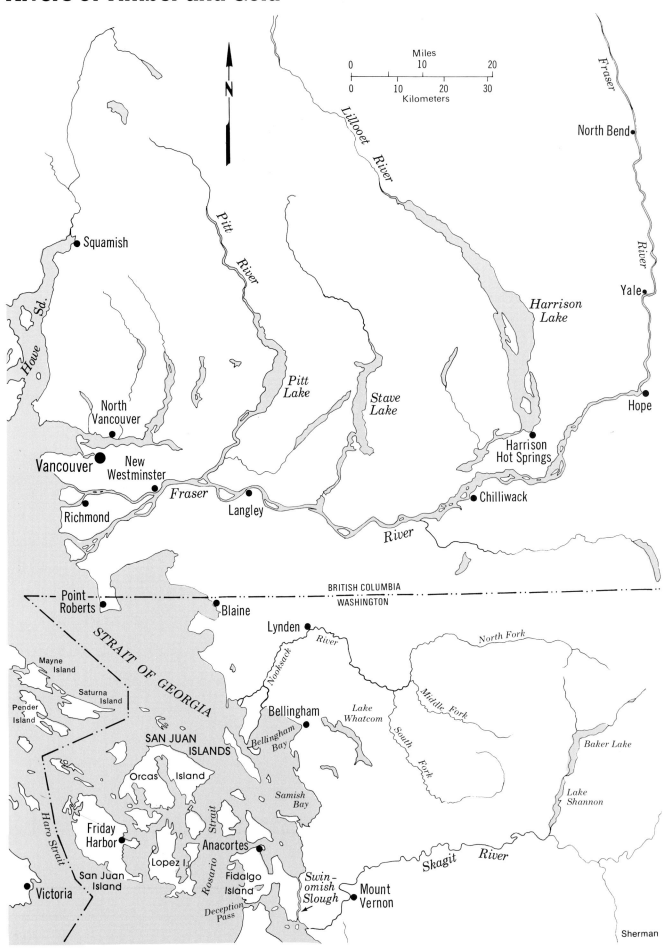

Miles
0   10   20

0   10   20   30
Kilometers

Fraser

North Bend

Lillooet River

Squamish

Pitt River

River

Yale

Harrison
Lake

Howe Sd.

Pitt
Lake

Stave
Lake

Hope

North
Vancouver

Vancouver

New
Westminster

Harrison
Hot Springs

Richmond

Fraser

Langley

Chilliwack

River

BRITISH COLUMBIA

WASHINGTON

Point
Roberts

Blaine

Lynden

River

North Fork

STRAIT OF GEORGIA

Mayne
Island

Nooksack

Saturna
Island

Middle Fork

Pender
Island

Bellingham

Lake
Whatcom

Baker Lake

SAN JUAN

ISLANDS

Bellingham
Bay

South

Orcas   Island

Fork

Lake
Shannon

Samish
Bay

Haro Strait

Friday
Harbor

Rosario Strait

Anacortes

Lopez I.

Fidalgo
Island

Swin-
omish
Slough

Skagit   River

San Juan
Island

Victoria

Deception
Pass

Mount
Vernon

Sherman

The Greater Columbia Country

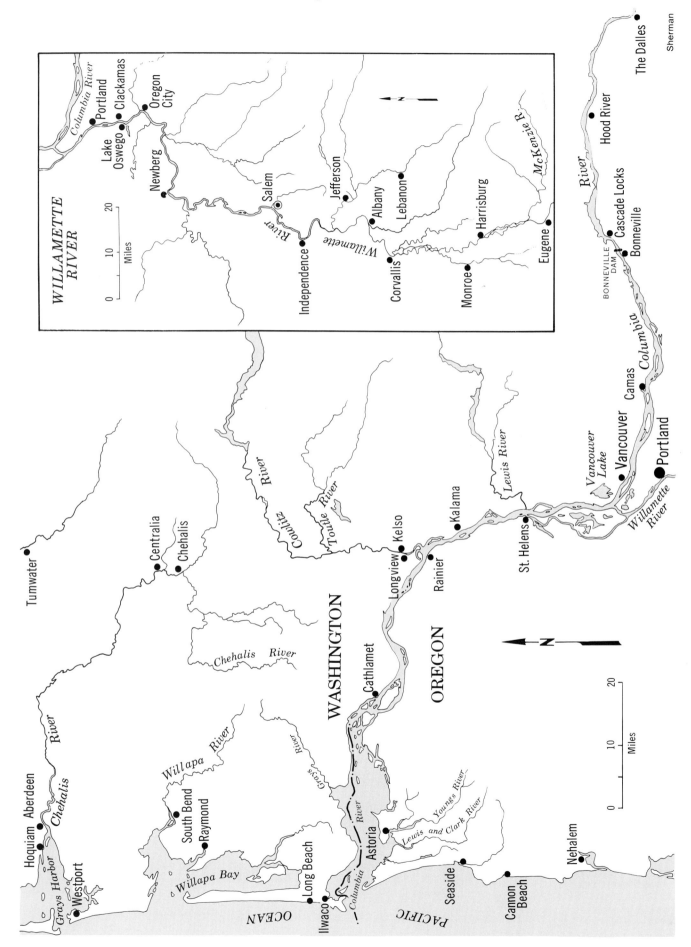

Index

Page numbers in italics indicate photographs or illustrations.

Aberdeen, 71, 83
accidents: *see* names of individual vessels
Acheson, Lois, president, Black Ball Transport, 90
Admiral Farragut; 249
Adventure, 6
Agate, Alfred; of Wilkes Expedition, 256
Agate Pass, named for A. Agate, 256; *239*
Agnes; Della Walck captain of, 90
Ainsworth, Capt. John C., 28-31, 32, 39; founds Oregon Steam Navigation Company, 29
Alabama, 210; *see also City of Victoria*
Alameda; hits Colman Docks, 136
Alaska, 24, 70, 101, 183; gold rush in, 74
\laska Commercial Company, 74
Alaska Steamship Company, 111
Alaska Yukon Pacific Exposition, 1909, 84 134, 139, 179, 221, 224
Alaskan 100-101, 137; design of, 101; photograph, *100-101*
Alaskan Way; construction of, 183
Alexander, H. F., 210
Alice May; use of boiler room as crematorium, 246
Alida, 94; photograph, *94*
Alki, 130, 186
Alki Beach, 162; photograph, *164*
Alki Point, 119, 120, 122, 191; lighthouse at, 19; Reliance; *runs aground off, 136*
Alliance; *as excursion vessel, 83*
Almota, 55; *54-55*
Alta Californian (newspaper); on *Surprise's* trip to Ft. Hope, 26
American River; gold discovery, 24
Anacortes, 128, 129, 134, 144, 197; stop for *Rosalie,* 106, 135
Anderson, Captain John, 194, 210, 221
Anderson, Matthew, 238
Anderson Island, 106, 135; wood for steamers, 92
Anderson Steamboat Company, 222, 225, 226
Ann Faxton; photograph, 46
Aquilo, 221
Argus, 131
Argyle, 106, 136
Arizona, U.S.S., 177
Arlington Dock, Seattle; T. Roosevelt arrives at, 122; photograph, 125
Arrow, 62
Arrow Lake, B.C., 27, 52; *photograph, 92-93*
Astoria (formerly Ft. George), 7, 29, 51, 154, 185
Atalanta, 221
Athlon, 122, 137, 249; photographs, *178-79*
automobile ferries; gradually replace Mosquito Fleet, 137, 141, 144-45, 151, 183, 200, 228, 229; photograph, *186*

B.C. Express; photograph, *26*
Bacon, Captain, 64; photograph, *65*
Bahada, 122
Bailey Gatzert, 49, 120; first to carry autos to Olympic Peninsula, 151; photographs, *48-49, 121, 150, 151, 152-53*
Bainbridge Island, 106, 131, 134, 135, 158, 162; as resort, 76; Hall Bros. shipyards at, 77; G. Vancouver first to use lumber of, 79; remains rural, 237
Bainbridge Landings (Beach), 158
Ball Riffles; *Bob Irving* explodes at, 34
Barkley, Captain Charles, 6
battleships; photograph, *174; see also* under names of individual ships
Bay Center, 83
Beach, Allen, 158
Beatrice; design of, 138

Beaver, H.M.S., 18, 36-37, 137, 164, 254; first steamer built for northwest, 8; mutiny aboard, 36; design of, 36; wreck of, 37; and fuel, 129 photographs, *36, 37*
Bel Geddes, Norman; designs *Kalakala,* 250
Belle, 55
Bellingham; 91, 96, 106, 126, 128, 129, 134, 135, 144
Bellingham, 136
Benecia, 79; photograph, *80*
Bergman, Nellie; christens *Garden City,* 88
Bering Sea, 246
Berton, Pierre; on Klondike gold rush, 25, 123
Binns, Archie, 117, 134
Birkland, Captain Torger, 131
Bishop, C.F., 200
Black Ball Line (PSN), 76, 131, 134, 214
Black Ball Transport; serves Victoria, 144
Black Prince; photograph, *157*
Blaine; cannery at, 128
Blakely, Johnson, 76
Blakely, 119
Blakely Island, 108
Blethen, Colonel Alden; on federal steamboat inspectors, 246
Blue Dick Berry; pilot on Fraser River, 27
Bob Irving; explodes at Ball Riffles, 34
Boeing Airplane Company; builds ferry at Vancouver, B.C., 232
Bon Marche; photograph, *192—93*
Bothell, 106, 135, 217, 221
Bremerton, 113, 131, 134, 176; T. Roosevelt visits navy yard at, 121, 122; tourists visit *U.S.S. Missouri,* 175
Bremerton (formerly *Kitsap*), destroyed by fire, 144
bridges; Puget Sound, 236-37
Brinnon, 106, 134
British Columbia, 24, 37, 62, 64, 111; *Beaver* arrives at, 36; and gold discoveries in, 44
British Columbia Legislative Building, 140
Brown, William, 31
Burrard Beaver, 241; photograph, *241*
Burton, 135
Businessman's Express; photograph, *20*

California, 24, 37; and gold discoveries, 40
California, U.S.S.; photograph, *177*
California Star (newspaper), 24
California Steam Navigation Company, 32; formation of, 41
Camano, 162; photograph, *162*
Canadian National Railroad; ships serve Victoria, 144
Canadian Pacific Navigation Company; founded by Irving, 99
Canadian Pacific Railroad, 27, 62, 137, 138, 143-44, 206, 207, 208, 210, 214, 215; liners of, 17; dominates Triangle Route, 139, 140, 143, 200, 209; institutes auto ferry service, 141; last run on Triangle Route, 141; ships serve Victoria, 144
Cannon, William; 7
"Canoe Express," 168
Cape Blanco, 101; *Alaskan* sinks off, 137
Capital City; struck by *Trader,* 161; *136, 161*
Carmack, George Washington; discovers Klondike Bonanza, 25
Cascade Locks, 150; photographs, *59, 60, 61, 152-53*
Cascade Mountains, 31, 47, 61, 67, 70; rapids in, 29; gold discoveries, 32
catamarans, 241; considered for use on Puget Sound, 242
C. C. Calkins, 221
C. C. Calkins Hotel; resort on Mercer Island, 222
Celilo, 39, 55; *Harvest Queen* goes over falls at, 50
Celilo, 119
Charles R. Spencer; races *Telephone,* 51; photograph, *150*
Chehalis River, 71
Chester, 73; design of, 73; photograph, *72-73*
Chili, S.S.; Flyer rams, 136

China; market for furs, 6; served by Empress Line, 138
Chinook, 212-13; design of, 212-13; photographs, *212-13, 214-15*
Chippewa; refit as auto ferry, 19, 200; greets Atlantic Fleet, 123; competes on Triangle Route, 139, 200-201; photographs, *182, 201, 203*
Christenson, Nels; and *Virginia V.,* 238, 239
City of Angeles, 141; photograph, *196*
City of Bothell, 218
City of Bremerton, 183; photograph, *20-21*
City of Denver, 88
City of Everett, 135; photograph, *252-53*
City of Kingston, 111, 120, 137; *140*
City of Long Beach, 196
City of Nanaimo; photograph, *143-44*
City of Puebla; photograph, *111*
City of Quincy; photograph, *95*
City of San Francisco; photograph, *240*
City of Seattle, 123, 137, 144, 158, 159; transports President B. Harrison, 120; visits Victoria, 143; design of, 158; becomes *YFB54,* 159; becomes *Magdalena,* 159; on Alaska gold route, 246; photographs, *111, 121, 158, 254;* drawing of deck plan, endpiece
City of Shelton, 91
City of Victoria, 210; facilities aboard, 210; photographs, *210-11, 234*
Clallam; sinking of, 136, 138, 190; photograph, *190*
Clan McDonald; first to have lighted cabins in Puget Sound, 88
Clara Nevada; fire aboard and grounding in Alaska, 246
Clark, Norman, 116
Clearwater River; gold discoveries on, 29
Clemens, Samuel (Mark Twain, pseud.), 31, 39; apprenticed under Capt. J. Ainsworth, 28
Cleremont, 37
Cleveland; drawing of, endpiece
Coffin, Captain Everett, 18, 18-19, 130, 236; and Klondike gold rush, 18; rams Colman Dock in *Flyer,* 186; photographs, *18, 19*
Coho, 144; photograph, *144*
Colfax; photograph, *64*
Collier, Harry; photograph, *131*
Colman, James; builds terminal, 131
Colman Dock, 130, 131-34, 183, 186, 236, 252-53; clock tower at, 131, 134, 136; design of, 134; accidents at, 136; busiest dock in Seattle, 249; photographs, *11, 87, 112-13, 134, 145, 179, 182*
Colonel Wright, 30
Columbia, 38
Columbia River, 7, 27, 28, 30, 31, 32, 36, 38, 41, 50, 51, 52, 57, 64, 66, 67, 83, 90, 95, 101, 117, 154, 157, 185, 239, 246; divided into Upper, Middle and Lower, 29; gold discoveries on, 39, 62, 99; racing on, 49; and obstacles to steamers, 58; freezes, 59; *George E. Starr,* 96; 116; Regulator Line offers excursions on, 150; photographs, *28, 30*
Columbia River Maritime Museum, 10
Commander, 149
Constitution, 9
Cosmopolitan Hotel, 61
Coupeville, 106, 109, 135, 162; photograph, *22*
Cowlitz River, 7, 38, 73
Cowlitz River Canoe and Bateaux Line, 38
Cunningham Wharf; photograph, *147*
Curtis, Asahel; photographs by, *79, 87, 164, 172-73, 188, 192-93, 201, 233*
Cutch, 246
Cyrene, 222; refit for Alaska Yukon Pacific Exposition, 224; photographs, *224, 226-27*

Daisy, 95
Dakota, S.S., 126
The Dalles, 29, 50, 57, 61; OSN steamers run to, 31, 32, 43; troops from quell Indian uprising, 55
Dalles City; photographs, *150, 151*
The Dalles Inland Empire (Merry), 30
Dalton (formerly *Capital City*), 161
Dart; destroyed by fire, 144
David, A. B.; owns *Fairy,* 9

Dawn, 221, 222
Dawson, Yukon Territory, 105, 161, 246, 247
De Huff, Peter; engineer aboard *Harvest Queen,* 50
De Launcy, Scott; Chief Engineer aboard *Clallam,* 190
Deception Pass; photograph, *228*
Deer Harbor, 106, 135
Delta King, 146
Delta Queen, 146
Demoro, Harre, 10
Denali, 111
Dennison, Charles; first mate of *Dix,* 191
Denny, David, 9
Denny Hotel, Seattle; photograph, *111*
Dewatto, 106, 134
Dimsdale; photograph, *236*
Discovery, H.M.S., 6, 79, 256
Dispatch, 254
Dix, 191; sinking of, 136, 191; photograph, *191*
Dode, 106, 134; Dora Troutman captain of, 90; design of, 106; rams *Flyer,* 136; photograph, *106-107*
Doig, Ivan, 10
Dolphin, as excursion vessel, 83
Dorpat, Paul, 10
Douglas Fir; 79; 158; 185
Dove; photograph, *118*
Driard Hotel, Victoria, 138
Duchess, 64; photograph, *65*
Dufferin, Lady, 62
Dunn, John, 8
Duwamish; fireboat, fights Grand Trunk Dock fire, 249
Duwamish Indians, 9
Dyea, 105, 245

Eagle, Lt. Henry; of Wilkes Expedition, 256
Eagle Harbor, 76, 77, 256
East Sound, 106, 135
East Sound House; photograph, *197*
echo boards; and navigational aids, 135
Eckhart, Captain W. R., 154
Edith, 68; photograph, *68*
Edmonds, 134
Edmonds-Victoria Ferry Company, 210
Edwards, Captain Michael; saves *Capital City,* 161
El Primero, 134
Eleventh Street Bridge, Tacoma; photograph, *130*
Eliza Anderson, 87, 137, 143; establishes steamer traffic on Puget Sound, 9; rams *Glory of the Sea,* 31; design of, 98; on Klondike gold run, 246; photograph, *86-87*
Elliott Bay, 131, 136, 175, 186; T. Roosevelt arrives at, 122; photograph, *139*
Elsinore; rescues passengers from *Margurite,* 194
Empress Hotel, 138, 215; designed by F. M. Rattenbury, 140
Empress Line, Canadian Pacific Railroad's line for North Pacific service, 138
Enetai (newspaper), 10
Enterprise, 71; photograph, *28*
Epler, John (Long John), 52
Everett, 88, 106, 109, 134, 135; T. Roosevelt speaks at, 122
Everett Yacht Club, 157
Everett IWW Massacre; *Verona's* role in, 90
Evergreen Fleet (Demoro), 10
Exact, 18

Fairhaven, 162; photograph, *162*
Fairy, 9; first American-owned steamer in Puget Sound, 84
Fanny Lake, 16, 34, 119
Feather River; and gold discovery, 24
ferries, 236-37; possible construction of modern foot ferries, 237-38; photograph, *237*
Finch, Captain D. B., 144; enterprising captain of *Eliza Anderson,* 97
Finch, Captain Duncan; owner of *Olympia,* 103

F. G. Reeve; abandoned in San Juan Islands, 144
Fleet Week, 174, 175, 176, 177
Fleetwood, 18, 83, 185
Fleishacker, Herbert, 210
Fletcher Bay; resort, 76
Florence K.; photograph, *192-93*
Flyer, 18, 19, 64, 130, 135, 137, 157, 185; and fuel, 129-30; accidents of, 136, 186; burned for metals, 144; design and speed of, 185; photographs, *35, 131, 139, 184-85, 186-87, 188*
Folger, Captain Isaiah, 18
Fort George (now Astoria), 7
Fort Hope, 26
Fort Langley, 7
Fort Nisqually, 7, 36, 164
Fort Vancouver, 7, 8, 37, 38, 164
Fort Victoria, 137
Fortuna, 221, 222
Fortymile, Alaska, 246
Foss Launch and Tug Company, Tacoma, 84; runs excursions, 168
Fox Island, 256
Fraser River, 7, 26, 29, 39, 44, 45, 50, 91, 139, 246; gold discoveries on, 25, 25-27, 62, 71, 99, 143, 181; photographs, *26, 27*
Friday Harbor, 106, 109, 128; 135; photographs, *108-109, 137*
fur trade; and early commerce in the northwest, 6

Gailbraith Dock, 192; *see also* Pier 3
Gassy Jack; pilot on Fraser River, 27
Gates, John; adapts hydraulic power to steamers, 33
Gatzert, Bailey; backs Joshua Green, 31
Gazelle, 88
Gazzam, Warren, 35
Gem, 88
General Frisbie, 149; design of, 149; photograph, *149*
George E. Starr, 96, 246; design of, 96, 98; transports President R. Hayes, 119; photograph, *96-97*
George Emery, 84
Georgiana, 157; photograph, *156*
Gibbs, William F., 212
Gifford, Benjamin, 57
Gill, Mayor Hi, 163
Gilmore, Lawrence, 10
Gleaner, 71; photograph, *70-71*
Glory of the Seas; rammed by *Eliza Anderson,* 74
Glosten, Lawrence; on influence of New England designs on Mosquito Fleet, 219
gold discoveries and rushes, 32, 40, 99, 111, 121; in California begins opening of west, 24-25, 146, 181; on Fraser River, 25-27, 39, 71, 142, 181; Boise Basin, 29; on Salmon River, 29; on Clearwater River, 29; J. Ainsworth profits from Fraser River, 29-31; and Cascades, 32; in Montana, 47; stimulates growth of riverboat steamer lines, 62; Alaskan, 27, 74, 161, 246-47
Goliah, 119
Gove, Captain Warren; owns *Fairy,* 9
Governor Newell, 90; photograph, *90*
Grand Trunk Dock, 131, 134; destroyed by fire, 249; photograph, *143*
Grand Trunk Pacific Line; competes with Canadian Pacific Railroad for Triangle Route, 139, 144, 209
Grant, 122
Gray, Captain Al, 154
Gray, Robert, 6
Gray, Captain William, 32
Gray's Harbor; mills help expand steamer traffic, 75
Great Northern Railway, 126
Great White Fleet; visits Pacific Northwest, 83, 127, 134, 172, 174, 181; photograph, *126*
Green, Joshua, 16, 17, 34, 162; career of, 16-17; develops steamer traffic on Puget

Sound, 34-35; owns La Conner Trading and Transportation Company, 96; on sale of *Chinook,* 213
Gulf of Georgia, 37, 256
Gustafson, Captain Ed; of Willie, 91

Hagemann, E.; on design of future ferries, 242
Haglund, Ivar, 11
Hall, Henry; founds Hall Brothers ship yard, 77
Hall, Isaac; founds Hall Brothers ship yard, 77
Hall, Winslow; founds Hall Brothers ship yard, 77
Hall Brothers ship yard, 77, 128
Harbor Belle; as excursion vessel, 83
Harbor Queen; as excursion vessel, 83
Harrison, Benjamin; visits Seattle, 111, 119, 120, 121; photograph of arrival in Seattle, *121*
Hartstene Island, 106, 135
Harvest Queen, 61; photographs, *50, 61*
Hassalo; races *Telephone,* 51; photograph, *102*
Hassalo II; runs Celilo Falls Rapids, 50
Hayes, Rutherford; visits Pacific Northwest, 96, 119
Haytian Republic, 120-21
H. B. Kennedy, 17, 135; photographs, *139, 178-79*
Heckman, Hazel, 92
Henry Bailey, 16, 34
Hester, Wilhelm, 81
Hill, Charles, 90
Hill, James, 126
Hill, Captain Minnie; first woman west of Mississippi River to hold captain's papers, 90
H. K. Hall, 81; launching of, 77; design of, 78; photograph, *77, 81*
Hogan, Daniel; photograph, *238*
Holly, 106, 134
Holyoke, 122
Hood Canal, 256
Hoodsport, 106, 134
Hope, 62
Hoquiam, 71, 83
Horluck Navigation Company; headed by Mary Nearhoff Lieske, 90
Hotel Dalles, 138-39
Hudson's Bay Company, 7, 8, 36, 37, 45, 103, 144, 164, 254
Humboldt, 122
Hume, Thomas, mayor of Seattle, 125
Hunter, Beatrice Jones, 252
Hunter, Louis, 252
Hutchinson, Bruce; on Victoria, B.C., 138
Hyak, 131, 135; abandoned on Duwamish River, 144; and summer excursions, 165; photographs, *12-13, 165*

Idaho; gold and mineral discoveries in, 25, 39, 61
Idaho, 88, 246; design of, 64
Idaho, U.S.S.; photograph, *175*
Imperial eagle, 6
Independent Ferry Company, 210
Indianapolis, 15, 18, 19, 110, 129; design of, 110; competes on Triangle Route, 139, 200-201; converted to auto ferry, 200-201; photographs, *20-21, 110, 200, 201*
Indians, 6-7; wars, 55; and canoe rentals, 168
Inland Boatmen's Union; and design of new ferries, 238
Inland Flyer, 122
Inland Navigation Company, 16
Inner Harbor, Victoria; photographs, *143-44, 214*
Inside Passage; to southeast Alaska, 37, 138, 246
Interlaken Steamboat Company, 225
Iowa, U.S.S., 88, 175; overhauled at Puget Sound Navy Yard, 175
Iroquois, 129; competes on Triangle Route, 139; refits of, 202; photographs, *201, 202-203*
An Irreverent Guide to Washington State, (Faber), 10
Irving, Captain John, 44
Isabella; lost at Columbia River bar, 7
Island County, 108

Island Flyer; struck by *Sioux,* 162
Island in the Sound (Heckman), 92
Islander, 109, 144, 232; photographs, *109, 237*
Isthmus of Panama, 24, 121

Jackson, Captain D. B., 95
Japanese Society; greets T. Roosevelt in
    Seattle, 122
J. B. Libby, 119
Jeanie; rams *Dix,* 191
Jeff Davis, 26
Jessie, 83
J. N. Teal; photograph, *61*
Joe Williamson Collection, 10, 150
John A. Sutter; and gold discoveries, 24
Johnson, William, 11
Joseph Supple Shipyard, 157
Josephine, 68; photograph, *69*
Julia, 37

Kalakala, 250; maiden voyage of, 19; excursion
    vessel of PSN, 139; designed by Norman Bel
    Geddes, 250; photographs, *177, 250, 251, 254*
Kangaroo; see Traveller
Kaslo; photographs, *2, 62,* and *back cover*
Kaslo, B.C.; maintains *Moyie,* 27
Kellogg, Captain Edward, 73
Kellogg, Captain Joseph, 73
Kellogg, Captain Orin, 73
Kiana Lodge; photograph, *239*
King County; operates ferries, 222, 232
Kingston, 106, 134
Kirkland, 121
Kitsap County Transportation Company, 144, 149
Kiyus; and gold discoveries, 29, 39
Klondike, 161, 246-47; gold discoveries in, 25,
    27; *Eliza Anderson* participates in gold rush,
    87; gold discoveries help end panic of '93, 123
Klondike; photograph, *240*
Klondike (Berton), 25
Kokanee; photograph, *62-63*
Kootenay, 52, 62; design of, 52; photograph, *53*
Kootenay Lake, 27; photographs, *2, 62-63*
Kootenay Lake Historical Society, 27
Kootenay River; gold discoveries, 62
Kulshan, 218, 234; construction of, 20;
    photographs, *20-21, 139*

LaConner Trading and Transportation
    Company, 96, 162
Lake Coeur d'Alene, 64
Lake Crescent, 106, 135
Lake Sammamish, 221
Lake Union, 221
Lake Washington, 121, 135, 218, 221, 226, 234
Lake Washington Ship Canal, 222
Lake Washington Steamboat Company;
    owned by J. Anderson, 221
Lake Whatcom, 106, 135, 194
Langley, 92, 106, 135
Lark; photograph, *84-85*
Leah, 246
Leonesa, 79
Lermond, Captain Percy; of *Dix,* 191
Leschi, 106, 135, 221, 222; headquarters for
    Anderson Steamboat Company, 226
Leschi, 229, 232; operated by Port of Seattle,
    232; photographs, *230, 230-31, 232-33*
Lewis, R., 95
Lewis and Clark Exposition, Portland, 150
Lewiston, 29, 39
Lieske, Mary Nearhoff; heads Horluck Naviga-
    tion Company, 90
Lilliwaup Falls, 106, 134
Lily, 45; photograph, *45*
Lister, Ernest, 15
Lister, Mrs. Ernest, 15
Lister, Florence; christens *Tacoma,* 15-16
Lloyds of London; rates *Tacoma,* 17; on *Flyer,*
    130, 186
Lopez, 106, 135
Lopez Island, 108, 128; photograph, *238*

Lorne, 122
Lot Whitcomb, 29, 38-39; launching of, 28;
    design of, 38; photographs, *27, 39*
Low, John, 9
L. T. Haas; photograph, *225*
Luna Park, 162; photograph, *163*
Lurline, 52; engine room of, 52; photograph, *52*
Lydia Thompson, 106, 135, 197; photograph, *102*
Lynch, Frank (Slim); on Grand Trunk Fire, 249

Madrona; resort, 222
Magdalena, 159
Magic; collides with *Camano,* 162
Magnolia; photograph, *192-93*
Magnolia Bluff, 175
Majestic (formerly *Whatcom*), 183
Major Tompkins, 7; first steamer on Triangle
    Run, 143
Manila, Battle of 122, 174
Manning, 122
Marion Street, Seattle; photograph, *158*
Marguerite, 194; runs aground, 194; photo-
    graph, *194-95*
Markham, Elizabeth, 38
Mary Moody; of Oregon and Montana Trans-
    portation Company, 47; photograph, *47*
Mary Tyler; 84
Maryland, U.S.S.; photograph, *177*
Matson, Captain Robert, 10, 221, 222;
    photograph collection of, 75
Maud, 68; photograph, *69*
May Blossom, 218; photograph, *216-217*
McClure, Captain Charles; captain of *Chip-
    pewa,* 200
McCullough, 122
*McCurdy's Marine History of the Pacific North-
    west* (Newell), 10; on wreck of Yosemite, 181
McKinley, William; assassination of, 122, 125
McLoughlin, Dr. John, 37
McNeill, Henry, 7
Meares, John, 6
Meeker, Ezra, 26
Mercer, 232; photograph, *232-33*
Mercer Island, 221, 222
The Merchant's Line; competes with OSN, 29
Merideth, J. D., 88
Merry, Thomas, 30
Merwin, W. K., 95; photograph, *95*
Miike Maru; arrives at Seattle, 128
Mikado, 88
Mill Town (Clark), 116
mills and milltowns; impact on opening Puget
    Sound and expanding steamer traffic, 32-33,
    34, 75-76, 126; and dependency on steamers,
    33, 116-17
Minnesota, S.S., 126
Minnie M., 88; design of, 88
Minto; on Arrow Lakes until 1954, 27; photo-
    graph, *27*
Mississippi, U.S.S.; photograph, *175*
Missouri, U.S.S.; at Puget Sound Navy Yard, 175
Mizpah; photograph, *84-85*
Mohawk; photograph, *192-93*
Monroe, Robert, 10
Montana; gold and mineral discoveries, 25,
    39, 47
Monte Carlo, 88
Monterey, U.S.S., 128
Montesano, 71, 83
Monticello, 75, 76, 135; photograph, *139*
Monticello Steamship Company, 149
Moore, Captain William; owns *Western Slope,* 27
Moran, Robert, 16, 247; develops assembly
    Line technique for building Yukon stern-
    wheelers, 246
Moran shipyard, 20, 238; photographs,
    129, 234
Morgan, Murray, 10, 116, 130, 237
"Mosquito Fleet," 15, 106, 122, 130, 137, 222,
    236, 237, 238, 241, 249; peak of, 116; devel-
    opment of, 128-29; design of steamers, 129,
    218-19, 219; fuel of, 129-30; serves farm/
    market trade, 130; demise of stimulated by

auto ferries, 144-45; origin of term, 252; crew
    compensation, 254
Moss, Captain Donald; photograph, *239*
Moss, Ted; photograph, *239*
Motor Princess; Canadian Pacific Railroad's
    auto ferry, 141, 144; photograph, *144, 208*
Mount Vernon; auto ferry, 141
Mountain Gem; photograph, *32*
Moyie; in Kaslo Museum, 27; retirement marks
    end of steamboat era, 254
Multnomah; design of, 38; photographs, *34,
    38, 84-85*
Museum of History and Industry, Seattle, 10
Mystic Seaport, Conn., 218

Naksup; photograph, *92-93*
navigation aids, 135
Neah Bay, 106, 135
Nebraska, U.S.S., 122; built at Moran shipyard,
    16, 246; photograph, *127*
Nevada, U.S.S.; photograph, *177*
New England; effects of designs on design of
    Mosquito Fleet, 218-19
New Jersey, U.S.S., 127
New World, 31, 32, 146; photograph, *147*
New York, U.S.S.; photograph, *175*
New York Sun; on Victoria, 139
Newell, Gordon, 10; on safety of Mosquito
    Fleet, 136; on end of Mosquito Fleet, 144-45
Nez Perce Chief; and gold discoveries, 29, 39;
    runs Celilo Falls rapids, 50
Nicholson, Captain Norman; of *S.S.
    Spokane,* 122
Nickum, George; on design and construction
    of *Kalakala,* 250
Nickum and Spaulding Company, 144, 241
Nisqually; design of, 130; photograph, *130*
Nome, 246; gold discoveries, 24, 161
North Pacific, 102, 246; design of, 98; defeats
    Olympia in race, 144; photograph, *102, 140*
North Vancouver #4; design of, 232; photo-
    graph, *232*
Northern Pacific Railroad, 33, 100, 116, 256;
    buys out OSN, 30; effects truce on Triangle
    Route, 139
Northwest America; first ship built in northwest, 6
Norwood; photograph, *118*

O'Brien, John (Dynamite Johnny); rams
    Colman Dock, 136
Okanogan, 62; and gold discoveries, 29; first to
    run Celilo Rapids, 50
Okanogan Lake, 199
Okanogan River; and gold discoveries, 39, 62
Oklahoma, U.S.S., 177
Olga, 106, 135
Oliver Wolcott, 119
Olympia, 87, 91, 94, 106, 119, 161; as port, 84
Olympia, 129, 143; defeated by *North Pacific*
    and removed from Puget Sound, 103, 144
Olympian, 100-101, 137, 144; design of, 98,
    101; breaks up in Strait of Magellan, 137;
    photograph, *101*
Olympic Peninsula, 6, 7; remains rural, 237
Oneonta, 50; design of, 31; photograph, *30*
Open River Navigation Company, 32
Orbit, 84
Orcas Island, 105, 135; agriculture on, 108;
    as resort, 127
Ohio, S.S., 247; design of, 247; photograph, *247*
Oregon, 24
Oregon, U.S.S., 121, 175; refit at Puget Sound
    Navy Yard, 176; photographs, *175, 176-77*
Oregon and Montana Transportation
    Company, 47
Oregon Railroad and Navigation Company, 95,
    96, 137; competes with Regulator Line, 150
Oregon Steam Navigation Company, 29, 30,
    31, 33, 39, 43, 55, 83; and success during gold
    rushes, 29-30, 39; strike after acquisition by
    Northern Pacific Railway, 30; purchases
    New World, 32

Otter; photograph, *143-44*
Outer Wharfs, Victoria, 135
Owyhee; and gold discoveries, 29, 39

Pacific Beach; as resort, 83
Pacific Coast Steamship Company, 111
paddlewheels; photograph, *33*
Pak Shan; drawing of, endpiece
Parker, Rev. Samuel, 164
Paterson, J. V., 17
Pawtucket, U.S.S., 122
Payne, J. Howard, 210
Peabody, Mrs. Alexander; christens
    Chinook, 212
Peabody, Charles, 35, 137, on *Kalakala*
    design, 250
Peace River; and gold discoveries, 62
Pend Oreille Lake, 47; photograph, *47*
Peralta; Kalakala built on burned-out hull of, 251
Percival Dock, Olympia; photograph, *84-85*
Perdita, 106; route of, 135
Perry, 122
Pethick, Derek, 37
picnics, 164, 165; photographs, *165, 170*
Pier 1, Seattle; photograph, *182*
Pier 2, Seattle, 252; home of Alaska Steamship
    Company, 113
Pier 3 (Gailbraith Dock), Seattle, 130, 131, 134,
    192; photograph, *179*
Pier 4, Seattle; photograph, *192-93*
"Pig War of 1859," 36
Pike Street Farmers Market; served by
    Mosquito Fleet, 130
The Pike Street Market (Morgan), 130
Pilgrim; and U.S. Navy visits, 172
pilots; on Fraser River, 27
Pioneer, 122
Pioneer Square, Seattle, 222; photograph, *125*
Politofsky, 74, 78, 120; on Alaskan gold run,
    74; photograph, *74*
Port Angeles, 202, 214, 254
Port Angeles Transportation Company, 196
Port Blakely, 161; sawmills at help expand
    steamer traffic, 75-76, 116, 128; Hall Bros.
    shipyard at, 77
Port Blakely Mill Company, 74, 75; closes to
    greet President Hayes, 119; closes in memory
    of lives lost on *Dix,* 191; photograph, *117*
Port Discovery, 116
Port Gamble, 37, 95, 106, 134, 135; mills at, 116
Port Ludlow, 106, 116, 128, 135
Port Madison, 79, 106, 119, 135
Port of Seattle; assumes cross-bay ferry run,
    159; operates ferries in competition with
    Anderson Company, 222; operates *Leschi,* 222
Port Orchard, 88, 256
Port Townsend, 20, 87, 94, 96, 106, 110, 128,
    129, 131, 134, 135, 136, 137, 138, 143, 183,
    190, 202; photograph of Fire Department, *119*
Portland, Oregon, 31, 43, 47, 49, 66, 73, 83, 90,
    102, 111, 151, 185; photographs, *50, 67*
Portland, 179; and Alaskan gold discoveries,
    32, 121
Portland and Vancouver Railway Company, 66
Potlach; summer festival in Seattle, 175
Potlach, 218
Poulsbo, 128, 131, 193; photograph, *118*
Prahl, Charles, 236-37
Prince David, 209; on Triangle Route, 139;
    design of, 140
Prince George; on Triangle Route, 139; design
    of, 209; photograph, *143-44*
Prince Henry; on Triangle Route, 139; design
    of, 140
Prince Robert, 209; on Triangle Route, 139;
    design of, 140
Prince Rupert, B.C., 130, *209*
Prince Rupert; on Triangle Route, 139; photo-
    graphs, *143-44,* 209
Princess Adelaide; photograph, *204-205*
Princess Alice; photographs, *143-44, 214-15*
Princess Beatrice; first Canadian Pacific Rail-

road steamer on Triangle Route, 138; photo-
    graph, *143-44*
Princess Charlotte, 104, 141; photograph; *214-15*
Princess Elizabeth, 141
Princess Irene; exploded during World War I, 198
Princess Kathleen, 141; photographs, *206, 207*
Princess Louise (formerly *Olympia*); returned
    to British Columbia and Puget Sound, 144;
    photographs, *103, 207*
Princess Margaret, 141
Princess Marguerite, 141; makes last run on
    Triangle Route, 141; photographs, *144, 204-205*
Princess Patricia, 141, 215
Princess Real, 6
Princess Victoria, 123, 138, 139, 140, 141;
    design of, 138; photographs, *140, 198*
Prosch, Thomas W., 120
Puget, Lt. Peter, 256
Puget Sound, 6, 15, 16, 32, 34, 35, 36, 37, 68,
    81, 84, 96, 100, 101, 106, 114, 119, 128, 157;
    discovery of, 7; strike on steamers on, 30; rac-
    ing on, 49; first export of timber, 79; ideal for
    commerce, 116; first steamer excursions, 164;
    population center, 236; residents view as moat,
    237; boundaries of 256
Puget Sound (Morgan), 116
Puget Sound Bridge and Drydock Company, 144
Puget Sound Day Line; subsidiary of PSN, 201
Puget Sound Excursion Line, 181
Puget Sound Freight Lines, 149
Puget Sound Maritime Historical Society, 10
Puget Sound Navigation Company (PSN), 16,
    35, 110, 136, 138, 183, 190, 196, 201, 234,
    237, 254; competes on Triangle Route, 139,
    144, 200-201; monopolizes auto ferry traffic,
    141, 144; purchased *Bailey Gatzert,* 151; takes
    over *Fairhaven,* 162; purchases Thompson
    Steamboat Company, 183; sale of to State of
    Washington, 213, 236
Puget Sound Navy Yard, Bremerton, 128, 175,
    176, 177; photograph, *176*
Puget Sound Vessel Traffic System, 256

Quartermaster Harbor, 92
Queen, 122
Queen Charlotte Islands, 27
Quimper, Manuel; charts Strait of Juan de Fuca, 6

Rabbeson, A. B., 9
Railroad Avenue, Seattle, 158; now Alaskan
    Way, 183; photograph, *182*
Railway and Marine News; on *Flyer,* 185
Ramsay, Alexander, 119
Rattenbury, Francis Mawson; designs Empress
    Hotel and British Columbia Legislative
    House, 140
Rattlesnake Pete; pilot on Fraser, 27
Red Collar Line, 64
Regulator, 60; photograph, *60*
Regulator Line; offers excursions on Columbia
    River, 150
Reliable, 83
Reliance; runs aground off Alki Point, 136;
    destroyed by fire, 144
Renton, Captain William, 76
Renton, 106, 135, 221
Richard Holyoke, 81, rescues survivors of
    Clallam, 190
Riggs, Captain Arthur, 73
Roanoke, 122
Roaring Land (Binns), 134
Roberts, Captain George; on *Clallam*
    sinking, 190
Robinson, 130, 186
Roosevelt, Theodore, 96; visits northwest, 119,
    121, 122-23, 123
Rosalie, 106, 108-109, 135-35; on Alaskan
    gold run, 246; photographs, *108-109, 109, 137*
Rosario, 106, 135
R. R. Thompson, 43

Sabino; photograph, *218*
Sacramento River, 26, 40, 146, 246; gold
    discoveries on, 24, 25, 99, 146, 181
St. Jo River, 64
Salmon River; gold discoveries, 29
Sammamish Slough, 217, 218, 221
San Francisco, 24, 25-26, 31, 79, 84, 111
San Francisco Chronicle (newspaper);
    on Klondike, 247
San Francisco Ferry Terminal; photograph, *147*
San Joaquin River; and gold rush, 24
San Juan Islands, 19, 26, 92, 106, 134, 135,
    190, 256; resort and excursion points, 88, 183,
    197; homesteaders on, 108; and apple pro-
    duction, 108; and salmon fishing, 109; and
    lime production, 109; and mutton production,
    109; first to depend on steamers, 109;
    rurality of, 237
Sandman; photograph, *84-85*
Santiago, Battle of, 122, 174, 176
Sarah Stone, 9
Savoy Hotel, Seattle; photograph, *192-93*
Scott, Robert; helps to beach *Capital City,* 161
Scott, Captain U. B.; owned and operated
    Telephone, 51; builds *Flyer,* 185
Sea Lion, 122; rescues survivors of
    Clallam, 190
Seabeck, 106, 134
Seaborn, Henry, 210
Sea-Land Corporation, 126
Seattle, 16, 20, 79, 84, 87, 88, 91, 109, 111,
    116, 131, 134, 137, 138, 183, 239; active port
    even during Great Depression, 113; visited by
    U.S. Presidents, 119-21, 122, 125; benefits
    from gold discoveries, 123, 246; part of Trian-
    gle Route, 138; City Council wants to rename
    Alaskan Way, 183; photographs, *102, 140,
    158, 161*
Seattle; consort of *Tacoma,* 16; photograph, *113*
Seattle, U.S.S., 173
Seattle Dry Dock and Construction Company, 15
Seattle Farmers' Market, 132-33
Seattle Mail and Herald (newspaper), 189
Seattle Museum of History and Industry, 151
Seattle Post-Intelligencer (newspaper), 163
Seattle Times (newspaper), 125, 163, 246;
    on christening of *Tacoma,* 15
Selkirk; photograph, *58*
Senator, 40-41, 211; transits Strait of Magellan
    for gold rush, 24, 146; design of, 40; photo-
    graphs, *40-41, 147*
Service, Robert, 246
Seymour, Frederick, 26
Shamrock; photograph, *83*
Shaughnessy, Lord Thomas; President of
    Canadian Pacific Railroad, 206
Shaw Island; agriculture on, 108
Sheridan, Lt. Philip H., 55
Sherman, William Tecumseh, 119
Ship Names (Kennedy), 254
Ships of the Inland Sea (Newell); on end of
    Mosquito Fleet, 144-45
Shoalwater Bay Transportation Company, 90
Shroll, Captain John (Hell-Roarin' Jack), 95
Sicamous, photograph, *199*
Sightseer, 222
Simpson, Aemilius, 7
Simpson, George, 7, 36
Sioux, 218; collides with *Camano* and *Island
    Flyer,* 162
Sitka, 36, 210
Sitka, 40; and Sacramento River Gold
    discoveries, 24
Skagit River, 31, 68, 157
Skagit and Snohomish, Puget Sound and
    Baker River Railroad, 157
Skagway, 96, 105, 246
Skeena River, 92; and gold discoveries, 62
Skinner, D. E., 111, 210
Smith's Island, 106, 135, 190
Snake River, 47; photograph, *46*
Snohomish City, 88
Snohomish River, 9, 68, 88, 106, 135

Snoqualmie; photographs, 112-13, 248-49
Snoqualmie Pass, 221
Snowden, Clinton, 25
Sol Duc, 218
Sophia, 92; runs aground, 136
S O S North Pacific (Newell), 136
Spakowsky, Michael, 253
Spaulding, Philip; on influence of New England
    on design of Mosquito Fleet, 218-19
Speel-est; Indian guide of Surprise, 26, 26-27
Spokane, 64
Spokane, S.S.; transports T. Roosevelt to Seattle,
    122, 125; photograph, 125
Sprackin, Captain William, 232
Spray; and gold discoveries, 29, 39
Starr, Edwin, 94; challenges Olympia for
    monopoly on Puget Sound, 144
Starr, Louis, 94; challenges Olympia for
    monopoly on Puget Sound, 144
State of Washington, 197; photograph, 118
Steamboats on the Western Rivers (Hunter and
    Hunter), 252
Steilacoom, 87, 106, 135, 143
Stevens, Governor Isaac, 9
Stevens, James; designs "walking beam"
    engine, 98
Stewart River; photograph, 92
Stikine River, 161; and gold discoveries, 27, 62
Stimson; photograph, 79
Strait of Georgia, 6
Strait of Juan de Fuca, 6, 7, 106, 123, 128, 135;
    photograph, 126
Strait of Magellan, 24, 110, 200; Olympian
    breaks up in, 101, 137
Stuart Island, 108
Stump, Captain Thomas; first to run Celilo
    Rapids, 50
Stuttering Bailey; pilot on Fraser River, 27
Success, 119
Supple, Joseph, 73
Surprise; first to ascend Fraser River to
    Fort Hope, 26
Sutter's Mill; gold strike at, 24, 40
Swan, James Gilchrist, 10
S. Wiley Navigation Company, 161

Tacoma, 15, 20, 84, 90, 92, 106, 110, 111, 120,
    131, 134, 135, 161, 168, 185, 239, 256; mills at,
    116; T. Roosevelt visits, 122; becomes Sea-
    Land port, 126; and trade with Orient, 128;
    photographs, 130, 171
Tacoma; 16, 17, 18-19, 67, 130, 218, 236, 237,
    239, 242; design of, 16; as excursion ship, 19;
    last run of, 18-19; cut up for scrap, 144; photo-
    graphs, 14-15, 16, 17, 19, 20, 20-21, 22, 139,
    234, 242, 252-53
Tacoma Ledger (newspaper), 121
Taft, William Howard, 134
Tanana River, 128
T. C. Reed, 71; design of, 71; photographs,
    70-71
Teaser; photograph, 95
Telegraph; rammed by Alameda, 136; photo-
    graph, 114
Telephone, 185; fire aboard, 51; races river-
    boats, 51; photograph, 51
Telicia, 36
Tenino; and gold discoveries, 29, 39
Tennessee, U.S.S., 177
Texas, U.S.S.; photograph, 175
Thompson, R. R., 30
Thompson River, 31
Thompson Steamboat Company, 183
Thorniley, William; publicizes Kalakala, 250
T. J. Potter, 32, 43, 49, 120, 154; races
    Telephone, 51; competes with Bailey Gatzert;
    undergoes refit, 154; photographs, 50, 154-55
Todd Seattle Shipyard; builds Chinook, 212
Topsy, 88
Trader, S.S., 161
Traveler, 9
Triangle Route, 138, 139, 140, 198, 207, 210,
    214, 215; last run on, 141

Troup, Captain James; takes Harvest Queen
    over Celilo rapids, 50; breaches Cascades, 55
Troutman, Captain Daniel; death of, 90
Troutman, Captain Dora Wells, 90
Turner, Robert, 10
Twelve-Foot Davis; pilot on Fraser River, 27
Tyee, 122

Umatilla, 61
Umatilla, 39; J. Ainsworth buys interest in, 29;
    photograph, 111
Umatilla House, The Dalles, 61;
    photograph, 61
Unalaska, 246
Unalga; helped fight Grand Trunk Dock
    fire, 249
Union City, 106, 134
Union Ferry Company, 149
Union Pacific Railroad, 61
United States Atlantic Fleet; visits Puget
    Sound, 123
United States Coast Guard; on definition of
    Puget Sound boundaries, 256
United States Pacific Fleet; photograph, 175
University of Washington, 119, 120; Northwest
    Collection, 11; students greet Atlantic Fleet,
    123; Department of Oceanography and defin-
    ing boundaries of Puget Sound, 256; photo-
    graph, 94
Utsalady; mills at, 116

Vancouver, George, 7, 76, 256; enters Admi-
    ralty Inlet, 6; first to use Puget Sound lumber,
    79; names Puget Sound for Lt. Peter
    Puget, 256
Vancouver, B.C., 137, 144, 183; part of Triangle
    Route, 138
Vancouver, 7, 66; runs aground, 7; design of,
    66; photograph, 66
Vancouver Island, 6
Vashon Island, 106, 128, 130, 135, 239;
    agricultural production, 109; rurality of, 237;
    photograph, 102
Verona, Gertrude Wiman is captain of, 90;
    design of, 130; photograph, 130
Victoria, B.C., 19, 37, 87, 99, 106, 110, 111,
    134, 135, 137, 139, 141, 144, 183, 190, 254;
    gold rush boom town, 138-40; as tourist attrac-
    tion, 143-44
Victoria Standard (newspaper), 62
Victorian, 102; on Alaskan gold run, 246;
    photographs, 102, 104-105
Villard, Henry; purchases OSN, 30; takes over
    ORN, 100
Vincennes, 164
Virginia III, 238; photograph, 238
Virginia IV, 238, 241
Virginia V, 218; sole survivor of Mosquito Fleet,
    238; construction of, 238-39; photographs,
    238, 239, 252-53
Virginia V Foundation, 239
Volcanic Brown; pilot on Fraser River, 27

Wake Up Jake; pilot on Fraser, 27
Wakeman, Captain Edgar, 26, 31
Walck, Captain Della, 90
Walck, John, 90
"walking beam" diesels; designed by J. Stevens;
    98; photograph, 98
Walla Walla, 61
Walla Walla and Columbia River Railroad, 61
Wallowa; on Alaskan gold runs, 246
Warren, Dr. James, 10
Washington, 186; photograph, 95
Washington, U.S.S., 172-73; design of, 172;
    career of, 173; photograph, 172-73
Washington and Alaska Steamship
    Company, 137
Washington Hotel, Seattle, 96; T. Roosevelt
    stays at, 123; photograph, 96-97
Washington State, 24; and gold discoveries,
    39; National Guard, 120; takes over Black Ball
    Line, 131, 134, 213

Washington State Department of Transportation;
    investigating number of vessel types for cur-
    rent service, 241
Washington State Ferries, 241; serve Victoria,
    144; succeed Black Ball Line, 236; financing
    of, 237
Washington Steamboat Company; competes
    with ORN, 95
Washington, Alfred; on Victoria, 143
Watt, Boulton, 37
Webfoot; and gold discoveries, 29, 39
West Seattle; photograph, 159
West Seattle; rams Seattle dock, 158;
    photographs, 20-21, 159
West Seattle Land and Improvement
    Company, 159
West Sound, 105, 135
West Virginia, 177
Western Slope; photograph, 27
Western Star; wrecked in Shelikoff Straits, 247
Westport; as resort, 83
Whatcom (now Bellingham), 26, 143, 197
Whatcom, 183; converted into auto ferry,
    City of Bremerton, 183; photograph, 183
Whidbey Island, 22, 130, 256; agriculture on,
    109; rurality of, 237
Whitcomb, Lot, 38
White, Mayor Harry, 120
White Collar Line, 35
White Pass and Yukon Railway, 105; operated
    Dalton, 161
Wide West, 33, 43; design of, 43; photographs,
    42, 43
Wildwood; launching of, 78
Wilkerson, Samuel; on northwest lumber trade,
    33, 116
Wilkes Expedition, 164, 256
Willamette; on Alaskan gold run, 246
Willamette River, 28, 71, 164; Telephone sinks
    on, 51; photograph, 67
William and Ann; lost at Columbia River Bar, 7
William Irving, 44; photograph, 44
William J. Patterson; photograph, 70-71
Williams, Theodore, 76
Willie, 91; photograph, 91
Wilson, Helen Stewart; christens U.S.S.
    Washington, 172
Wilson, Senator John, 172
Wilson, Woodrow; visits Seattle, 174; photo-
    graph, 174
Wilson G. Hunt, 9, 27, 87; on Sacramento,
    Columbia and Fraser Rivers' gold rushes, 99;
    design of, 99; photograph, 99
Wiman, Captain Gertrude, 90
Winslow; cut up for scrap, 144
Wittelsy, Richard, 161
wood; as fuel for steamers, 79;
    "wooding up," 92
Wright, George, 87, 103
Wright, John, 87
Wright, Thomas, 87
Wyoming, U.S.S., 175

Xanthus, 221

Yakima, 108
Yakima; and gold discovery, 29, 39
Yesler, Henry, 79
Yesler Mill, 183; used as steamer waiting
    room, 131
Yesler Wharf; photograph, 95
YFB54 (formerly City of Seattle), 159
Yosemite, 37, 123; on Sacramento and Fraser
    River gold rushes, 181; photographs, 24, 147;
    (wrecked), 181
Yuba River; and gold rush, 24
Yukon River, 45, 128, 241; gold rush on,
    129, 247
Yukon Territory, 62, 161, 246

Zephyr, 88; photograph, 95

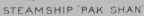

STEAMSHIP "PAK SHAN"

DODWELL, CARLILL & CO.,

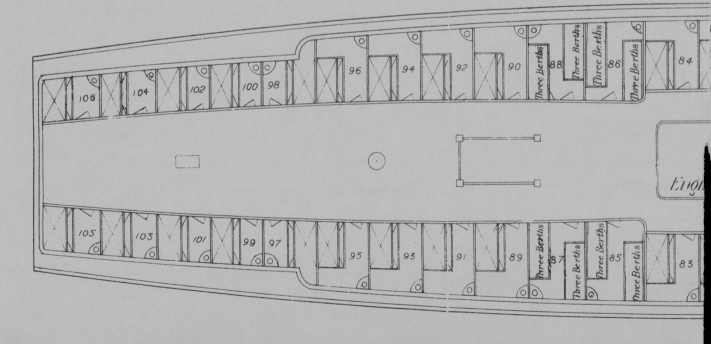